MISSING
THE
TAG

B. D. GATES

OTHER BOOKS IN THE SERIES

BISHOP'S RUN

DOUBLE PLAY

While I encourage you to read the first two books in the Bishop's Run series, it is not entirely necessary, as you can pick up the basic threads of the stories here.

To all who have been with us,
and to all who join us now--
we're reaching the tipping point.
The danger is close.

How many lifetimes I would live, to find and fall in love with you.

"Hey, how was the beach? Wow, girl, you got a tan," Penny said to Tess, taking her in as she mounted the stairs of the carriage house porch. Hatch followed, smiling, and the hugs all around were quick but warm.

"It was beautiful. Really, and so nice to get away," Tess smiled at the two.

I was in the kitchen prepping steaks for the grill, stopping to give Penny a hug and a kiss. "Hello, hello! Glad you could come!" I shook hands with Hatch. "You look good, Hatch."

"Feeling much better, thank you. Penny's been taking good care of me."

The two smiled at each other.

It has been just a little over a month since Hatch had surprised everyone, especially Penny, when she turned up at the wedding.

Oh.

Yeah.

The wedding.

Tess and I.

We're married.

It's going well so far.

Our honeymoon was a week at the beach, an unexpected wedding present from my boss, Dr. Sharon Biggs, a veterinarian here in Tenley, and her wife, Carole. We'd had to delay the trip until Tess could schedule the time off from work.

I wish I'd been there to see her tell her captain that she had recently married and was requesting a week of vacation for her honeymoon.

Tess said that Captain Huff had burst out laughing, but she shut that down when she showed him her left hand, now adorned with her wedding band--the twin to my own-- telling him who she'd married and when. She said that the emotions that passed over his face were priceless in how quickly they came and went, and that she wasn't sure that he wasn't having a stroke at one point, his face had gotten so dark.

See, Captain Huff and I are not exactly on the best of terms to start with, and he obviously believes I'm a bad influence on Tess.

I think the main thing is that he wasn't in the loop. No one--well, Tess, actually--had stopped long enough to inform him that she and Penny were chasing Darren Nichols and his crew into Richmond that Saturday night. So when the state news services called and began questioning him about the 'joint DEA-Tenley PD Task Force' and the Richmond PD rescue of a member of that force, he was caught a bit flat-footed.

Of course, he was as slick as any small-town politician, spinning answers designed to show his department in the best possible light, but it had obviously strained him. He looked a bit worn after the story fell off the news cycle.

I'm not knocking Captain Huff by any means, he loves Tess like a daughter. He's known her for nearly fourteen years, has watched her grow into an exemplary police officer, a by-the-book detective that he could count on to handle situations appropriately and within the constraints of the rules and regulations.

An "officer's officer," as it were, one that he had given a lead role in his detectives' division.

Now, she was a loose cannon, full of surprises and snap decisions, and he did not know how to rein her in.

Regarding her request, though, he had offered up his congratulations, wished us the best, and granted her the week of vacation.

So, with the exception of our time at the Virginia shore, we've been working on the adjustment two people make when moving in and sharing the same space.

Fortunately, we'd already spent a lot of time here together, when I'd first arrived in Tenley to begin my new life as Lisa Baxter--I prefer just 'Baxter,' please--with Tess was in charge of my WITSEC protection detail.

She'd actually been the one to unpack my things, to make the carriage house my home, as it were, while I slept off the drugs I'd been injected with before being transported from the Baltimore hospital to Tenley that rainy night. She'd been there with me for days, maybe weeks, before I'd realized her presence, the pain medications and occasional tranquilizers dulling my senses nearly to the point of disconnection from my surroundings.

When I finally gained real consciousness, I found her warm and caring, and kind. And charming. And funny. And sweet.

And on one particular morning, as she cooked my breakfast, to celebrate the removal of the cast on my arm, I found her pretty.

Wait.

I found her beautiful.

And after getting to know her, learning her history, maybe also a little damaged.

I know.

Who isn't, right?

I'd like to tell you that it was easy getting to where we are now, but I'd be lying.

The fact that we are here, together, and married, is nothing short of a miracle or two, and more than one story would have to be told to explain exactly how we--all four of us-- got to this place in one piece.

We *are* here, though, seemingly against all odds, and now Tess and I are figuring out how to join two households in the remodelled one-bedroom carriage house behind that turn-of-the-century Victorian one block off of Main Street in Tenley, Virginia.

We had decided to make the carriage house our home after having a discussion of sorts, one that occurred over days, with me really just simply listening while Tess talked. Her house was the last physical connection she had to her parents and I let her work her way through that decision on her own.

It really wasn't for me to say whether or not she should keep it, whether or not we should live in it, because the new life she wanted was wherever she thought she'd be happiest, and I would follow her wherever she led us.

With Miz Maggie's blessing, of course, as she owns the property, we all, including Miz Maggie's live-in significant other, Jared, share in the upkeep of the houses and grounds.

This is truly communal living at its finest.

2

We were outside now, Penny and Tess sitting at the table, Hatch on the steps while I put the steaks and vegetables on the grill, keeping an eye on the flames. Hatch had poured the wine and it was quiet while everyone sipped from their glasses, enjoying the late August evening and taking a minute to just breathe.

"How long before school starts?" I asked Hatch, breaking the silence.

"Ten days," she replied, smiling.

"You ready?"

She laughed at that, but with a groan, too. "I never, ever, thought I'd be counting off the days until school started again. I thought I was done with that when I graduated from the Academy."

"Maybe it'll be different this time, since you're on the other side of the desk," Tess assured her.

Hatch nodded at that.

"So, when does summer ball end? Labor Day weekend?" I was wondering how long Biggs was going to continue the pick-up games. Knowing her love for softball, she'd keep on playing all the way to Christmas, and maybe even right on through to the start of next season if the winter was warm enough.

Penny nodded, confirming Labor Day as she laughed. "You know Biggs. She'd sleep in the dugout if she could talk Carole into it."

Hatch nodded at that. "Carole's got her hands full between Biggs and Justine."

"Justine." Penny's lip curled with the name. I looked over at her and she saw the questioning look on my face.

"She's...just...ugh."

I turned and looked at Hatch with "What the hell?" written on my face.

Hatch leaned forward, smiling and stage-whispering, "Penny doesn't like Justine." Then she cut her eyes back at the woman sitting at the table.

Penny crossed her arms. "I don't trust her."

"You don't trust her. Why not?"

"I don't know, there's just something about her." Penny's scowl accentuated her statement and I laughed at that.

Tess chimed in, leaning forward. "Okay, honestly, I don't care for her much either."

Now, I've never heard Tess say anything like that about anyone, so that caught my attention. Hatch seemed a bit surprised by it, too.

"Tess!"

"Well, what? I don't trust her, and I don't like the way she looks at you and Hatch."

"What I'm sayin'," Penny nodded, pointing at Tess. "She looks at y'all like you're snacks and she's hungry."

Hatch and I locked eyes and we burst out laughing.

"Who's your little honey bun?" Hatch chuckled. She stood up and stepped across the porch, picking up Penny's empty wine glass and kissing her on top of her head before moving into the kitchen for refills.

Tess was deep in thought, her mouth pulled sideways. "It's not just that," she added to her earlier comment, "she's just...something's not right. I don't think we have the full story."

Okay, so let me say this right here. If Tess has learned anything in the past two years, it is that she cannot take things at face value. She no longer assumes anything to be simply what it is, and I may have had a lot to do with that.

"What do you mean?" I asked.

"I think...I think she's like you."

"What?" Now that was unexpected. "Uh, 'like me' in a good way, or in a bad way?'"

She looked at me, trying to find the words and having a bit of a struggle. "I can't tell."

It was my turn to scowl and she tried to explain what she was thinking.

"I thought I knew who you were, why you were here, and I was so wrong about you, Bishop. I was wrong about everything."

"Tess, there was no reason for you to think that I was anything more than an average witness that needed protection. I didn't tell you the truth and that wasn't fair to you."

She smiled at that, but it was a little pained at the end, and I wondered what else she thought she'd missed about me.

"Yeah, I knew something wasn't right about your sorry ass," Penny chimed in and I shot her a cutting look. She pursed her lips in an 'oops' sort of way and leaned back in her chair. Hatch came out and handed Penny her replenished glass, and she took a big gulp.

I wondered if Tess thought I might still be keeping secrets from her.

3

Hatch took the tongs from me and flipped the steaks before taking her seat on the steps again. She had picked up the tension in the air and took it upon herself to start a new topic.

"While you were gone, Penny and I did a little shopping," she began. "We were looking for a lamp to go next to the loveseat, and we noticed a new little boutique in that strip mall over on Andrews Street. Just guess what we found."

Okay, I'm not one for shopping in general, boutique shopping in particular, so I left it up to Tess to try and answer, but not before asking what happened to the lamp.

"Hatch kicked it off the table and broke it."

"What?"

"It was Penny's fault, she hit a tickle spot and I didn't have control."

"Oh, lawd, okay, let's just...continue," Tess laughed as we both shook our heads and rolled our eyes.

"Are you sure you don't want to guess?"

"I'm sure. Tess, you sure?"

"Yep. Tell us, Hatch, what did you and Penny find?"

"Purses. Lots of designer purses. Out on display. And I took a look around and saw some cardboard shipping boxes in what I guess used to be a changing room. I'd swear they're some of the same ones that were at Charlie's."

She pulled out her phone and opened the pictures gallery, showing me pics of the boxes she'd found. I took the phone from her and zoomed the shot to get a better look.

Charlie Pierce's store was a combination pawn shop and discount warehouse, selling used goods and stock overruns at below market prices. It had been closed after Darren Nichols and his crew were arrested in Richmond, with Charlie sitting in the county jail awaiting trial for his involvement as a co-conspirator. He sold the store for cash, trying to make bail and falling short, and the store had reopened with a new name under new management.

After seeing the boxes in the boutique, curiosity had gotten the better of Hatch, but she couldn't make her way into Charlie's former store to have a look, not knowing who owned it, or if there might be someone in there willing to settle a score for Charlie or Darren Nichols.

She sent Penny in to handle the recon, telling her where the boxes had been stacked when she and I had last seen them. Penny scouted the entire store, including the attached garage, now a sort of outdoor showroom with pitched tents and children's backyard gyms, reporting that there were no boxes matching the descriptions Hatch had given her anywhere inside, nor were there any purses for sale.

I'd moved to the grill and was taking up the steaks, handing off the platter to Hatch while I slid the foil-wrapped vegetables over the flame for a blast of heat.

Tess had followed Hatch inside to get the potatoes out of the oven and to toss the salad one more time. I looked over at Penny.

"Did you take a good look at the merchandise at the boutique? What do you think?"

Her forehead was puckered as she considered what I'd asked. "Honestly, I'm no pro at knock-offs, so I really can't say. I did some research and I know what to look for now, but I'm still not sure I'd be able to spot the differences."

I nodded at that.

"What about shoes?"

"Nope. Just purses."

"Hm."

"Yeah."

"Who owns the boutique?"

"I don't know. Maybe we start there?"

"We don't know if those bags are counterfeit, or if they're actually the ones from Charlie's store. Or if the owner knows who the hell Charlie is. I can't even say for sure that the boxes are the ones we saw in the flea market. So, we just need to step back and take a breath, you know?"

She nodded at that as she stood up and I handed her the tray of vegetables to carry into the house.

As I scraped the residue from the grill, I had to wonder if Tenley was a regular ol' hotbed of criminal activity, or was I imagining it.

And is it just in my nature to go looking for trouble?

Tess tightened the belt on her slacks and smoothed out the creases in her white blouse as she gazed at her reflection in the mirror, noting the second pair of eyes on her from the bed.

She smiled at the reflection, a bit shy. "What are you doing?"

"Watching my wife get dressed," I answered, then added "Thinking about undressing her."

"Too late," Tess replied. "You had your chance, you blew it."

I got up from the bed and pulled Tess to me. "But you smell so good," I whispered, delivering light kisses on the soft skin below her ear.

Tess leaned into me, her arms draped around my shoulders. "So do you."

Tess nuzzled my neck, then touched her lips to it.

"Hm. Salty." She sighed. "We've got to stop, I'm going to be late."

"You know you don't really want me to." I growled.

"That's not fair, you talking all low and husky like that, you know what your morning voice does to me." Tess whispered, pushing herself away from me as my lips traced her jaw, my fingers still playing with the top button of her blouse.

She put her hand on mine, wrapping her fingers so that I couldn't work that button free. "I have to go," she whispered.

I laughed then kissed her on the lips. "Okay, okay. So, Detective, can I make an appointment with you for this evening, then? I'd like to have some really hot sex, then take you out to dinner. Or vice versa. Your choice. Are you available?"

Tess considered my request, the edges of her mouth pulled down into a frown. "Gee, I don't know, I'm pretty busy these days."

"Oh, really? Too busy to spend some quality time with your wife?"

"Well, I'll have to juggle a few things, but I might be able to squeeze you in."

I feigned hurt. "Squeeze me in? Ah, well, the honeymoon's over, isn't it? Guess I'll have to find my pleasures somewhere else, with such a busy wife."

Tess narrowed her eyes, smirking at me. "You just try it," she cautioned.

"Yep. I can see it now. The age-old story. My wife is too busy to see me."

"You!" Tess playfully pushed at me, sending me a step backwards.

I laughed, shaking my head. "Yeah, see, you don't want me anymore."

"I don't want you any less," Tess corrected.

She looked at her watch, absentmindedly spinning the wedding band on her finger. "Okay, sweetheart, you'd better get a move on, too."

"I'm going. I'll see you tonight," I said as I turned and headed for the shower. "I love you."

I poked my head back into the room, but Tess was already gone.

"Good morning." Captain Huff addressed the room of patrol officers and detectives at roll call. He waited as the room quieted before he continued. He didn't have to wait long.

"This morning begins the first day implementing the use of body cams by the Tenley Police Department officers, as well as the recording of detectives during on-scene investigations. This is in addition to our CSI division and we are utilizing this technology to assist in the transparency of our actions in our operations as law enforcement officers.

"The use of this technology is not punitive, it is to provide a clear and concise record of interaction by the Tenley PD with the general public. I see this as a tool we will use to educate the public as well as officers employed by this agency in community relations for the betterment of all.

"That is all. Be careful out there. Dismissed."

As the room cleared of the patrol officers, the detectives as a group moved to the desks at the front of the room. Penny came running in, taking a seat next to Tess, who looked over at her, a bit puzzled.

"Hatch," was all the woman said in a low whisper, shaking her head and rolling her eyes. "Her timing is terrible sometimes, but gawd, once she starts something, I just...can't..."

Tess's eyes widened when she realized what Penny was referring to.

"What? Don't look at me like you've never had morning sex, Tess Hayes, I've seen you come in here looking like you just need a good nap to top it all off."

Tess's lips tightened into a straight line at that revelation.

Penny continued on, digging deep into her pack for a pen and notepad. "Baxter was all about the morning sex, I think that's her peak time, frankly,weekend sex would last half the day and...oh, sorry, is this making you uncomfortable?" She had glanced over and caught the look on Tess's face.

"It's..." Tess waved Penny off, her reply just one more thing left unfinished this morning regarding Bishop and sex. She scowled at the notepad in front of her and sighed.

"What?" Penny tried to coax more out of Tess, seeing the serious look on the woman's face. The answer wasn't forthcoming and she tried again. "What's going on, Tess?"

Tess shook her head, still looking down. "It's just...it's been hard finding time the past couple of weeks. We were at the beach only a month ago, and now it's like, I don't know. We've both been so busy lately and...we seem to just keep...missing each other."

Penny had put her chin in her hand, and now she rubbed it in a thoughtful way. "So, the honeymoon's over."

Tess looked at her. There was no way she could know that Bishop had said that very same thing earlier this morning, albeit far more playfully.

Penny squinted at Tess, the other woman's reaction letting her know that she was dead-on with her assessment. "Honey, that's not unusual. We all have that problem at some time or another, we're busy, our schedules conflict, we're hardly in the same place at the same time and when we are, we're exhausted and we fall asleep. And yes, it's frustrating, but it doesn't last, it will get better, I promise. You two were probably going at it like rabbits at first and now..."

"Penny!"

"You know what I mean, Tess, I'm just saying that the way it's been is not a good measure of where the two of you are right now. It's really not realistic to think that you could maintain that level of intimacy without pushing other things aside."

Tess weighed Penny's words and found herself silently agreeing with her. It had all been just like Penny'd said, she and Bishop had spent a lot of time in bed and not doing much else and they'd gotten used to that, especially since people had stepped back and given them space.

Now, though, the honeymoon really was over, and they both had responsibilities and expectations to be met and it seemed like it had all come crashing down on them at once.

She pulled out her phone and texted Bishop, asking her if she was free this evening, she wanted to take her out.

I was smiling as I tapped out the message to Tess and sent it off into the ether. Dr. Biggs saw it.

"Well, that's a happy grin."

"Yep. I've got a date tonight."

Dr. Biggs laughed at that. "Anyone I know?"

I played along, nodding. "You've met her."

"Oh, I hope it's the pretty one, with the chestnut hair and the gun on her hip."

"That's the one!" I laughed. "You know I love'em armed and dangerous!"

I considered that statement. I certainly do seem to have a type, when you think about it.

"So, where are you taking her?"

"She's taking me. And I have no idea."

"Oh, boy, now that does sound like fun! Do you need to leave early to get ready? You know, to do your hair, your make-up?"

"Ha ha. Unless she's taking me somewhere that we've never been before, I think I can get away with 'casual and clean,' and she goes for the natural look."

Biggs nodded at that. "Well, I am so glad you two are trying to make a go of it," she laughed.

Meg came into the surgery and flicked the x-ray into the viewbox. We all stood and studied the light and shadows on the film.

"Dating is scary," I offered.

"Compared to most other things, yes, it is. Glad I don't have to do it anymore."

Meg turned with a questioning look at Dr. Biggs.

"It's good, thanks, Meg, I'll buzz when we need another," Dr. Biggs answered her unspoken question and Meg left the room.

"Yeah, but we kinda did things a little backwards," I continued, looking over the instruments on the surgical tray. "We got married before we ever really dated."

"Oh, you two dated, just not in the usual sense."

I considered that. Even though it was Tess's job to stay with me, it had become more like a nightly date where we ate and watched a movie or tv shows together on the couch in the carriage house. And we continued to do that after the round-the-clock surveillance ended, culminating in a real date to the softball cookout, Tess asking me to go with her, the first time the word 'date' was ever actually used between us.

I sighed at that. If I could, I'd turn back time to that night, I would do things so differently, knowing that what I was feeling as I held her in my arms was real, and reciprocated.

I just didn't want to be 'that' lesbian.

I'd been caught out before, and it's hard sometimes, to know if what I'm feeling from a woman is real, or if I'm projecting--is this a friendly hug or does it mean more?

Being wrong had strained a few of my friendships with women in the past, so I tended to err in the opposite direction, keeping the relationships safe.

So, even though Tess was in my arms that night, and the whole world had gone silent in that moment, I'd still mentally held her at arm's length, not wanting to misread any intent on her part.

I'd done exactly that, though, and I lost her anyway.

That evening, we had a lovely meal at Gene and Hettie's restaurant, this one sounding a much happier note than the last time. Hettie had noticed our wedding bands, and the edges of her mouth turned up when she did, but she made no mention of it, with Gene likely oblivious to such things. She brought us a carafe of wine, personally chosen to complement our meal, but I also think it was her way of congratulating us without drawing the attention of anyone who might object to our marriage.

The evening drive home was pleasant with the Jeep windows down and the radio on. It was tuned to the local radio station, WWTR, when we heard the announcement about a pop-up shop happening at an empty storefront in downtown Tenley, starting at nine o'clock the following morning and lasting through Saturday evening. The event would showcase designer handbags and shoes.

I took my eyes off the road for a few seconds to look over at Tess. "You have *got* to be kidding me."

She slowly shook her head, her lips pursed a bit in thought. "Bishop."

She said it in a way that was almost like a warning.

"What?"

"I see those wheels of yours turning."

I laughed at that, shook my head. "Doesn't it make you wonder? I mean, that's a bit of a coincidence, don't you think?"

She didn't say anything to that.

"Look," I started, about to make a case for going to check it out.

"Bishop! No! You're not a police officer any more."

"Tess, do you honestly think you'll ever stop being a cop? After you've put in your twenty, and as a detective no less, do you think you can just turn it all off and walk away?"

She considered that. "I don't know, but it doesn't matter, as far as you're concerned, because you're not a police officer anymore, you're Dr. Biggs' vet tech, you're *Lisa Baxter*, for gawdsake. You've got to let that other life go!"

I snorted a bit at that.

As if it could really be that easy, to just forget an entire lifetime as if it had never existed.

"Bishop, please don't."

I bit my lip and didn't answer.

She was insistent. "Please don't go looking for trouble. Promise me."

She was holding my hand as it laid on the gearshift and she gave it a small squeeze. Then she leaned over and softly pressed her lips just below my ear, lightly humming when she felt me shiver. She went back for seconds and I leaned into her, her kisses leaving a trail down to my shoulder.

She moved her hand to my lap, stroking against the inside of my thigh, giving it a gentle squeeze.

I sighed, as much for the way she was making me feel as for the way I felt about making such a promise to her.

"If you want trouble, I'm right here," she whispered, her lips against my ear, her breath hot. "Take me home, I'll give you all the trouble you can handle."

Now that was trouble I couldn't resist.

Tess walked into the department and tossed her keys on her desk. Penny came in behind her with one of the patrol cameras in her hand as she headed for her own. She nodded to Tess as Tess sighed, dropping into her chair.

"Problem?" Penny asked, glancing over at Tess as she rattled the mouse to wake her computer.

"I don't know. Maybe. Did you hear about the pop-up shop happening..."

She didn't have time to finish before Penny was holding up her hand, the universal signal to stop not lost on the police officer.

"Yep. Last night. On Silke's show. Hatch practically fell off the couch trying to turn it up in time to hear it. Started the talk about the pocketbooks all over again. I had to remind her that she wasn't a DEA agent anymore."

Tess shook her head. "Lawd, the same with Bishop."

Penny smiled at that. "They sure are kinda like two peas in a pod, aren't they."

"From the same mold."

"Like sisters."

Tess nodded. "Which reminds me, I haven't done much on our little search project for Bishop in the last couple of months, have you?"

Penny laughed. "You mean 'Project Jillian?' No, nothing, I've been swamped with work and getting Hatch settled. Maybe we can plan on spending a little time on it now that things are slowing down."

Tess nodded at that. "I wonder if Hatch would have some insight into the record keeping in Baltimore."

"Oh, I'm not telling Hatch, and you shouldn't either. She'll run her mouth to Baxter."

"Hm. You're right, good thinking. If we just happen to pull it off, it would ruin the surprise. I do have one idea I want to try, I think it could work, or at least it might point us in the right direction."

"Cool. Let me know what you find."

The two women nodded to each other and started their day.

I was bent over the whelping box, trying to get one of the pups to latch on to its mother and have its lunchtime feeding when someone pressed up against me from behind and wrapped their arms around my waist.

"Alright, now, stop, you'll push me in on the puppies." I laughed as I pushed back from the low wall, then half-turned, expecting to find Tess making one of her surprise visits to take me to lunch.

"Whoa! Shit! Justine!" My hands automatically went to her hips as I backed her away. "What are you doing?"

Her innocent smile never changed. "Just came to see the puppies. Hello, puppy."

The door to the kennel squeaked open and Justine took another step back, her eyes narrowed and her smile now more of a smirk. Tracey loped around the corner and headed over to the sinks with a box of shampoo.

"Hey, Justine. Checking out the puppies? They're getting big, aren't they? Such cute babies."

"Yeah, cute's the word," she laughed, looking me up and down.

Damn.

This girl was bold.

I sidestepped her and headed out to the supply room.

She followed.

"Aren't you supposed to be in class?"

She was propped against the shelf system I was pulling supplies from, not quite in my space but close. "Not today. My instructor gave us a free period. I'm done for the afternoon."

"No homework? A project? Papers to write?"

"Well, my goodness, Baxter, you sound like my aunt. No, I do not have anything I need to do. I came by to see if Meg wanted to go to the pop-up shop happening downtown, and I'm just waiting for her to finish her chores."

"The pop-up shop. The one with the pocketbooks?"

"Yeah. Pocketbooks, shoes, maybe some belts, scarves, who knows. Nothing you'd be interested in, I'm sure."

Huh. If she only knew.

I nodded anyway.

Meg poked her head in. "Let's go, I've only got my lunch hour," then turned and left.

Justine pushed off from the cart. "See you, puppy."

I just shook my head. "Huh."

I piled the kennel pads onto the rolling cart, biting the inside of my lip as I watched Justine walk through the lab area and out to reception and the front door.

The more I considered it, the more I really did want to check out that merchandise.

I headed back to the kennel and cleared leaving with Tracey, then grabbed my jacket and keys, firing up the Jeep and pointing it towards downtown.

10

"Well, Baxter! What a surprise!" Justine smirked, spotting me as I walked through the store entrance, she and Meg having only made it just past the first displays. Meg was checking out a rather large red satchel, turning it this way and that before inspecting the inside.

"Look, it's sectioned and has zippered compartments!"

The two women were appropriately awed and when Meg read the price tag, she nearly had a stroke.

"That's not possible. This tote usually lists for five hundred dollars or more online and in the stores. This is only three hundred before the thirty percent discount." She looked at Justine with an animated jaw-drop.

Justine nodded, smiling. "And I have a coupon for another ten percent off, if you want to use it. We could just pay for everything at once and I can give you my share in cash."

"Deal."

I had moved on into the store, wandering like I was lost, and I kind of was, a bit. I found myself looking at the wallets.

In what seemed like no time, Justine stole up next to me. "Now what is a girl like you doing in a place like this?"

She was not stupid by any means.

"Well, Christmas is coming, so I thought I might find something to surprise Tess with."

So, that wasn't exactly true, but it sounded good.

"Hm." Her mouth crooked a bit at that. "Did you really marry her?"

I blinked at that. "Yes. I did." I held up my left hand, my band glinting in the light.

"If you say so."

"What?"

"Does she carry a pocketbook?"

"No."

"So, pockets. Bet she wears suit-style slacks and jackets, jeans on the weekends."

I nodded at that.

She didn't answer, just reached past me and handed me a thin leather wallet.

"If women's slacks have pockets, they're usually cut very shallow, they wouldn't hold anything bigger than this. She wants something to carry a little cash, a credit card or two, and her drivers license. Am I right?"

I nodded. The wallet Tess used was almost exactly like that, but its edges were rounded and worn, the leather cracked and drying out. I think she kept it mostly because she hadn't been able to find another one like it. I checked the price tag and did the math.

Not bad for a Christmas present.

"Okay, this is nice. This'll do." I nodded and smiled at Justine. She took the opportunity to nod and smile back, reaching over and rubbing my upper arm, pressing her thumb into my muscle.

"So will this," she whispered, leaning in, her hand still on my upper arm. "Very firm. Very nice." Her eyes were bright and she was watching for my reaction.

I took her wrist in my free hand, but she dug in a bit. "I'll bet you're really strong."

I was about to tell her she wouldn't find out, but I was interrupted.

"Baxter!"

Penny.

"What's going on?" She walked up on the two of us as Justine relaxed her grip on my arm, turning her hand so that she brushed her fingertips across my palm, her touch feather-light as she let go.

"Shopping." I answered, knowing that that really wasn't the answer to the question she was asking. "Christmas."

Penny was skeptical, and it was written all over her face. She side-eyed Justine for cause. "Well, if it's for Tess, she'll be here any minute, she's taking a call outside."

"Thanks for the heads-up. What do you think of this? For Tess?" I showed her the wallet, trying to placate her.

She nodded. "Okay. Yeah, that's nice. She'd like that."

I nodded, replicating her head movement, then saw Tess coming through the door. She had stopped and was scanning the layout, spotting Penny, her face lighting up in pleasant surprise when she saw me. One second later, the surprise was still there but less pleasant when she settled on Justine.

I glanced at Justine, noting what I considered to be a rather self-satisfied look. Justine caught my eye as she reached over and took the wallet from me.

Tess made her way to us and we hugged hello, exchanging a quick kiss.

"What a surprise."

The flatness of that statement conveyed the fact that she'd likely reconsidered her initial happiness at seeing me with the discussion we'd had last night before sleep.

Sitting up in the bed, facing Tess, I had crossed my heart, swearing that I would not do exactly what I was doing.

That I wouldn't go looking for trouble.

And now, standing in that store, next to Justine, made it seem as if I'd just served up a double portion for Tess's consideration.

She sighed. "You promised."

I ducked my head. I felt like I had chipped off a piece of her trust, breaking my word to her. "I'm sorry."

"Hm." She turned her attention to the young woman next to me. "So, Justine, how's school?"

Maybe she was being cordial or maybe she didn't want to discuss this any further, for now. I knew, though, that it would not be forgotten.

Justine had watched our conversation, a bemused expression on her face, but now she totally engaged Tess with a smile. "Fine. I have the afternoon off and dropped by the hospital to see if Meg wanted to do a little shopping. Baxter decided she'd tag along."

Well, damn. That wasn't entirely true.

Penny looked at me, her expression unreadable.

I have to think that Justine knew exactly what she was doing, she seemed to be enjoying my discomfort.

"Speaking of Meg," Justine added, as Meg joined us.

"Hey, y'all! The bargains are incredible--look at these bags!" She had three totes in her hands and was wearing two shoulder bags. She turned from side-to-side to show us.

Penny said "May I?" and took the one Meg offered her. She held it up close to see the designer mark, examined the stitching, then opened it up and ran a hand through the interior. "Huh."

Tess was watching her. "Well?"

Penny turned the bag in her hand, pondering, then shrugged and said "I have no idea," as she handed the bag back to Meg.

Justine gazed at Penny like she was sizing her up.

Penny wasn't sure how to answer the questioning look Meg was giving her, without letting the cat out of the bag, so to speak, and she ended up just smiling and saying "Nice bag."

Meg nodded. "I think that's the one I'm getting." She looked at Justine. "Ready to go?"

"Yes. I found this great little wallet, isn't it cute?" She held up Tess's Christmas present for Meg to have a look. "Let's check out. Good seeing you," she said to Tess and Penny, then "Bye, Baxter," with that same smug-damn smile as I watched her walk away.

Maybe I stood watching a little too long, I was at a loss with Justine taking the wallet with her, but when I turned back to Tess and Penny, I found them both looking a bit stern.

Penny went first. "What the hell are you doing with her?"

And I had no real answer for that, with Tess standing there.

"You *promised.*" Tess repeated it so quietly but the tone of disappointment was profound.

And that cut like a knife.

I couldn't look at her. I had no apology to give.

She turned and walked out.

Penny, being Penny, punched me in the shoulder, then followed Tess.

Damn.

Damn.

Damn.

Damn.

11

That afternoon, I was in the kennel washing food bowls when Justine came in and lifted herself up onto the counter, perching right next to me at the sinks, her head above mine.

"Someone's whipped."

"What?" I looked up from my work. She was leaning over me, eyes narrow, that damn smile on her lips.

"You heard me."

I shrugged and shook my head.

"I've got something for you," she announced in a sing-song way, holding up a small plastic bag, letting it dangle between us.

"Is that Tess's wallet?"

"Well, it's mine now, but I might let you buy it from me. For the right price."

I knew where this was going but I had to ask. "Oh? And what would that be?"

She just scoffed. "Baxter, you are not as thick-headed as you want me to believe."

I opened the spigot to heat the soapy water. "Keep it."

"Now, now," she continued, "you might want to think about this. I dare you to go back into that store and see if you can find another wallet like this one. I just don't think you have the balls to defy your *wife*."

She said the word almost like a slur, the challenge a taunt in itself.

"I love my wife."

My firm conviction seemed to be nothing more than fodder for her reply.

"Baxter, please. I don't care. This is not about love, or your wife."

She reached down into the water, dipping under the surface to stroke the inside of my forearm, the hot soapy water letting her hand glide with ease up to the bend of my elbow and down again. She leaned close to me, whispering, "This is about you. You love women. Especially when they're hot and wet for you. Like I am right now."

I pulled away from her.

I was finished with the chore, and with this conversation, and I pulled the plug on both, rinsing off under the running water as the sink drained. I turned to face her as I dried my arms and hands.

"*I love my wife.*"

"Whatever." She dropped onto the floor, moving closer to me, nearly touching, looking up into my eyes.

"Think about my offer, Baxter. You really shouldn't pass me up." She turned and sauntered to the door, knowing that I was watching her go, adding a little swing to her gait, accentuating her round, firm bottom. She broke into a smile as she held the door for Tess about to enter, carrying two cups of coffee on a to-go tray.

Geezus. Time is just not on my side at all today.

"I brought a little...peace offering." Tess indicated the tray but was watching the door close behind Justine, and I smiled, a bit weakly, and maybe it was really more like a grimace, as I grabbed paper towels and dried the countertop, opening the drawer underneath and sweeping the bag with the wallet into it as I did.

"Well, thank you, ma'am, that's more than welcome right now." We met and I wrapped my arms around her, giving her a soft kiss.

She leaned up, kissing me in turn. I hummed and pulled her closer, both of us sighing as we leaned against each other.

"Don't be mad at me," I whispered.

"I'm not mad, just...disappointed."

Please, can anyone tell me why that word is so much worse?

She took a step back, breaking my hold, patting me lightly on my arm, but looking away, changing the subject and handing me my cup of coffee. She looked across the kennel at the door. "So, does she spend a lot of time here?"

"No." Maybe my answer was too quick, too dry. Tess looked skeptical, her head tilted and her eyes a bit narrow.

What is it with these women that they don't believe anything I say?

And then I gave that a second thought.

"She just turned up today, I really hardly ever see her."

Tess nodded at that but the skeptical look remained. "I just...don't trust her." She shrugged her shoulders.

Well, I was certainly not going to tell her she had good reason. "I know."

I sipped my coffee. It burned my tongue a bit, but I figured that was karma.

Huh. And here I was expecting just cream and sugar.

Honestly, I felt like I was in a hole, and that I couldn't breathe, with Tess being upset and Justine being...well, Justine.

I heard a little whimper, wondering for half a second if I'd actually made that sound, but then it escalated into lots of whimpers, then the full cries of hungry puppies waking up and wanting their afternoon feeding.

"C'mon, come see the puppies," I took Tess by the hand and walked her over to the whelping box in the end kennel.

"Oh, look, they're beautiful! Can I touch them?"

"Sure." The mama had been sunning herself outside but joined us as soon as she'd heard her babies' cries. She stepped into the box and settled in, the puppies scrambling, climbing over each other for access.

Tess laughed as she watched the tubby little monsters swarm their mother.

My claustrophobic feeling began lifting with that.

I mean, come on.

Puppies.

Who can be mad when there are puppies?

12

The radio was on, low, tuned to WWTR. There were lit candles, fresh sheets on the bed, Rosie and Sophie had soup bones to work on out on the porch, and Tess had joined me in the shower before leading me by the hand into the bedroom, pushing me down and straddling me, kissing me long and slow, skimming her hands up my arms and into my hair.

She knew that she was having an effect when I involuntarily stretched as she found her way between my legs, her hand languid in its movements as she brushed against me, alternating her fingertips with her palm.

"You feel so good," she murmured as she moved down my jaw and lightly touched her lips against my throat.

Tess has a finesse in her kissing that I have never felt before, and it can completely incapacitate me. Her lips on mine are pure pleasure and she delivers them in increments, like kindling a fire--never too much or too little, just a soft warming, gently adding tinder until I am fully on fire.

I groaned under her. She continued, sliding down, kissing and sucking, her warm hand still on me, moving and kneading.

She made her way between my legs, teasing me with the lightest of touches, her warm breath adding to my own heat. The first full kiss from her hot mouth caused me to suck in my breath and I was taut underneath her. I was panting with my want for her, and it was rapturous when her mouth found me.

Her moans were vibrations as she held me, her arms encircling my thighs. Knowing me like she did, she responded to my movements with those of her own and she built me up and held me on the edge before delivering the coup de grâce that finished me.

She laid with her head on my thigh, gazing up at me, her eyes bright.

"I will never get tired of doing that to you," she whispered.

I laughed. "I will never get tired of you doing that. My god, Tess, I can't move."

Now she was laughing. "Good. Then my plan is working."

"You have a plan? For what?"

"To send you to sleep with a smile on your face."

"You do that anyway."

"Well, this smile is always a little different."

"Because you've rendered me senseless. A happy idiot."

"Yeah, that's the look."

She moved from between my legs and settled up against my side, reaching across and picking up my arm, letting it fall in a flop back onto the bed.

"You are relaxed."

I nodded. I couldn't deny it.

She leaned over me and laid a lazy kiss on my lips. "Are you getting sleepy? Because if you want to go to sleep, that'd be okay."

"You're sweet. I just need a minute."

She looked so pleased when I said that and I laughed. "Don't be so smug."

"I can't help it. Oh! Our song!"

A love song was playing and I listened to the words. It had been popular while we were apart, when she was in Richmond, and it was a story of lost love and an aching heart.

"Our song? We have a song?"

"This one."

"Tess, that is not our song. It's sad."

"No, it's not. It's about finding that one love."

"That's sweet, but her love is unrequited."

"And ours is not."

"So what does our love have to do with this song?"

"Listen to it up to the third verse, it's us."

"He's in love with someone else."

"But up to the third verse, she's singing about a love that transcends the distance between them."

"There's distance because he's in love with someone else."

"Bishop!"

"Look, he didn't love her to start with. I never stopped loving you, Tess, no matter how far away you were."

"And that's what the first three verses are about. She never stopped loving him. 'Every night, you're in my dreams, you're the love I can't set free.'"

"So, we have three-quarters of a song."

She laughed. "Okay. I'll take that."

She leaned over and kissed me. I wrapped my fingers in her hair and held her to me, taking my time as I explored her mouth, her breath hitching when I softly stroked her back with my free hand.

We broke apart and she looked down at me and smiled. "Caught your breath, have you?"

I just nodded as I rolled her over.

13

The local radio station, WWTR, is located inside the Communications Department of Whitmore Community College, and it is manned by the students taking courses for degrees in multimedia and broadcast journalism, to provide hands-on training and experience.

The students in the utilities trades curriculum maintain the electrical wiring, designing power sources and circuits while brigades of welders and construction students monitor the broadcast tower and transmitter for repairs.

The station has been broadcasting for nearly fifty years from a farm on the outskirts of Tenley before the original owner/operator passed away. The family sold the station license to the college, along with all of the equipment, record albums, and recording stars' memorabilia in the station building, a massive amount of that dating from the 1970s.

It was a live-radio fan's wet dream and the college catalogued the lot and then sold it in pieces and parts to collectors the world over through an internet auction website.

The station is licensed to broadcast from sunrise to midnight, the low-level signal output ranging maybe 40 listening miles on a crystal clear night. It can get drowned out by the big stations in Richmond, Virginia Beach, and Norfolk, but it's the Tri-Counties' station and most everyone has their radios tuned to it.

Since the college took over, the various music genres have been corralled into three and four-hour listening blocks, but the program that runs from eight p.m. until sign-off on weeknights is the one that everyone agrees on.

That program is 'Silke in the Night,' and its star has a voice like...well, like silk--soft, smooth, and oh, so sexy.

Silke has a way of cozying up to that radio mic like she's snuggling up next to you, talking low in your ear, you can practically feel her hand slip into yours as she talks about the music she's playing, telling odd facts and anecdotes about the bands, the singers, the songwriters, about meeting them on their tours.

During the first hour of the show, she opens the station phone lines, taking requests from her listeners and making up a playlist, telling the Tri-County world who had requested the song and who it's being played for in her lead-in to the music.

She can bring tears to your eyes with her dedications, especially of the loves lost or from long ago, but balances the mood of her listeners with a lighthearted story of a happy ending with the next request.

It's the hottest show in town.

14

Carole Dailey-Biggs met Silke, whose real name is Erika Bentley, as the newly-hired Chairman of the Communications Department at the college, during the first staff meeting before the start of the Fall semester.

"Hi, Carole Dailey, right?" Erika introduced herself, shaking Carole's hand as she did. "I was told to see you about using the tennis courts, maybe finding a partner?"

They'd spent a minute or so talking about reserving the courts and players rankings, then another hour chatting in general after Carole had mentioned her wife.

Erika appeared surprised. "You're married. To a woman."

"Yes." Carole stood a little taller, squaring her shoulders, preparing to defend her marriage to Biggs.

Erika recognized the change in Carole's demeanor. She lowered her voice. "Oh, no, relax, please. I didn't mean to...I'm sorry, no, I'm just relieved."

"Relieved?"

"That I'm not alone."

Carole immediately understood what she meant and she smiled. "You are most certainly not alone."

They made their way across the campus to what was now generally referred to as the Comms building, Carole taking a seat on the small couch in Erika's office while Erika put on a pot of coffee.

Erika was from Georgia, from one of the moderately-sized cities, and had only recently graduated from the state college located there. She had been involved in radio since she was in her teens, starting with a local weekend afternoon show aimed at the area's high schoolers, then progressing to presenting the morning newscasts after graduation.

It was never just a job to her, and it was more than a hobby--it was her passion. Going on to university and getting her B.A. was the logical next step. Becoming the chairman of a Telecommunications department in a community college in southern Virginia was not something she'd intentionally set her sights on, but the opportunity had presented itself at the same time her four year relationship imploded, and so she moved to Whitmore, Virginia, into a new apartment and a new life.

She'd settled in nearly three months prior to the start of the semester and, after the newness of it all had worn off, found herself sitting alone in her living room far too many evenings, with little to do or see.

As the start of the semester approached, the station broadcast tests were done, passing with only minor tweaks required, and she had found herself with more free time than she'd expected.

There had been a few offers of coffee, or lunch, or dinner and a movie from the older male students, but they were most definitely not her type, and she gently shook them off with minimal fuss.

A rather large, tall woman in their midst had caught her eye, but she quickly learned that Stacey Pierce was married with three teenagers, so that was that.

Now, though, here was a tennis coach who was married to a veterinarian sitting on her couch and telling her all about Whitmore and Tenley and the softball league her wife had put together for the women in the Tri-County area.

She smiled, encouraged by her life choices for the first time in days as she felt the darkness lift.

15

"You take in people like I take in stray pups," Biggs commented, out of the shower and dressing in fresh clothes for their dinner guests.

"Maybe," Carole laughed. "You should have seen her face, though, it absolutely lit up when I invited her."

"I know you, Carole Dailey, you're a sucker for a lost waif."

"She's no waif, Biggs, she's the chairman of her department. Besides," she continued, surveying her appearance in the mirror as she sampled various earrings, "I think she was thrilled to have the night out. She spends her weekday evenings at the station and she's been home alone on the weekends, so I think this is a perfect opportunity for her to meet some women in the community and maybe make some friends, if nothing else."

Biggs was nodding her head to that. "It wouldn't hurt if she was to meet someone she hits it off with, though, would it."

That wasn't a question and Carole didn't take it that way.

"Right. Exactly. Wouldn't hurt a thing."

Biggs just smiled. Her wife, the matchmaker. "So, what time does this shindig start?"

"Dinner is at seven, but people will be arriving around six or so."

Carole spritzed her perfume in the air, then stepped through it. Biggs sniffed, then growled low and closed the distance between them, pulling her close.

"Not now, you'll wrinkle me," Carole laughed, wrapping her arms around the woman's shoulders.

"Not if I don't lay you down," Biggs replied as she backed her against the wall.

Carole laughed and pulled Biggs tight against her.

They had time.

16

Nearly ten days of unseasonably warm, dry weather made for a beautiful late October.

Carole looked out over the back yard at the clusters of women scattered about the seating areas and smiled. Dinner had been a relaxed affair, the shrimp boil was delicious, and the desserts were a sweet ending to the seasoned main course. There was laughter from the various conversations, a perfect mix for the evening.

"You're quiet tonight," Penny commented to Jacks as she joined her sitting on the brick steps leading up to the terraced lawn. She saw Jacks glance across the patio at the pretty woman talking to Biggs and Mary Helen, a local high school teacher, then look back down at her dessert.

"Oh! I get it," Penny whispered. "Go talk to her, Jacks."

"About what," Jacks replied. "The sale on corned beef this week?"

Penny jerked back at that. This was new. And she didn't like it. Not from Jacks.

"Jacks Daughtry, don't you dare," she whispered sharply. "Don't you dare compare yourself to any of these women and think you are less than them. In fact, how dare you talk about my friend Jacks like that. She is smart and kind and multitalented and I don't ever want to hear you say anything like that again. Do you hear me?"

Jacks just shrugged her shoulders.

"I won't have it, Jacks."

Tess heard Penny's harsh tone and looked over at the two, seeing Penny's earnest look and Jacks's hunched shoulders. She smiled at Bishop and the other women in her group, leaving them to join Penny and Jacks.

"What's going on? Jacks, what's Penny giving you a hard time about?"

Penny didn't give Jacks time to answer. "She thinks she doesn't compare to the women here," she quietly informed Tess.

"Penny..." Jacks cautioned her in a low voice.

"It's true." Penny was incensed.

"Jacks, no, why would you even," Tess caught the quick nod of Penny's head towards the three women on the other side of the patio and immediately assessed the situation. "Oh. I see."

Penny looked at her and nodded.

"Just go talk to her."

"That's what I said," Penny informed her. "She got all snarky with me and that's when I got mad."

Tess sipped her wine and thought for a minute. She knew Mary Helen from previous get-togethers, and she was honestly a bit of a bore, but she'd only briefly been introduced to the third woman, learning that her name was Erika and that she worked at the college with Carole.

She suddenly reached down and took Jacks by the hand, pulling her up and wrapping her arm through hers, then walking them across the space that separated the two groups of women. Penny watched, surprised, then tagged along behind them.

"Hi, hey, y'all, what a beautiful evening," Tess remarked as they joined the three women. "That was a terrific dinner," she acknowledged to Dr. Biggs. "Just great. Hi, I'm Tess Hayes-Baxter, this is my friend, Jacks Daughtry."

Mary Helen nodded and smiled at the two newcomers as she took a sip of wine, but the third woman reached over and shook hands with Tess and Jacks. "Erika Bentley, nice to meet you." She looked at Tess. "So, you're hyphenated. Baxter. That Baxter?" She pointed towards Bishop standing in another group with Carole.

"That's my wife," Tess said proudly.

"Are all of you married?" Erika wondered aloud.

"No! No, no, not all, not at all," Tess replied. "Jacks here isn't married. Uh, Mary Helen? Are you married?"

Mary Helen shook her head at that.

"I'm not married." Penny added her two cents.

Tess laughed. "You and Hatch might as well be."

Penny looked thoughtful. "Yeah, you're right."

"So," Tess stalled as she quickly searched about for a topic of conversation. "We were just talking, over there, about the...ah, the tennis tournament and who's going to win the Grand Slam this year." She noticed Erika's eyes light at that and plowed ahead. "Jacks, who did you think would win?"

Jacks stood staring at Tess, caught a bit off-guard, and it took a few seconds, but then she offered her answer and it wasn't the reigning champion. Mary Helen scoffed at that, but Erika tilted her head in thought.

"Hm. So, you think that she hasn't really come back from that shoulder injury, do you?"

Jacks shook her head. "No, I don't. She loses power in her serves over the course of the game, and her backhand is weak, too, that's why she's not going to make it to the finals this year."

Erika nodded. "I thought the same thing, watching her in this morning's match. So you think Sweeney has a shot at the title?"

"I think she's going to be the player to watch for the next ten years if she doesn't get injured."

"Wow." Erika smiled at that.

"She's young, she's disciplined, if she can stay out of trouble, she'll be the one to beat."

"You know, I was really impressed with her, too. Do you play?"

"A little," Jacks replied. "I've been taking lessons from Carole when we both have the time."

"Chess is Jacks's game," Penny interjected. "She's a wizard at chess."

Erika was delighted to hear that. "I play chess, but I haven't had anyone to play with, so I've been playing online. It's not nearly as much fun. Maybe we could...would you be interested...?" And she tilted her head, gazing at Jacks.

Jacks stood looking at her, the delight registering on her face. Penny kept her eyes on Erika but lightly nudged at Jacks's foot, tapping her into answering.

"Yes! Yes, of course, I'd love it!"

Erika nodded at that, smiling. "I'm usually busy during the weeknights, with my show and all, but I'm free on the weekends."

It only took a few seconds, and then Jacks was all wide-eyed with awe. "Oh my god, now I know...you're Silke."

"Shh, don't say that too loud," Erika chuckled. "I like my anonymity. That'll be our secret," she cautioned the rest of the women.

"Oh, sure, of course," Jacks replied, all of the women nodding, except for Mary Helen, who looked upon them with a bit of wonder, obviously not a die-hard listener.

Tess stepped back, a little pleased with herself and the way things had turned out, and she scanned the groups for Bishop, who had wandered off somewhere.

17

I exited the bathroom and was starting down the hallway when someone rushed me from the side and pushed me into a bedroom, closing the door.

"What the hell?" I blinked, trying to adjust to the dark, but I recognized the voice.

"Hello, puppy."

The light on the dressing table clicked on and she stood in front of the door, arms crossed and smelling like liquor.

"You're drunk."

"I've had a few drinks, but I'm not drunk. I know exactly what I'm doing."

"Then you know you shouldn't be doing this."

"You really don't want me. Really?"

"Dammit, Justine, I'm married. I love my wife!"

"Did I say anything about love? About leaving your precious wife? Gawd, Baxter, you don't have to love someone to fuck them."

"I'm not doing this." I moved towards her and the door. "Get out of my way."

"Baxter, just think about it. I'm giving it all to you, every bit of me, any way you want me."

She grabbed my hand and pressed it to her breast, lightly swaying under it. "Doesn't that feel good to you? Sure feels good to me."

I felt her nipple harden beneath her blouse and I pulled my hand away. "Justine. Stop. Now."

"Just think about what I'm offering you." Her voice took on a low, husky quality. "It won't be one-sided, baby, I want to do you, too. I've been told I have a very hot mouth."

She caressed my arm, her fingers lightly grazing up to my elbow then back down again.

"Justine, let me out."

"Fine, Baxter. I'll let you go this time, but just this once. You know where to find me if you change your mind. I'll be right here, thinking about you. Think about *that* while you're out there standing next to your wife."

She opened the door and pushed me out of the room.

"See you, sugar," she laughed as she closed the door.

I shook my head and turned.

And saw Tess standing at the end of the hall.

18

She turned and walked away, steps ahead of me, snatching up her glass of wine as she passed it on the kitchen island, exiting the open French doors to the patio, her posture ramrod straight. I didn't need to see her face to know that she was upset.

I stood at the island, watching her move past the small groups to take a seat on the brick steps, leaning against the retaining wall beside her and taking a sip from her glass, her eyes downcast. Hatch made her way over, sitting down next to her, her lips moving, then Tess shaking her head and keeping her eyes averted.

"Hey!"

Startled, my hand hit the stack of cocktail napkins, sending them up into the air, Penny breaking into a laugh as they rained down onto the floor.

"What's got you so jumpy?"

I bent down and began picking up the white squares, Penny joining me, looking at my face as we combined them and began sorting them into a more respectable-looking pile.

"Baxter..." She waited for an answer to a question she didn't have to ask, we'd spent too much time together for me to ever try to keep anything from her.

"I'm in trouble and I don't know what to do about it."

"You mean about going to the pop-up shop? Because I can tell you that Tess was mad, but not as mad," she directed an erratic finger wave at me, "as all that."

I shook my head, my voice low. "Not that. It doesn't help that I've already upset her, but this is for something I didn't do."

"What?"

About that time, Justine entered the kitchen, taking on a smug smirk as I looked over at her. She poured a rum and coke, her eyes moving from the glass, then to me and back again.

When she finished, she shook her head, making disparaging noises as she walked out the doors and onto the patio, joining Carole and Biggs talking with Mary Helen and another woman just outside.

Penny watched all of this without a word and now she stood there squinting at me. "Just what the hell was that all about?"

"That's why I'm in trouble."

"What did you do?"

"Penny, I didn't do anything, but I think Tess thinks I did, and I don't know what to do about it."

Penny looked out at Hatch and Tess sitting on the steps. "She sure doesn't look happy."

"I know. What do I do? What would you do?"

She refilled her wine glass while she considered an answer to that, then nodded in Justine's direction and said, "Stay away from her," before she made her way out and across the patio to Hatch and Tess.

Well.

That really wasn't all that helpful.

19

"Take me home."

Her face was stark, pale.

"Tess..."

"Take me home, Bishop."

"It's early, the party..."

"You do not want to have this conversation here, Bishop, trust me."

I ran my hand down my face, nodded. "We should at least say goodnight."

We made our way around the patio, said our goodbyes to Carole and Biggs, Tess making no excuses for the early hour, merely saying how much we enjoyed it and thanking them for their hospitality before she shut down for the trip home.

Penny, sitting with Hatch, watched us as we made our way out.

That ten-minute ride was long and so, so quiet.

The girls were happy to see us, bouncing and barking until Tess gave them the hand signal that would hush them. It was something she'd rarely done before, and they picked up on the undercurrent of tension. We walked into our kitchen and she nodded towards the table.

I was about to be interrogated.

My blood was running cold, and I found myself shivering, but I tried to lighten the mood.

"Tess, shouldn't I have an attorney present?"

She put up her hand. My signal to be quiet.

"Is there something going on between you and Justine?"

"No."

"Bishop, you'd better not be lying to me."

"Tess, I'm not."

"Then please explain to me why I keep finding you with her."

"She's...she's...got a thing...for me."

"She has a thing for you. And do you have a thing for her? Is it mutual?"

"No, Tess. No! Not at all!"

"And you're not doing anything to encourage her."

"Tess! Why would you even think such a thing?"

"Because I keep finding you two together! What were you doing in that bedroom with her, Bishop?"

"I was trying to get out of that bedroom, Tess."

"How about on Thursday in the kennel?"

"Nothing there, either."

"And at the shop?"

Okay, so maybe that was where her distrust started. I had, after all, made a solemn promise and crossed my heart, swearing I'd not go poking around the pop-up event.

That I would forget my life as a cop.

"Tess, I'm sorry. I'm sorry I broke my promise to you about the shop, my curiosity got the better of me, but that's the only promise to you I have ever broken. I swear!"

Damn.

That was weak.

"You lied to me once, Bishop, how do I know you're not lying about everything?"

"Tess, you know that I'm not lying about Justine--I'm not. I would never cheat on you--you're my wife, we're married. That's the unbreakable vow!"

She had turned away from me. I couldn't see her face, I couldn't read her feelings, and I was shivering with the fear that my marriage was in danger.

I spoke quietly. Softly. "Tess."

I stood up, she heard the chair scrape the floor, and she turned, tears in her eyes.

"Did we go too fast, Bishop? Did we get married too quick? You were traumatized by what had happened to you in Richmond, there's no way you weren't. Not to mention Baltimore."

She stopped, the words seemed caught in her throat. "Did you ask me to marry you to make it all go away? To substitute something happy for something terrible?"

That took my breath and I had to stop to catch it.

We stood staring at each other.

I struggled finding my voice.

"Tess, I asked you to marry me because I want to be married to you. Pure and simple. No ulterior motives, no salve for the traumas of my life. The things that happened to me before I got here, and the things that happened after, were nothing compared to the loss of you. Nothing wrecked me like losing you, Tess. And I don't ever want to go through that again, I never want to lose you again, so I married you.

"I couldn't bear the thought of living one more day of my life without you in it. That's all I was thinking when I asked you to marry me, Tess, that you would always be here, that we would be together. Why would I fuck that up?"

It was Tess who was shivering now, her arms crossed tight against the tremors and I went to her, wrapped my arms around her, tucked her tight against me.

"Tess, I love you. I love you."

We went to bed that night, holding each other tight, an unresolved current of tension floating between us. I could feel it in the air, I inhaled it with every breath.

Did she really think that our marriage was a sham?

20

In the blink of an eye, Thanksgiving was upon us.

Now, let me tell you, *that* was a dinner.

We were all invited to Miz Maggie's and Jared's house for the biggest spread I have ever seen. The best surprise, though, was to see Kane and Christy come through the front door, and I'd swear Hatch and Kane were both crying when they finally let go of each other.

Though it's not typically a Thanksgiving sort of drink, Jared served up his special margaritas with everyone feeling the joy by their second ones.

And that was when Kane and Christy announced their engagement.

I think we could all be heard yelling about that in Whitmore.

21

The following Saturday evening, I picked up Hatch and Jacks and the three of us headed over to Whitmore for supper at a Mexican restaurant we liked. Tess and Penny had gotten called to a crime scene.

They'd been really busy lately, but the holiday season is like that--too much 'family time' really brings out the worst in some people.

So, we're in the Jeep, the radio's on WWTR, and when Jacks tells me to turn it up, there's a commercial announcing another pop-up event starting today and lasting through the weekend, only this time it's in Whitmore. I look at Hatch, who's already looking at me, and we're both thinking the same thing.

Great minds think alike, right?

Now, up to this point, I've kept my promise to Tess, I've stayed away from the pop-ups occurring two, sometimes three times a week in empty shop spaces in Tenley.

We learn that the shop is in the same shopping center as the restaurant.

And maybe Hatch and I should never be left alone together.

I look over at her, she's already looking at me, and we don't have to say a word. We just know.

Hatch leans toward me so that I can hear her over the road noise. "You realize that if Tess or Penny hear about this, we're in big damn trouble."

We both look at Jacks in the back seat.

Hatch shifts between our seats to talk to her. "You can't tell the girls about where we're going."

"Uh, we're not getting dinner?"

"Well, yeah, but first we're going to go..."

"Shopping for Christmas presents," I said, cutting off Hatch before she can say anything even remotely close to "checking out counterfeit goods."

"Oh, cool, count me in," Jacks smiled. "Never gonna turn down the chance to shop for Christmas presents."

"But it's a secret, so no telling," Hatch reaffirmed.

"Right, right, I get it."

I looked up at Jacks in the rearview mirror, nodding that she understood.

"Cool."

And thus it was agreed.

22

This event took up twice the space of the last one, and with a much bigger turnout, too. The three of us moved off to the side when we walked in, surveying the scene. The smell of leather really is a bit intoxicating to me, and I sniffed the air, my attraction to the scent undeniable.

Standing there, taking in the racks and hanging displays of pocketbooks and purses, I felt a mild discomfort as I looked around, but I think it was because I was definitely out of my element.

Hatch and Jacks were looking around like they'd wandered into the wrong party, too.

"Uh, okay, so..."

"Do you know what we're looking for?"

"Not a clue."

"Oh, look, portfolios--" Jacks headed over to the stand covered in a variety of leather-bound notebooks as well as briefcases and planners.

"Wow, these are nice." Jacks had picked up a day-planner and opened it, looking through the calendar and address book. She put it down and selected a legal pad cover.

I ran my hand over a briefcase, the cool smoothness a pleasure.

Jacks looked at the tag. "Not bad. And these are really good knock-offs."

Hatch and I looked at each other.

"What?" We both turned to Jacks.

"They're not real."

"How can you tell?"

"I knew they weren't from the start. Do you see any signs advertising famous name brands? And look at this." Jacks opened the leather binder. "See how the leather is kinda pulled in this corner? You wouldn't notice just glancing at it, but it's skewed, not a perfect rectangle, and the stitching overlaps the tiniest bit at the finish. A designer item is perfect, and this is not."

"C'mere." She walked over to a display tree with handbags and took one off the hook. "Look closely at the insignia. That's not a 'C,' that's a 'G,' and it's thicker than the real deal to distract you. Also," she had opened the bag and ran her hand inside. "The lining is the tiniest bit loose in one of the corners. That would never pass quality inspection if it was real. And they're all missing the tags, there aren't any designer labels on any of these products, inside or out."

"How do you know this?" I wasn't challenging her knowledge, I sincerely wanted to know how she knew what to look for.

"The first summer my parents kicked me out, I went to New York with a friend and we worked on Canal Street in Chinatown. You can learn a lot about Shanzhai in three months."

"Shanzhai." Hatch and I repeated the word.

Jacks kept her voice low, conspiratorially. "Knock-offs. Look-a-likes. These," she smiled, gesturing at the merchandise, "these are good ones. Really good."

So, with Jacks' confirmation, we'd found out what we wanted to know, there was no point in hanging around.

"Well, then, c'mon, y'all, let's go," Hatch directed. "I'm starving."

"Wait, I want to get this for Erica for Christmas," Jacks interjected. "Or, one like it, without the obvious flaw." She shook her head. "I can't unsee that."

She turned and went back to the first display and began sorting through the planners. "Aren't y'all gonna get anything?"

As productive, knowledge-wise, as all of this had been, I hadn't done any shopping, and even though these goods were counterfeits, they'd still make nice presents.

"Yeah, let me take a look around."

Hatch nodded at that and we both turned and went our separate ways.

A few minutes later, as I was looking through the wallets and billfolds, someone jostled me.

Justine had edged up beside me. "You won't find another one you want as much."

"Another?"

"Hm. Wallet. Were you thinking something else?"

"Are you stalking me?"

"Hardly," she laughed. "I'm working here."

"Define 'working.'" I smirked, but kept my eyes on the wallets.

"Baxter." This was a breathy whisper and she leaned against me, wrapping her arm around mine, her fingers lightly stroking the back of my hand.

"Justine," I growled, low. "We are just not going to happen. Ever."

She huffed at that but she moved away, then abruptly turned on me.

If you can see a storm in someone's eyes, then I was definitely in for a hurricane. Her voice was low as she laid into me.

"There was only one wallet like that one. If you want it, take it. I don't care. I just want to have a little fun, Baxter, that's all, but I've wasted enough time being turned down by you. A girl can only take so much, then she starts taking it personally. It's fine. Whatever. I want you to know that you're missing out, though, so you can just go to hell and take your *wife* with you."

She turned on her heel and stalked off.

I watched her walk away, that saying about scorned women suddenly echoing in my head. I got the feeling that this was going to all come back and bite me on the ass.

In retrospect, I had no idea how close I was to the truth of that.

Hatch came around the opposite end of the shelving. "You okay?"

"You heard that, huh." It wasn't a question.

She nodded, her lips pressed tight.

We met up with Jacks waiting for us by the door, and moved on outside. Hatch handed over the sling bag she'd bought, knowing Penny's love of leather, for Jacks' approval.

She smiled and nodded, saying 'good eye' as she handed it back.

I sighed as we walked down the sidewalk to the restaurant.

Hatch looked over at me, shaking her head.

"Don't worry, Baxter, it'll be fine. I'm sure it'll all blow over."

I nodded at her attempt to reassure me, but if you've ever been in a hurricane, you know that they do not just blow over.

And you should never ignore the calm before the storm.

23

It took time, but with a great deal of hands-on care, Tess and I moved past the Justine debacle.

Tess made a phone call to the local real estate agency, setting an appointment to put her house on the market. She followed that with one to the local thrift store, scheduling a time for them to pick up the things she no longer wished to keep.

The next evening, we were in her house, sorting through all the things she'd acquired through the years, choosing what to keep, what to donate, and what she wanted to burn out of frank embarrassment, though that was mostly clothes that had gone happily out of style.

Having only known her in her persona of 'detective,' I couldn't imagine Tess following any sort of fashion dictate, and yet, here it was, proof that she was inclined to dress in the hot outfits of the day.

"Oh, please, put this on, I want to see it," I said, throwing a hot-pink half-tee and black tights in her direction. She picked them up and looked at them, scowling a bit as she considered the pieces.

"You know, there's nothing wrong with these." She threw the clothing into the box going home with us.

"Oh, yay!" I applauded her choice.

"Hello! Anyone home?"

I had heard the rumble of the rental truck as it backed into the driveway, and I called out to Hatch and Penny.

"Back here!"

Then they were standing at the doorway, looking into the room, both a bit wide-eyed at the boxes and the high piles of clothes scattered over the floor and the bed.

"Have a bit of a habit, there, Tess?" Hatch quizzed her with a smile.

"No more than anyone else," she sighed. She picked up the clothes from the chaise lounge in the corner. "Could y'all start with this?"

Hatch and I nodded and made our way through the piles and boxes. We each took an end and started working our way out of the room with it.

Penny had moved over to the bed and picked up a blouse. "Well, this is cute," she said, looking at Tess. "Are you keeping it?"

"Penny, don't help her, she'll never part with any of it if you decide something's cute or pretty or whatever," I laughed, shifting the weight of the chaise as we maneuvered it through the doorway. "And we don't have that much room."

As Hatch and I made our way out the front door, we met an older woman, blonde hair coiffed and she was dressed to the teeth, stepping up onto the brick porch and moving aside while we juggled the chaise through the narrow passage.

"Hello, I'm Cecelia Turner, with Tri-County Real Estate. Is Tess Hayes here?"

Hatch and I nodded our hellos, and I directed her towards Tess's bedroom. She stepped inside, taking a moment to look around the living room and kitchen before disappearing down the hallway.

Tess gave her a tour while we loaded more boxes, and they discussed updates and staging and how these things would affect the selling.

As Tess signed the agent's contract, I heard Cecelia telling her that Tri-County Real Estate would be more than happy to purchase the property outright if it failed to sell within ninety days of the initial for-sale date.

About two hours later, we had unloaded the boxes and the chaise at the carriage house, thanking Penny and Hatch with dinner at Johnson's before going home and starting any actual unpacking.

After feeding the dogs and filling Smokey's bowl, I found Tess sitting on her chaise, now angled into the far corner of the living room, the small table and lamp next to it having been brought from her bedroom as well. I stood looking at her, happily ensconced, and then I squeezed down onto the chaise with her.

"It's a little tight."

"Well, it's really only built for one, you know."

"That's no fun."

"You know what they say, a woman needs her own space. Or something like that."

I laughed. "Yeah, it's something like that." I kissed the side of her head. "Happy?"

"Very."

"I'm glad." I sincerely meant it.

"You happy?"

"I am the happiest I have ever been."

"And I'm so glad to hear that."

"Tess, you should know that I would search for you in every lifetime and I would die sad and unfulfilled if I didn't find you."

She looked at me, her smile so sweet, and then she kissed me. "We'll just have to make sure you find me then. We need a word or phrase, so that when you hear it, you'll know."

I laughed.

We didn't get any more unpacking done that night.

We didn't decide on a password, either, and, looking back, maybe we should have.

24

I wish I could say that the days leading up to the holidays were quiet in the kennels, and in the hospital in general, but that would be a lie.

Tracey and I were up to our hips in pets needing baths and trimmings before their owners' houseguests arrived.

By the end of November, we were exhausted, and I think Dr. Biggs could see it, because that next week, we had a part-time employee added to the roster.

Guess who.

Yeah, I didn't think you'd need a hint.

Apparently, Justine was available to assist us on the days she wasn't working for the high-fashion stores in the rush leading up to the big gift-exchange day known as Christmas. At least she was on her best behavior and was actually pleasant to work with, but that may have been because Tracey was always with us.

Or she really had given up on pursuing me.

We all shared duties in the kennel, no one was above doing any of the daily chores that were required to keep the facility in tiptop working order, from hosing out the runs to laundering the pads and towels, changed daily, to washing instruments and packing surgical trays for sterilizing in the autoclave in the supply room.

I was in Central Supply dividing out those instruments into their respective packs when Justine came in looking for more work since she'd finished cleaning the grooming area. She stood by my side and watched as I pulled the various surgical tools from the pile on the cupboard and placed them onto the tray I was packaging.

"How do you know what goes in each tray?" she asked.

I glanced over my shoulder at her. "Can you reach that?" I nodded towards the clipboard on a hook on the wall in front of us.

She pulled it down and looked at it.

"See the lines that aren't marked through? Those are the trays we used in surgery and treatments this week, so I know that I need to make three surgical trays and four skin trays. Now, flip that sheet and underneath is a list of instruments that Dr. Biggs wants in each of the trays, so that's your guide."

"How do you know the instruments?"

"Oh, now that took a bit of doing. Meg taught me the names and then it was just memorizing. Saying the names and holding them in my hand while I washed them up helped."

She nodded at this.

"Do you want to do a tray? I could start you off with a skin tray, they're the easiest."

She smiled and nodded at that and I gave her instructions while she made up the pack, both of us repeating the names of the instruments as she pulled them from the pile.

By the second tray, Justine was rolling on her own, had made up a bit of a song using the melody from "The Twelve Days of Christmas,' about clamps and 'snips,' a word we use for scissors, and we were both laughing by the time she was following my movements in folding the thick blue paper wrapping and securing it with autoclave tape.

She finished the smaller trays, and I handed off my last surgical pack to give her that experience as I filled the shelves of the autoclave.

Our work finished, we were standing in the hallway between the supply room and the lab.

"I've got to go, I'm working the store in Whitmore at six," Justine smiled up at me. "It's been fun, thank you for teaching me. Have a good evening."

"You're welcome. You, too," I replied, nodding and smiling in turn.

And then she left me there, walking through the lab and out to Reception.

I stood for a minute, considering our interaction, my forehead furrowed as I replayed the last hour with her. Dr. Biggs came out of her office and nearly bumped into me, neither of us paying attention.

"Whoa there, Baxter. What's wrong?" Her head was tipped as she took me in.

"Nothing." I shook her off. "Absolutely nothing." I turned and headed down the hall to the kennel, still pondering.

25

So I didn't object when Dr. Biggs sent us to Whitmore that Thursday to pick up some extra crates and pads for the upcoming Rabies Clinic. The clinic was going to be held on Saturday, it's a low-cost option designed to protect the county pets from rabies, but it also allows residents the opportunity for a casual assessment of their animal for any health issues.

We were picking up the supplies from Dr. Tedder's office, it was something the two vets did to offset costs to the host clinic clients on the bi-monthly rotation. Not everyone could afford a crate to transport their animal but if they signed an agreement to return it after use, they'd get their critter inoculated for the low, low price of five bucks.

Biggs had only had one client 'forget' to return the rented crate, but he surrendered it to the Sheriff's Deputy who'd turned up at his door the following Monday and it was all good.

I called Tess to tell her I was going to Whitmore for Biggs. She told me to swing by the house and pick her up, that we'd get dinner while we were there, and I paused just long enough for her to figure out that I wasn't going alone.

"Look, never mind, forget I mentioned it. I'm tired, anyway, it's been a long day. I'll see you when you get home."

I could feel the cold through the phone.

"Tess, there is nothing going on between Justine and me."

"It's fine, Bishop. Be careful. I'll see you tonight." The call disconnected.

I slapped the clamshell shut.

Justine and I went to Whitmore.

And then everything turned upside down.

26

Tess sat up with a start, blinking as she peered into the darkness of the carriage house living room. Rosie and Sophie were fast asleep. She thought she'd heard the creaking of the porch steps and she got up to look, pulling Bishop's flannel shirt tight around her as she made her way to the kitchen.

It was just a dream.

She pulled the collar to her nose and inhaled, taking in the scent of the woman she loved from the cloth, feeling her despair deepen.

"Where are you?"

That was a question she'd been asking for nearly thirty-six hours.

When Bishop hadn't gotten home by midnight that Thursday night, she'd called Dr. Biggs, who was instantly concerned, putting Justine on the phone with Tess. It was a tense conversation between the two women, but Justine advised Tess that she and Baxter had run the errand, and that Baxter had left the clinic parking lot the same time she had.

Ending the call, Tess felt that, while she did not trust the girl in general, she had no reason not to believe her now, with Justine sounding just as concerned as Dr. Biggs.

She and Bishop had been down this road before, on another night that Bishop hadn't come home, but this time felt different.

Making the necessary calls to put a search in motion, Tess chastised herself all the while, realizing that she'd gotten too complacent in the past two years, she'd practically forgotten that there could still be people out there looking for Bishop-- people who wanted her dead.

People willing to go to any lengths to make that happen.

She shivered, unable to shake the feeling that she'd truly lost her.

That Bishop was gone.

The night sky was fading as the sun began edging its way into the day and Tess knew that more sleep was not worth pursuing.

While preparing a pot of coffee, her phone buzzed, rattling the teaspoon next to her cup.

It was Hatch. Tess snatched up the device and swiped the screen in one motion.

"What!"

"What? Tess?"

"What have you got?"

"I got a hit on a 'Jane Doe' in the Whitmore County Hospital matching Baxter's description, possibly involved in a beating and found at the bottom of one of the city's overflow culverts late yesterday afternoon."

"Hatch, is she...is she dead?"

"No, no, she's alive, but she's unconscious. Want to ride over and take a look?"

27

The light was bright, flashing back and forth, and I was blinded by it, unable to see around the yellow spots now burned onto my retinas. Someone was holding my eyes open, moving the light from one to the other, and I tried to pull my head away, out from under their intrusiveness.

"Easy."

I heard the word, it was almost a whisper, the person holding the light was close and trying to calm me, as if I could bolt from my position under their fingers. I wasn't panicked, I was mad, this *hurt*, the light was too bright and this person was too heavyhanded for my liking. I held still all the same, knowing I was really in no position to argue.

"That's it. Good. Can you hear me? Understand me? Nod your head."

I guess I did because I was rewarded with another verbal headpat.

"Good. Okay. Can you talk? What's your name?"

"Bishop."

It couldn't have been more than a light whisper, my throat was so dry and my lips were chapped.

"I'm sorry, I didn't get that. Can you try again?"

"Bishop." This time I felt like I was shouting, but only because I was annoyed and I wanted to go back to sleep. My head ached and it hurt to talk loud enough to be heard.

"Well, Miss Bishop, it's nice to meet you. I'm Dr. Sampson and I've been waiting for you to wake up. You've had a really good knock on the head. Can you squeeze my hands?"

I felt her fingers in my hands, they were warm compared to mine, and I did the best I could, netting another "good" from the doctor. I tried to look around but my eyelids were heavy and the overhead lighting made it too painful.

"Alright, then. Still, you're doing much better and I'm glad for that. Tomorrow, I'll write orders for you to be moved to a room on the hall, it won't be so noisy and bright, okay? I'll see you first thing in the morning. Have a good night, Miss Bishop."

"Just Bishop," I replied, but I don't think she heard me.

28

Minutes later, the light was back in my eyes and I raised my hand to push it away.

"Well, now that's really promising. Good morning, Miss Bishop, I see you had a good night."

It was morning already.

Impossible.

"Miss Bishop, can you open your eyes and look at me?"

Call me 'Miss' again and I'll do more than that.

I managed to open one eye and squint in the direction of the doctor's voice.

"Hi." She smiled at me. "Both eyes, please?"

Okay, she's pretty. Nice to look at.

Maybe I should try harder.

I turned my head and looked at her through two slits, blinking with the pain of it.

"Hey, there you are! I know this is hard for you, but you're doing really well, we just need to get you up and going, okay? That's the plan, just so you know. We're going to move you out to the floor this morning and then we're going to get started on your therapy programs. I want you to work really hard with the therapists, okay?

I nodded.

"Good. Have a good morning, I'll see you later."

Not long after that, I had the sensation of air moving over my face and I opened my eyes and watched two or three of the recessed hallway lights pass overhead. The bed bumped and jerked and I bit back some really harsh words for the people steering it as it was parked in my new address.

The nurse gave me a half-spoonful of ice chips, waited for me to swallow, then put my call bell in my hand before she retreated.

It was dark and quiet and I sighed in relief before quickly returning to sleep.

"Hi, Miss Bishop! How do you like your new room?"

I cracked an eye at the overly-enthusiastic good doctor. "It's just Bishop."

"Well, I sure heard that! Okay, 'just Bishop' it is, then."

We went through all the examinations we'd done in the past and Dr. Sampson seemed pleased with my progress. She was commending me when the nurse came in and interrupted us, turning her back to me and whispering to the doctor.

"Really? Oh, sure, but let's keep it short, okay?"

She leaned over to me, looking rather pleased. "You have some visitors."

Uhm. Okay.

Dr. Sampson was watching when the three women walked in, apparently looking for my reaction to them as more evidence of my improving condition. I sat blinking, turning my head from the three to the doctor. The brunette had a police badge clipped on her waist.

When she stepped up to the bed and took my hand in hers, I expected her to introduce herself.

Imagine my surprise when she leaned in and kissed me on the cheek.

"Wow. Well, uh. Wow. Okay." I nodded, blinking.

"Bishop...we were so worried. Everyone will be really glad to hear that we found you. Captain Huff had every law enforcement agency and wild-life service in the Tri-County area looking for you." The woman stroked my arm, her other hand still in mine.

The familiarity on the officer's part was most certainly odd, but to say I had questions was an understatement. I squinted, one eye closed as I looked up at her. "Who's Captain Huff?"

She tilted her head, puzzled, but she didn't answer, her eyes were searching my face as I pressed on, looking for answers. "What about Captain Pike?"

"Bishop, Huff is my captain."

"Okay. And Pike is mine."

None of this was making any sense, but I had to know one thing.

"Did you get him?"

No one answered.

"Did you get Krieger?"

Dead silence. Seconds passed. No one moved.

"Well? Did you?" My head was pounding now. I wanted answers.

I needed them.

"Bishop." The police officer was concerned, her eyes searching my face. "Tell me where you are."

What is the deal?

"I'm in the hospital."

"Yes, but what city?"

"Baltimore."

Her eyes widened at that, and she paled, her voice quiet with her next question. "What year is it?"

And my answer sent everyone over the edge.

Dr. Sampson's concern was apparent. "Do you know who these women are?"

I shook my head. "No. Am I supposed to?"

The distress on the brunette's face was hard to look at. The shorter woman with curly brown hair stepped to the edge of my bed.

"Baxter, that's not funny."

I tipped my head. "It's Bishop."

"C'mon, Bax, cut it out."

She was pissed. The tall blonde wrapped her arm across the smaller woman, pulling her back against her.

"Why don't we all just let Bishop rest now, hm?" Dr. Sampson directed everyone out into the hallway, following behind them and closing the door.

I had a feeling I had just flunked a very important test.

30

"Okay, so what's going on here?"

Dr. Sampson had led them down the hall to a vacant consultation room, closing the door behind her. She crossed her arms and focused her look on Tess, who then gave a brief overview of Bishop's history, after confirming confidentiality on the part of Dr. Sampson.

The doctor listened, nodding as Tess reached the end the telling. "That would certainly explain the old scars we noted in our initial exam. So she's been in hiding for the past two years?"

"Well, not exactly. I mean, yes, she's been hidden from the people in Baltimore, but she hasn't...exactly...been...living a quiet life...exactly." Tess grimaced as she admitted that.

Hatch nodded at that. "Jolene Hatcher, DEA. We got into a little trouble this past summer breaking up a drug-smuggling operation and it may have put us on the radar of some very angry mobsters. Since she was found in what would be considered a body-dump scenario, I think we may be dealing with someone who had every intent in killing her but was interrupted."

Tess shivered at that but was nodding her head in agreement.

Penny, keeping quiet for far too long, cut right to the chase.

"She's lost two years time. She thinks Krieger is still alive and that it's the beating he gave her that she's waking up from. What are we going to do about that, huh?"

This woman had a full wind in her sails. "She doesn't remember us, she doesn't remember killing Krieger, she doesn't remember marrying you, Tess, she doesn't remember any of it! How do we fix that, Doctor?"

Dr. Sampson was shaking her head. "Bishop has only just awakened and started talking. I'm just as concerned as you. Moreso, frankly, since this may indicate a complication that is occurring as we speak.

"I'll schedule a stat scan to be done and we'll proceed from there. Now, you should know that this is still going to take time to resolve itself, there's nothing I can do personally, no magic pill, we just have to wait for the concussion effects to wear off and hope that her memory returns. You're certainly welcome to remind her of the things she's forgotten, but don't be discouraged if she challenges you or refuses to believe you, though, especially at first."

The doctor's face told of her concern. "It's simply a matter of time."

She didn't have the heart to tell them the rest--that Bishop may never reclaim those lost memories.

31

Over that day, my headache improved to the point of being a solid 'nagging' on the pain scale, a big reprieve from the 'excruciating' it'd been when I had first awakened. My IV was removed, I was brought food and drinks at regular intervals, and I had constant company at my bedside.

Tess, the woman with the badge, was apparently in charge, a detective from the small town of Tenley, east of my current location, which I was told was Whitmore, Virginia. Now, I'm from Baltimore, so how I got here was my first question, the second being just exactly why a small-town police force had taken such an interest in my well-being.

And yes, there was the matter of two years' lost time.

I made the detective prove the date and my location by showing me a current newspaper.

"I was assigned to your protection detail when you were sent to Tenley two years ago by the Witness Protection Service and you've been living under the assumed name of Lisa Baxter there. You work for Dr. Sharon Biggs in her animal hospital."

"Lisa. Yuck." I shuddered at that, then "I work with animals?"

She nodded.

"Cool." I smiled. "I like that."

She smiled in turn but it was a little sad, too. "I'm glad. I thought you might when I arranged it."

I looked at her, squinting, my forehead a little knotted as I considered that.

"You live in a renovated one-bedroom carriage house behind a...well, a mansion, really, on a corner lot in the town of Tenley, about twenty-five miles east of here."

"Omigod, wait! Rosie--and Sophie! Smokey!"

She smiled again, that same sadness creeping into the edges of it. "They're there, they're fine, everyone loves them. Miz Maggie and Jared are looking after them until we get back."

"Tell them to leave a light on for them at night," I started.

"Because they don't like the dark," Tess finished. "I know."

Have we had this conversation before?

She had reached over and patted my hand as she said it. The comfort of her touch surprised me and I found myself looking up at her, blinking, taking in her features.

She looked back at me, her gaze steady, unwavering.

"One more thing, Bishop." She stopped, as if she was considering what would follow. I tipped my head, a sign conveying my listening.

"We're married."

32

I squinted up at her, trying to read her face, waiting for her to crack at the sheer audacity of it, knowing that, of all she'd told me, *that* was the lie.

You know, like the game--two truths and a lie.

And then I burst out laughing with the ridiculousness of it, but the lightning bolt that shot through my head made me choke and I slumped onto my side, groaning with pain.

"Bishop!" Tess was up now and circling the bed, reaching for me, her cool hands on my face and neck.

I quieted as the waves receded, loudly exhaling each breath.

"Bishop," she whispered. "Are you okay?"

I shook my head just enough for her to feel it.

"Do you need the nurse?"

"No," I gasped. "No, just give me a minute."

I moved to sit up and she helped guide me back onto the pillow. My eyes were shut tight until the last of the throbbing subsided. I blinked them open, still squinting at her, and still a little tickled in spite of it all.

"What?" Tess saw my smirk.

"That last one. That was rich!" I would have been chuckling if it didn't hurt so bad, but I could still grin.

The hallway door opened and we were joined by the detective's two friends.

"What's so funny?" The shorter girl, Penny, smiled at us.

"Your friend here is trying to test me and catch me out, mixing up truths and lies. She just told me we're married."

I turned back to the detective. "Look, sweetheart, if there's one thing you need to know, it's this--I am *not* the marrying type. You'll have to come up with a better lie next time."

The two newcomers to the conversation turned to each other, sharing a similar surprised look--eyes a little wide, mouths round.

The tall blonde found her voice first. "Uh, Baxter? That one's true. I was there. You and Tess are married."

I squinted at her.

Penny was nodding as well. "I was there, too."

"Prove it."

Tess wrapped her arms around her waist. "Our marriage license is at home. In a frame. On our bedroom wall."

"Our bedroom wall..."

"Yes."

"*Our* bedroom wall."

"We're married, Bishop. We live together. We sleep together. We have every night...except..."

"Except what?"

"Except for the last two nights after you went to Whitmore for Dr. Biggs and then disappeared."

"So just how long have we been married?"

"Nearly four months."

"Happily?"

"Well. Uh. Yes. For the most part."

"Huh."

See how she hedged that answer? That's worth investigating. Let's see if I've maintained my status quo regarding relationships.

"What were we fighting about?"

Here, the detective cast her eyes to the floor, almost as if there was some shame on her part.

"I thought you were cheating on me. That you were lying to me. That we'd gotten married for the wrong reasons."

My mouth fell open at that.

We'd hit the trifecta.

"Well. Damn."

She nodded.

"So," I ventured, "was I? Cheating? Lying?"

"No. There was another woman, you were spending a lot of time together, but no."

"You're sure."

Tess nodded. "Hatch, here," and she pointed to the tall blonde, "filled me in on what you had told her, what she'd seen going on. I just took it to heart because we'd decided to get married so quickly."

I couldn't resist and I snickered. "Why did we have to get married so quickly? Did I enlist and I'm shipping out? Is one of us pregnant--and that would not be me, by the way..."

Her lips were a straight line as she shook her head. "We're not having kids."

Yeah, okay, so that caught me off-guard.

She was right, I don't want kids. Apparently, she doesn't either and the fact that she said 'we' means we must have discussed that at some point.

Okay.

Well.

Crap.

Maybe she was telling the truth.

33

Later that afternoon, I was questioned by two uniform officers from the Whitmore Police Department regarding the events leading to my hospitalization. They seemed none too pleased that I couldn't remember any details, including why I was in Whitmore to start with. That seemed to piss them off, but I'm used to that and I took it all in stride.

Tess, on the other hand, took offense to their line of questioning when they insinuated that I was involved in illicit activity because I was found in a less-than-stellar part of town. She was cold and short in my defense, reminding them that I was the victim in this matter and if they had proof of my engaging in criminal activity then they needed to put me under arrest, state the charges, and read me my rights.

I found myself taken by surprise at her standing toe-to-toe with the Whitmore boys in my defense. I think I smiled the tiniest bit about that, and just maybe that smile was a little smug.

Good call, Bishop, marrying this one. She's tough. Gotta respect that.

The two men looked at each other, the younger one rolling his eyes a bit, and then the older of the two laid his card on my bedside table, instructing me to call him if I remembered anything. I nodded at that, and they left the room.

Tess stood next to me, her hands on her hips, concern on her face and her head cocked a bit.

"Well. You were awesome." I was smiling at her, and I took the opportunity to study her a little more closely, catching the look on her face. "What?"

"Is it like this for you all the time?"

"Is what like this for me?"

"Just...the way men treat you."

Now it was my turn to be puzzled.

She went on. "The way they talked to you. That wasn't just officers being officers, they were rude. And then, there's Captain Huff..."

I had nothing to compare that to. I honestly did not know what she was talking about. I shrugged my shoulders. "Sorry, but that was all pretty standard."

"Gawd, no wonder you're an asshole."

My eyes went wide at that. "Hey! You haven't known me long enough to call me an asshole!"

"I've known you for two years, Bishop, and I married you anyway."

She smiled sweetly at that, then leaned over and kissed my cheek.

For once, I didn't know what to say.

So.

I didn't say anything.

34

I slept through most of Sunday, my headache still nagging but with less intensity. People were in and out of the room, staff and visitors, and I'd crack an eye at intervals when I heard the detective whispering to them, noting the different people and recognizing none of them.

I was discharged by Dr. Sampson on Monday afternoon after agreeing to follow up with her if I had any changes in my condition. She spoke by phone with a friend of Tess's, a nurse, before releasing me into the custody of the Tenley detective and her friends, satisfied with their assurances regarding my continued care and well-being.

I watched the conversations as they happened around me, a bit pissed, frankly, that no one had consulted me and what I wanted. I also knew, though, that if what the detective had told me was true, my animals were in Tenley, along with all my belongings, and if I was going to get back to Baltimore, I'd have to backtrack through Tenley first.

The trip took about thirty minutes, and I spent a good amount of time with my eyes closed against the bright sunlight. We rolled into town, eventually turning onto the main street, and I looked about as best I could as we traveled through the downtown shopping and business district. We drove past the town commons with the large gazebo at the center of the well-cared-for park, benches and statuary scattered here and there.

With quick glances, I took in the Victorian-era homes, the rare Greek-revival mansion squared on its lot. They all seemed to hunker too close to the sidewalks, leaving only narrow lawns between their front doors and the white cement, the town's original cart paths giving way to pavements laid for automobiles, two-way traffic, and street parking.

It was typical of the hundreds of towns scattered throughout the southeastern United States, their Chambers of Commerce all touting the benefits of small-town living in their visitors' bureau brochures.

Tess had been stealing glances at me, I was pretty sure she was hoping that what I was seeing would jar loose my memories. We turned onto a side street and drove down the short block to the stop sign at the intersection, opposite a massive home set back on a double lot. The wrap-around porch was shaded by hundred-year-old oak trees abutting the sidewalk, the roofline of the carriage house behind it visible at the opposite end of the picket fence wrapping around the property.

I shook my head when I caught her looking, and she crossed the intersection, pulling to the curb at the gate outside the smaller house.

"That's yours," she said, indicating the red Jeep parked ahead of us. There was a fair amount of scratches and scrapes and dents and I tipped my head as I considered its condition.

"Runs like a top," Tess answered the question I was just about to ask, and I nodded and sighed, grateful that it wasn't a lemon that needed constant work.

I opened my door and in seconds Rosie and Sophie were at the gate, barking and shrieking as they do when I've been gone too long. I laughed out loud at my girls, setting off another round of throbbing headache as I leaned down to pet them and accept their anxious kisses.

Tess was smiling as she followed me through the gate, both dogs bouncing and barking their greetings at her as well. She handed me her key ring with one key singled out, and nodded towards the back door, then headed across the wide expanse between the houses, towards an older woman coming down the back steps of the main house.

The dogs went through the doggie door as I unlocked the bolt and I walked through the mudroom into a cozy little kitchen, a small bar dividing the cooking area from the table and chairs in the recessed bay window overlooking the back yard. I could see Tess still talking to the woman and I moved on through to have a look at the rest of the place, hugging and petting the girls as I went.

The short hallway opened into a nice-sized living room, comfortably appointed with a couch, tv, small end tables with lamps, a chaise lounge jutting from the corner at the far end of the room. Two doors opposite the living room led to the bedroom and the bath, which also had a second door allowing access from the bedroom.

Moving through the doorway into the bedroom, I was taken over by the light touch of perfume, familiar because I had spent a good while in a closed car with the woman who wore the scent, and as I looked around the room, my eyes landed on the framed document hanging on the wall opposite the bed.

It was indeed a Certificate of Marriage, my WITSEC name and hers inscribed in a flowing cursive, and I rested my hand on the frame as I read the date.

35

She was standing in the doorway, Rosie and Sophie with her, I could hear Smokey howling his cigar-smoker caterwaul from the kitchen, telling me he knew I was home and he wanted treats and petting to make up for being left alone with the girl dogs.

"Do you believe me now?"

I grimaced at that, turning to face her. "I didn't not believe you," I lied.

She shook her head. "You absolutely didn't believe me."

I sighed. "You're right. It's just...I mean...I'm sure you're a lovely woman, don't get me wrong, Detective, and maybe getting married is not so deep in the realm of impossibility for me, but I just...I have so much on my plate right now."

"No, you don't, Bishop. What you're remembering happened two years ago, it's in the past."

"Not from where I'm standing."

"Bishop."

"Listen, Detective, I've got information, things that I need to take care of. They're dirty, all of 'em, and it's huge, the people involved, you have no idea..."

"*Bishop.* They think you're *dead.* You can't go back to Baltimore. Ever. They'll shoot you on sight."

Now I was shaking my head, which was starting to pound again. I walked to the bed and sat down on the edge, rubbing my eyes.

She took a seat next to me, her cool hand on the back of my neck a welcome presence and I sighed with the sensation.

She was quiet now. "Look. It's been a long few days, you're hurting, and we've got work to do, but let's take tonight off and start fresh in the morning."

I nodded. I was tired, in pain, and unable to reconcile my life in its current state.

"Are you hungry? How about some scrambled eggs with tomatoes, and cinnamon toast for dessert?"

"That's my favorite."

"I know, Bishop." She patted my knee. "I know."

Oh.

Yeah.

Because she's my wife.

36

We had an early supper, then I took a shower, washing away the smell of the hospital clinging to my hair and skin.

Living with another person would be an adjustment for me, to say the least.

Tess had opened the door to place a fresh pair of boxers and a T-shirt on the counter and I jumped and pulled the towel over me like a schoolgirl. Her eyes widened and she immediately apologized, backing out and closing the door.

And then there was the matter of the sleeping arrangements.

We sat on the couch, Rosie on my lap, Sophie on the floor beside me, and I petted them both while I reassured Tess that neither of us should sleep on the couch, that we could safely share a bed without her waking up with me on top of her.

I don't quite know how to describe the look on her face, one eyebrow raised, her lips pursed a bit. If she had something to say about that, she kept it to herself.

I went to bed not long after, leaving her sitting in the chaise lounge, reading. I know she was tired and I really think she would have liked to have gone to bed the same time I did, but wanted me to be comfortable enough to fall right to sleep. I woke up later that night with her next to me, her hand under my left butt cheek.

I let it stay there.

37

The next morning, Tess had us up and dressed and at the Tenley Police Department. We were meeting a detective from Whitmore, Curtis Dennings, who'd been assigned to investigate the circumstances of my disappearance or abduction or whatever it was that caused me to end up at the bottom of that culvert.

Tall, dark-haired, built like the quarterback he used to be, the man literally swaggered into the Tenley PD conference room, accompanied by Detective Joe Fowler, who was working my case from the Tenley side. Actually, Fowler and Tess were teamed up for this one--a continuation, more or less--of their earlier assignment of watching over me when I was first brought into Witness Protection.

I don't think Fowler liked Dennings much and I don't suppose it was because Tenley High, his son's team, lost the championship game to a blown call favoring their Whitmore rivals, Tess offering up that info later. It seemed a little more personal, as if letting this dog onto his turf had Fowler's hackles up, especially since it seemed that Dennings was hellbent on pissing on Tenley PD territory.

The Whitmore detective started off within seconds of tapping the record button on the screen of his phone, identifying the four of us, noting my waiving of legal representation, the date, and our location before throwing questions at me, one after the other. The problem was that I had no answers for him, and I don't think he liked that. He thought I was lying and he grew agitated trying to shake my story.

After five minutes of "I don't know," and "I can't recall," Dennings reached his limits. "So, you have no recollection of the events of the night in question. You have no idea why you were in Whitmore, why your vehicle was parked at Baljean's, or how you ended up in that ditch nearly a half-mile away."

"That's right."

"I don't believe you. I think you're lying."

"What? Why would I do that?"

"I don't know. Are you protecting someone?"

"I'm not protecting anyone. Hell, I don't even know anyone here."

"What?"

"Do I need to slow it down for you, Detective? Listen carefully. I'm from Baltimore. And I don't know anyone here." I looked at Tess, and then at Fowler. "He doesn't know?"

"Know what," Dennings sneered.

"I've been told I have amnesia."

"Well. That's damned convenient."

"Actually, it's been a real pain in the ass, if you must know."

Now it was Dennings' turn to look at Tess, then at Fowler, then back at me.

His face pulled into a rather obnoxious-looking smirk.

"You've lived here for two years." That smirk became a sneer as he pointed at Tess. "You're--hah--you're 'married' to Tess-- to Detective Hayes. But you don't know anyone here. Do you think I'm stupid, Ms. Baxter?"

"Detective, I don't believe I've known you long enough to give an educated answer to that question, frankly, but I'm certainly more than willing to put my first impressions of you on the record."

He was red-faced now, and his anger came off him in waves.

Fowler stood up. "Okay, I think that'll do it, Dennings."

The look Dennings gave Fowler was disbelieving, he was thoroughly pissed that Fowler was shutting him down. He answered through gritted teeth.

"I'm not through."

"I don't care."

They stared at each other for a beat.

"Fine."

Dennings stabbed at the red button on his phone, then grabbed it up, stopping only long enough to kick his chair back under the conference table.

"I'm done--for today--but keep yourself available for further questioning, Ms. Baxter."

Fowler followed him out.

I looked at Tess and smiled. "Oh, boy, is he pissed." I pantomimed dusting off my hands. "My work here is done."

She shook her head and rolled her eyes.

But she was smiling.

38

As soon as we got home, I made coffee, then sat down with Tess at the kitchen table. Calling what would follow "Memory School," she first handed me my wallet, found in the Jeep console, and my keys, collected from my jeans pocket by the hospital staff.

I noticed a key on my ring that was heavier and bigger than my house key, and Tess told me that it unlocked the front door of Dr. Biggs' animal hospital. I nodded at that.

I looked through the leather bifold, examining the Virginia driver's license and noting WITSEC had obviously used the Maryland picture on file when creating my new identity. Following that was a credit card, likely for emergencies, and the proof of insurance for the Jeep.

I counted the thirteen dollars in the money section and smiled. That has always been the amount I carry in cash, for as long as I can remember. Some things never change.

Nothing was missing and I was more than certain robbery was not the motive for my attack.

There was also a small black-and-white photo of Tess and me standing close, our hands clasped together, eyes on each other, our faces conveying what I can only describe as frank reverence. It was beautiful to look at and I spent more than a few seconds taking it in.

When I looked up, Tess quickly glanced away, she'd been watching, and I saw what I interpreted as hopefulness disappear, to be replaced with a grim determination.

Tess opened a case file box she'd filled with folders and notebooks before we left the Tenley Police Department, and I now learned that it contained my Witness Security file, the Tenley PD file of her daily reports regarding my case-- starting with the night I arrived in Tenley--and a file labeled "Whitmore Airport Field Reports."

She began with the Witness Security file since it was the initial file in my case, originating in Baltimore. It was her intent to lay out all of the information in a chronological trail of breadcrumbs leading up to the file containing reports of the incident at the airport.

She also had a plain white binder with my biographical information as Lisa Baxter in it and when I opened it, I was surprised to see my handwriting in the margins of the pages, apparently from the first time I had studied the details of my new life.

The detective presented the daily reports she'd filed, each one describing my early days here, adding her own comments that she couldn't commit to in writing--the specifics of how the personal nature of our relationship had evolved over time.

"You were aggravating and irritating and a real torment to me," Tess laughed, her green eyes sparkling. "That was after you came around, began regaining your strength--gawd, you were so hurt. But you were also sweet and kind and endearing and funny and I'd never met anyone like you before."

She stopped, smiling at me and shaking her head. "Oh, we had our differences, to be sure, but there was nothing about you that scared me so much as what I felt for you when I saw you standing in this kitchen the day after you didn't come home from softball practice."

"Where was I?"

"Penny's."

I held my arm out shoulder high. "Penny?"

"Yes."

"Were we together then?"

"No, not at all, but I was supposed to keep track of your whereabouts, I was supposed to know where you were at all times, and I didn't. I was afraid that...someone had found you."

"What was I doing at Penny's?"

And then I realized the most obvious answer to that question, and my face conveyed my sudden surprise at that. "Oh. Huh."

She nodded. "I was afraid you were dead. And that I would never find you...I would never know for sure..."

I swear I could see the concern, the fear in her eyes, even after all this time, and a chill passed through me. She was scared I was dead and I was out getting laid.

I felt a certain shame for that, but exactly why, I don't know.

"I'm sorry."

She nodded. "You promised you wouldn't ever fall off my radar again."

"Did I? Fall off your radar again?"

"You did. Four days ago."

Damn.

I blew a breath.

"I'm sorry."

"Bishop, you don't need to apologize. I'm sure you didn't intend to disappear the other night--at least, not willingly. I--I mean--*we* can't ever forget why you ended up in Tenley."

She was telling me that no matter how much time has passed, I should never stop looking over my shoulder.

39

At one o'clock, Tess decided we'd take a break and get some lunch, telling me we were going to the Pharmacy.

I looked at her a little quizzically, not quite sure I'd heard her right.

"Don't worry, you love it," she assured me, and I just nodded at that.

We sat at the counter just inside the back door, Tess directing me to the first stool while she took the second.

"Hi, Bernice."

"Hi, Tess, hi, Baxter! You want the usual?"

"Yes, please."

Well, that sure made ordering easy on me. I looked at Tess, and she smiled at the wondering look on my face. She patted my leg. "You get it all the time, it's your favorite."

I nodded. What could I do? At this point, she knew me better than I knew myself.

And when I finished my burger and fries, along with a few of her onion rings, I nodded and smiled at her as I pulled a mouthful of thick vanilla milkshake up the straw in my cup.

I swallowed. "So, we come here a lot?"

"Oh, couple of times a month, you eat lunch with Dr. Biggs here every other week or so."

My mind was a complete blank, I couldn't envision Dr. Biggs at all, and there wasn't even a glimmer of recollection in having any lunches here with her.

Tess must have seen that thought cross my face, breaking through, because she leaned over and set her hand on my thigh. "It's okay, Bishop, you're okay. It just takes time."

She sounded so certain in her belief that my memory would return, I felt like I was betraying her in some way by not snapping to and recalling all of the past two years immediately and in whole.

She was still smiling as I let my gaze wander over her face, as I took in the soft pink coloring of her cheeks, the shape of her lips, her chin raised toward me in her self-assured way. I could see how she had caught my attention, she was beautiful and strong and the most honest and open woman I have ever encountered.

Her green eyes glittered as she smiled and looked back at me. I was struck by a warmth that rose from deep in my chest, flushing through my torso and down my arms and legs.

The air was suddenly a bit warm, my breathing a little faster as I wondered what it would be like to kiss her, to take a taste of her lips.

"You're probably ready for a nap," she remarked, her concern apparent as she assessed my heated response to her as simply my being stressed.

Oh, I was stressed all right.

"Are you feeling okay?"

"I'm fine."

I was not fine.

I was thinking that I wanted to do more than kiss her, I wanted to take this woman to bed, make love to her, make her feel better.

Make her promises I couldn't keep.

40

That evening, we had a visit from the nurse, Tess's friend Ginnie, who came to examine me and report her findings to Dr. Sampson.

Ginnie is in her mid-fifties, I'd say, dark blonde hair held back with a scarf, wearing an old Linda Winston concert T, jeans, and slip-ons, and is very approachable in a laid-back sort of way. We were introduced in the kitchen and she wasted no time in taking me straight back to the bedroom so that she could perform her tests.

I took my place on the bed as she pulled her pen light and stethoscope from her bag then stepped to the bedside, smiling as she leaned over me. Her first questions as she shone the light in my eyes confirmed for her that I knew what day it was, and where I was, and that my speech was clear and strong.

We went through all of the motions that Dr. Sampson had put me through and then Ginnie changed her course a bit.

"Do you remember me?"

I shook my head.

"Oh, don't worry, I'm not surprised, I was just curious. I didn't see you much after Tess started taking care of you."

"Tess took care of me? When?"

"When you first got here. You were in a bit of a fix, really, malnourished, busted up, not moving around much. I got you started with protein shakes, then Tess began cooking for you."

Huh.

"I've known Tess a long time, since the night her dad was killed. Joe, my husband, and Whyte, his partner, worked his case. Joe brought her home to me that very night, she's like a daughter to me, and I suppose she'd say I'm as good as a mother to her, since she didn't have one growing up. I've never known her to be so taken with someone like she was with you, you really threw her for a loop."

"Her dad was killed? When? How? And what happened to her mother?"

"Lawd, Bishop." She pulled back from me, her forehead knotted with concern. "You really don't remember shit, do you?"

For the first time since I woke up, I felt almost ashamed for not remembering.

"No, I don't."

I think she heard the regret in my voice because she patted me on the leg and gave me a little smile.

"Give it time, sweetie. I will tell you, though, that she loves you with all her heart, and I wasn't at all surprised when she called from Richmond and told me she was coming home to you."

"Richmond. What was she doing in Richmond?"

"Honestly? Finding out that it was a life with you that she wanted."

She smiled a soft, sweet smile, her eyes crinkling. "I'm glad you took her back, I was a little scared you wouldn't, and that she'd be missing one more person in her life."

"Took her back. So, she left me?"

"Yes, she left you. And you can get mad about that all over again if you want, you can be hurt, but she came back for you. Because when all is said and done, it's you she wants."

I can't tell you how I felt hearing that.

Did I really think that I was just going to blow through here on my way back to Baltimore without causing some heartache and pain in my wake?

I didn't know our history, I didn't know her.

Most of all, I didn't know myself.

Who the hell had I become in the last two years?

And why was I thinking that the woman Tess fell in love with, the woman she married, was a much better person than me?

41

That next morning I woke with Tess lying against me, her head on my shoulder. It was warm, and comfortable, and I laid there listening to her soft breathing, taking in the scent of her and I felt a sudden longing for something I couldn't name.

I loved Tess enough to marry her, something I had never considered with any other woman in my past. Typically, my relationships were shallow, superficial--good times to be had by one and all, and not always landing in a bed.

The last time I'd lived with a woman, it had gone badly and I was glad for the end because I couldn't keep living with her disappointment in all the ways our relationship did not satisfy her.

I wouldn't marry her.

But I had married Tess.

And I laid there thinking that maybe this 'Lisa Baxter' was not the selfish jerk I am, she was ready and willing to make that leap into holy matrimony with this woman who had obviously reached in and touched her heart.

Had touched *my* heart.

As Lisa Baxter, I had pledged my love to her, had made her my wife, became her wife as well, both of us beholden to each other.

Till death do us part.

And that's quite the question, isn't it.

Where did Lisa Baxter go when I lost my memory?

42

I must have dozed off, and when Tess woke up I was a little startled as she moved away from me, swearing a bit under her breath.

Had she established boundaries that I wasn't aware of? Did she make them after walking in on me in the bathroom, realizing that I had no memory of her--of us--and it would only be considerate?

"Good morning."

"Hi. Sleep well?"

"Yes, thank you."

The formality was killing me. Her too, I think. She seemed a little sad.

"What are we doing today?"

"How do you feel? Want to run some errands with me? I can always bring you back if it gets to be too much."

"Okay, sure."

We spent the morning doing exactly that, picking up groceries and dry cleaning, small household items like lightbulbs and batteries from the combination hardware and all-around general store, stopping back at home to unload our purchases before getting lunch.

We drove out to Johnson's, a restaurant specializing in home cooking situated on the four-lane highway on the edge of town.

"Whew!" Tess pushed away her plate and leaned back in her chair. "I'm stuffed."

I smiled and shook my head. I had watched her eat a double serving of meatloaf and mashed potatoes with gravy, green beans, fried okra, a biscuit to sop up the remaining gravy from the empty plate, and two glasses of sweet tea.

Where the hell did she put it?

"What?" She looked at me, a small smile on her face. "Don't you say a word, Bishop, I've watched you do worse plenty of times," she laughed.

I looked down at my plate. She was right, I really couldn't say anything, I'd had half a fried chicken, the mashed potatoes and gravy, green beans, and cole slaw, and I'd left no real remnants for any scavengers to fight over.

And I certainly couldn't argue with her. This food was Sunday-Lunch-on-the-Church-Grounds kind of cooking, where you'd best not take more than you could eat under the disapproving glares of the mothers and grandmothers who would not-so-silently rebuke you if you wasted their good food.

I laughed and nodded. "What's next?"

"Well," she started, drawing out the word a bit, "we need to pick up dog food out at the hospital."

It took a few seconds to realize she meant the animal hospital. "Where I work?"

She nodded.

"Okay."

43

She drove us back into town and we were in the animal
hospital parking lot in a few short minutes.

I looked at the squat building, the front covered in shingled
cedar wood facade, the back two-thirds bricked and then
cinder block at the back for what I assumed was the kennels.
It was landscaped with a small green lawn to the side of the
front door, likely there for the nervous patients who needed a
quick stop before they went inside.

The receptionist, an older woman dressed in standard office
attire, met us at the door, throwing her arms around me and
pulling me tight against her. I was afraid she was going to
bend the glasses on the chain around her neck, but they
disappeared into the crevice of her large and surprisingly
firm bosom.

It caught me off guard, this familiarity, I wasn't used to being
embraced with such intensity. Actually, I wasn't used to
being embraced at all, so I wasn't quite sure how to respond.

"Baxter! You look good, how are you feeling? When are you
coming back to work?"

I was a bit tongue-tied, not knowing the answer to her
question or even who she was, frankly, but I made a show of
being glad to see her. "I'm feeling better, thank you. I don't
know when I'm coming back."

I looked at Tess for help.

"Ginnie Fowler is following her for Dr. Sampson, she'll be the one to give the OK, Marilyn," Tess informed her, giving me the woman's name as she answered.

Marilyn squeezed me one more time then let me go. "Dr. Biggs is in her office, I'm sure she'll be glad to see you." She walked around the counter and picked up the phone, punching a number. "Baxter's here."

She nodded and hung up. "Go on back," she smiled.

"Thank you," Tess replied. She lightly took my upper arm and steered me through the door beyond the counter, walking us through what looked to be a lab area to the hallway beyond.

We turned left there and met a short woman in blue scrubs and a lab coat coming out of the office, with a smile that made me smile, and I knew in that instant that she was one of my people.

"Baxter!"

But I didn't recognize her.

44

I think she knew it.

There's a ritual between butches. When two butches meet, we shake hands, and we do it whether it's been a week, a month, a year, or a decade since we've seen each other. It's universal and it is as comforting to us as a hug would be to anyone else.

We clasped hands, hers was firm and warm, a glad-to-see-you sort of grip, while mine was more of a very-nice-to-meet-you in return and I think that if she felt that, it didn't show.

We followed her back into the office, Tess and I sitting across from her as she took her seat behind the desk. It was very comfortable, we were all smiling, and Dr. Biggs cut right to the chase.

"Tess tells me you're having some trouble with remembering the last two years. Can you tell me which parts?"

"Uhm, well," I started, then made a full confession. "All of it."

Dr. Biggs looked at Tess, who dropped her eyes. "You don't remember any of the last two years?"

"Not a bit."

"So, in your mind, you've never met me before today."

"No."

Dr. Biggs glanced at Tess again, then looked out the window. Her gaze was thoughtful, and we waited only a few seconds before she turned back to us.

To me.

"I took you on as a kennel assistant two years ago after I interviewed you for the position, as a favor to Tess. You learned the routines and procedures quickly, and in time, I took you into surgery to train you myself. You were good with the animals and you enjoyed your work. You fit in here nicely and became an integral part of this hospital. I wasn't aware of the extent of your memory loss but perhaps if we were to start you back at the beginning, in the kennels, your muscle memory will trigger something and help you recall the time you've lost."

Tess was nodding, they both seemed to agree with that, so it surely surprised them when I asked "Can I think about it?"

The silence in that room was striking, I don't think they'd considered that I would turn down the offer. I quickly added "just for a day or two," mostly to fill that uncomfortable void I'd created.

"Yes. Yes, of course." Dr. Biggs nodded, smiling, "you have my numbers, just give me a call when you decide."

I stood up, Tess and Dr. Biggs following my lead.

"Oh, we need dog food," Tess remembered as we stepped out of the office. The door at the opposite end of the hallway opened and a cute young blonde-haired woman came through, stopping dead in her tracks, eyes round as she looked at our little group.

"Tess, can you give me a minute? Justine, help Baxter get a bag of dog food, would you, please?" Dr. Biggs reversed their course and led her back into the office, Tess looking over her shoulder at me as Dr. Biggs closed the office door. The instant it shut, the blonde grabbed my wrist and pulled me into the room marked Central Supply.

"Baxter!" She hissed. "What the hell happened to you? Why did you go back to the store?"

I looked at her, I had no idea who she was or what she was talking about, but she knew something.

She was my first lead.

I followed her to the shelves holding the bags and cases of food, recognizing the large blue bag on the bottom, it was the same as the one in the carriage house mudroom. Finding it rather heavy and that I was still sore, I struggled a bit to get the forty-pound bag up onto my shoulder.

"What store?" I whispered.

She blinked and the expression on her face was one of puzzlement. "What do you mean, 'what store?'"

"I don't remember."

Her eyebrows raised at that, opening her eyes wide, and I nodded to reinforce what I'd said.

"You don't remember. Anything?"

"Honestly? I don't even know who you are."

"Omigod. You really have amnesia? Seriously?"

"Yeah, seriously," I nodded. "Look, I need to talk to you, but I don't have time right now."

I had questions and I wasn't sure I wanted Tess around while I asked them, but off the top of my head I didn't know how I was going to work that out, Tess didn't seem inclined to let me out of her sight.

I'd have to ditch her somehow.

"We need to meet somewhere we can talk. Justine, right? Give me your number."

She smiled, a bit smug. "I put my number in your phone a month ago."

Now it was my turn to be surprised. Suddenly, Tess telling me she thought I was cheating made sense. And I'm thinking that Justine was the 'other woman.'

"Okay. I'll text you when I can get free."

She smiled. There was a devious little curl to it that was impossible to miss. "Sure. See you then, puppy."

Over her shoulder I saw Tess come to the door, her green eyes a bit narrow as she looked at the two of us standing close together.

Oh, gawd. Was I a cheater?

"Okay, I've got it, thanks," I said to Justine as I rearranged the bag on my shoulder and made my way to Tess. Dr. Biggs saw us to the reception area, all of us calling goodbyes as we exited to the parking lot.

I stood looking at the front of the building, trying to will any memory of the hospital I might have to show itself as I waited for Tess to pop the trunk.

"What did she want?" Tess asked--a little sharply, too, I noted.

"Who is she?"

I leapfrogged over her question in reply, and I felt a little sick at how quickly I had decided on deception as a diversion tactic.

Tess nodded, apparently reminding herself that if I didn't know Dr. Biggs or Marilyn, I wouldn't know her, either. "That's Justine, Carole Daley's niece. Carole is Dr. Biggs' wife."

So, I just may need a scorecard here.

"She's the reason we fought."

Oh.

Boy.

I was right.

45

Biggs was home, had showered and changed and was sitting on the side of the bed when Carole came into their bedroom.

She could see the veterinarian's face reflected in the bureau mirror and she frowned a bit as she went to sit beside her.

"Bad day?" Sometimes Biggs had to say goodbye to animals she'd known and loved in her practice and it was never something she took lightly.

"Tess and Baxter came by today."

"How's she doing?" The look on Biggs' face was disturbing.

"Carole," Biggs swallowed and looked up at the ceiling, choking a bit. "I've lost my best friend."

"What?"

"She doesn't remember me."

Carole held Biggs as she wept.

46

That night, I dreamed.

It was a jumble of people whose faces I couldn't see, blonde hair, and falling. I jerked awake as I hit the ground, Tess awake right behind me.

"Hey. What's wrong?"

She rubbed my arm. I kept my eyes closed. "I'm okay. It was just a dream."

My head ached a bit and I groaned as I turned over, away from her. "I'll be alright."

I swear I could feel her eyes on me, and I feigned returning to sleep to keep from talking to her about it.

The next morning, I was up before Tess, and I stood in the kitchen, drinking coffee and petting my kids, including Smokey, who'd decided to allow the occasional stroke on the top of his head. We were both watching a cardinal on the porch railing outside the window, and I briefly questioned whether that redbird could see us through the window, if he actually knew just what a tease he was to Smokey.

I may have had eyes on the bird, but I was thinking of Justine and how to text her, wondering if I had a phone and where it might be. I wasn't even sure it was in the house, to be honest, but I came to the conclusion that, if it was, the most logical place would be Tess's work bag.

It's one thing to search the bag of someone I've arrested, but I just didn't seem to have the nerve to go digging into my new wife's personal property.

I steeled myself and took a breath, then picked it up. I was admiring the smoothness of the leather as I ran my hand over its side, and I had the odd sensation of déjà vu. I stood there, eyes closed, holding the bag, trying to tease out the thread of the memory it was invoking.

It felt important, especially since I was strangely excited by it, and that wasn't because I have an unresolved leather fetish.

"Bishop...what are you doing?" Tess came into the kitchen, a quizzical look on her face.

"I'm...ah, I'm...looking for my phone, I thought you may have it."

Not a lie.

"Oh, of course, I should have given it to you sooner." She crossed the kitchen and took the bag from me, digging into a side pouch and handing me an honest-to-god flip phone.

I blinked at the old clamshell case and then I looked up at her. "You're kidding."

"No, I'm not, I promise."

"Maybe it's time for a new one, this thing's at least five years old. That's ancient for tech, you know."

She looked at me with an odd sadness, the edges of her mouth bending down in the slightest way.

I flipped it open and noted the blinking battery symbol at the top of the screen. "It's dying."

"You keep the charger over here," she said, taking the phone from my hand and getting the cord out of the last drawer under the counter, plugging everything up. In seconds, a chime sounded.

"There. So, I guess you've made a decision about working for Dr. Biggs?"

In that instant, it all came together.

Taking the job would give me the freedom to find the answers I'm looking for.

I smiled at her. "Yes. Yes, I have."

47

It was Thursday, I had three more days before I would be released from the medical supervision of Ginnie and Dr. Sampson, and I was chomping at the bit, ready to go to work at the animal hospital, but more on point, to get started on my investigation.

It was a struggle to tamp down my eagerness to be cut loose from the restrictions placed on me by Tess's constant watch.

We continued with Tess's Memory School and I used the sessions as a fact-finding mission, not just in filling out the two-year gap, but to also try to suss out the Baltimore connection I seemed so sure of but couldn't recall.

Tess wasn't the only teacher in her curriculum. We were joined by Penny Harris, who assisted in the telling of what they both referred to as the 'Airport Incident,' Tess handing me the vest with the two slugs still embedded just off its center.

There'd been a shoot-out.

I had killed Krieger.

They both watched that sink in. I squeezed my eyes shut, working hard to recall why I thought it so important to get back to Baltimore if whatever I was onto now didn't involve him.

Had I found another link to the Company that I can't remember?

48

I think Tess hoped that my hearing Krieger was no longer in this world would bring an end to my wanting to return to Baltimore.

But all of that was only the first half of the story.

Her discomfort was palpable as she told of leaving me that morning for Richmond, assuming a matter-of-fact sort of telling--trying, I think, to diminish the impact her leaving had had on me.

She referred to my being in WITSEC as my 'do-over,' my second chance, a brand-new start with a clean slate in a world that didn't forget, and I surmised that she was looking for her own opportunity to begin a new life without a history.

Without her history. One that didn't involve a dead mother and a murdered father.

I sat there trying to feel something. Anger, pain, what a lover left behind should feel--anything, really--but I couldn't capture any emotion at all. My memory loss had removed any trace of care or concern for what she'd done.

Tess had left someone else that morning. Not me.

Penny was looking back and forth between us, squinting a bit as she watched.

If she had an opinion, she kept it to herself.

49

The kitchen door of the trailer banged open, Penny slamming it shut after passing through, dropping her bag on the stool and walking around the bar to Hatch standing at the stove.

"Hey, babe," Hatch leaned down and kissed the woman as she pulled her into a one-armed hug. Penny wrapped her arms around her waist, pressing her face against Hatch's chest. "You okay?"

"I don't know."

"Bad day?"

She didn't answer at first. When she did, her voice was muffled. "Hatch, I don't think they're gonna make it."

Hatch set down the spoon she held and took Penny in both arms.

"Tess and Baxter?"

Penny nodded, her face still buried. "Baxter's gone."

Hatch didn't say anything.

"I don't know who this woman is."

Then she leaned back, looking Hatch in the eye. "And I really don't think I like her."

50

Tess had poured the coffee into mugs and carried them outside, the afternoon was chilly but clear with a warm sun, and she handed one to Ginnie already seated at the table on the porch of the carriage house.

"If she doesn't wake up, I'll come back, it's not a problem," Ginnie said before taking a sip.

"Sorry, Ginnie, she was playing a video game when the headache came on."

"I'll make a note of it, that's not uncommon. Do you have any more information on what happened to her?"

"Nothing. She can't remember anything and we can't ask the public for assistance because she's in Witness Protection. Showing her picture around or on tv might attract attention from the wrong people. You remember what happened the last time a picture of her got out."

Ginnie nodded at that. "Well, that kinda ties your hands, doesn't it."

Tess sighed. "I wish there was a way I could help her remember."

"I think you're doing very well with the history lessons. Just keep doing what you're doing, every little bit helps. So," she went on, the change in the topic of conversation signalled by that one word, "how are you two doing?"

Tess knew what Ginnie meant and she took time answering, her eyes wandering over the gardens between the two houses. Ginnie, always assessing and measuring, leaned back and sipped from her mug while she waited.

She knew Tess well, that her answer was forthcoming but that it would not be good given that it was taking time.

"We're two strangers sharing a house."

Ginnie nodded, her lips pursed as she considered that statement.

"I mean, she looks like Bishop, she talks like Bishop, but..." Tess was shaking her head. "I look in her eyes and she's not there. She doesn't recognize me. The woman I love, the woman who loved me...she just isn't in there anymore, Ginnie. And I don't know what to do."

She turned and sat sideways in her chair to look at the woman. "Should I stay here with her? Or should I move back into my house? Is it fair to expect her to stay married to me when she doesn't even know who I am?"

51

That evening, we had company.

Miz Maggie brought a basket containing jars of tomatoes and packages of yellow squash from her large freezer. I smiled at that, knowing that canned store-bought tomatoes don't even come close in flavor to the home-grown kind.

She smiled at me in turn then reached over and gently pulled at a hank of my hair hitting the collar of my shirt.

"Time for a cut, Lisa."

Lisa?

Tess, standing behind her, pursed her lips and shook her head. She could see that the "Lisa" had surprised me, and she was signalling me to keep still at that.

"Uhm, yeah," I nodded, then corrected myself. "Yes, ma'am, I guess it is."

"Meet me in the garden tomorrow at eleven, we'll get you all trimmed up."

Tess, looking pointedly at me and nodded her head.

"Yes, ma'am."

With Tess directing me, I felt like a five-year-old taking instructions from a parent in how to deal with a grown-up.

Miz Maggie smiled and headed for the door, calling 'goodnight' over her shoulder.

Tess and I responded in kind.

"She's going to cut my hair." I ran my hands through it, pulled at the curling ends on my neck.

"She's been cutting your hair for the past two years. And she knows how you like it. You'll be fine." Tess patted me on the arm in a reassuring manner as she passed me with the basket of vegetables, taking them to the freezer and making room on the shelves.

The anger hit suddenly, out of the blue.

I had spent the last four days being told what to do, what to eat, where to go, and practically what to say and I'd had enough. I turned and snagged my keys and phone and headed for the door.

"Bishop! Where are you going?"

"Out." I grabbed my coat as I opened the door and made my way down the steps. By the time I got to the gate, there was some distance between Tess and me.

"But...you can't."

"Why not?" I yelled over my shoulder.

She had followed me through, moving at a fast trot, grabbing me by the arm as I got up into the Jeep. "Where are you going?"

I looked down at her. "I don't know. Am I under house arrest, Detective?"

She seemed surprised to be holding my arm and she released it. "No. No, of course not, it's just...you don't know where you are, you could get lost."

"I learned my way around here once, I can do it again."

I cranked the Jeep, put it in gear, and left her standing in the street.

52

Penny had run to the grocery for Hatch and was heading down the highway towards home when she came up on Baxter's Jeep in the right-hand lane, noting that Baxter was alone.

She sighed. "Oh, what fresh hell is this?" she thought, pulling up parallel with the driver's door of the Jeep, tapping her horn, and then waving at Baxter.

Baxter looked down at her, the recognition flashing across her face, followed by a hesitant wave.

Penny motioned for her to pull over. She dropped behind her in the lane and they both pulled off onto the shoulder.

Baxter was out the door and walking towards Penny's vehicle. Penny had exited hers as well and they met in the space between the rear of the Jeep and the front of the classic MGB.

"So...what's up, hotshot?" Penny loved the woman she knew as Baxter, always would, and she knew her better than anyone in Tenley could.

"What do you want?"

"Where ya goin'?"

"Why?"

"Because it would be good to know."

"It's none of your business."

But damn, here was that other woman.

"You're right. It isn't." She thought for a second, then, "Why don't you come out to the house and have dinner with me and Hatch? Hatch is cooking."

Baxter stood blinking at that.

"Or not." Penny wasn't going to stand on the side of the road and beg, it was too damn cold for that. "I just thought that if you had any questions that needed answering, I could help you. Otherwise, I need to get home, so..."

And she left it at that, turning on her heel and getting back into her car. The warmth inside felt good and she paused to thaw a bit before putting the sports car in gear. Baxter had watched her, they were looking at each other through the windshield, then she climbed back into her Jeep as Penny pulled out onto the highway.

Normally, she would have shifted through the gears and reached cruising speed in a matter of about eight seconds, but she held off and watched her rear-view mirror. The front of the Jeep appeared in the reflection and began closing the distance between them.

Baxter pulled up to within three car lengths, and copied Penny's moves into the left-turn lane at the break in the median, following her onto the two-lane road that would lead to the lake and Penny's house.

53

The crunch of gravel and the headlights sweeping over the property announced their arrival as they made their way to the trailer set back nearly a quarter mile from the blacktop, hidden from prying eyes behind a curtain of mature pine trees and scrub undergrowth.

Baxter parked next to Penny and got out, looking around with a sense of wonder as she took it all in. The trailer was nestled close to the tree line at the top of a gentle slope down to the water, a dock visible at the end of the footpath. Nearly halfway to the water was a firepit with chairs and an outcropping of rock on its far side finishing the circle.

"This is beautiful. I'll bet it's awesome in warm weather."

That statement pierced Penny's heart and took her breath.

Baxter had practically lived here, had enjoyed everything that the property, and that she, personally, had offered her for nearly a year.

And she remembered none of it.

Penny realized that she now knew exactly the pain Tess was feeling. "It is. You're gonna love it. You'll see."

They made their way up onto the screened porch and Penny opened the door, waving Baxter through before following her in.

"Baxter! Hey! Good to see you." Hatch, sitting on the loveseat, reading, stood up to greet her. The two women shook hands, both smiling politely.

Baxter looked around, taking in the beauty of the living area and the kitchen, stepping over to the far wall to look at a framed magazine photo hanging there.

Hatch heard Penny suck air through her teeth as Baxter stiffened, inches away from the photo before turning to look at her.

"That's me."

"Yes."

54

I stood staring at the picture. If I'd had any doubt, any disbelief about anything these women had been telling me, it was all snuffed out by that picture.

Hatch reached over and took me by the arm, guiding me to the loveseat, still holding on as she lowered me onto the cushion.

"Easy, pal."

I looked around, blinking.

Penny pushed a short glass of brown liquid into my hand, passing one to Hatch as well before taking up her own from the counter. "Cheers."

We all three drank, and I gasped as the bourbon burned its way down before exploding in my stomach.

"There you go, now you've got a bit of color," Hatch remarked. "Hungry? We've got pot roast."

I looked up at Hatch and nodded.

55

Penny excused herself, heading down the hall to the bedroom, closing the door behind her as she hit the speed dial.

She started talking when the call was picked up. "Hi! Did you lose something?"

"Penny?"

"Yes, Tess, and I have your wife here, I found her out on the highway and coaxed her to my house with Hatch's pot roast. What's going on?"

"Oh, thank god," Tess sighed. "Penny, I don't know what to do for her. I don't know how much of this is from the concussion, but she's frustrated and aggravated and I think I'm just getting on her nerves."

"Okay." Penny paused, and the connection was quiet while she thought about that. "What if you give her some space and go back to work?"

"What if she takes off for Baltimore?"

"Then we'll put out an APB. Do you really think she'd do that, though?"

"That's just it--I don't *know*. I don't know what she'll do, what she thinks, what she wants. I don't know *her*, Penny." Tess's voice dropped nearly to a whisper. "She is not the woman I married."

Penny knew that feeling. "Yeah...well, then...you might not like this, but hear me out. Maybe you need to put your marriage aside for a while, it might be part of her agitation. Baxter doesn't know you--hell, she doesn't know anyone--but I know Baxter, and maybe I know this current version of her better than you regarding her issues with commitment."

She paused again, thinking, then "Tess, if you want her to relax and get to know you, you're going to have to start over."

"How do I do that?"

"Date her."

"What?"

"*Date* her. Like you would anyone you're interested in. Y'all just need to go out, get to know each other."

"You're right--that is ridiculous."

"Look, it can't hurt. Take her out to dinner, a movie, dancing. Baxter's a good dancer." She laughed at that. "She's a dirty dancer."

"Where can two women go and dance around here?"

"Well, there is a dance club. But I can't talk about it."

"Why not?"

"Because the first rule of Dance Club is you don't talk about Dance Club."

"Oh, come on."

Penny laughed. "Okay, I'm kidding about that, but a friend of mine does have a warehouse in Whitmore and she throws these very awesome parties for donations to pay her rent. All hush-hush, though, because no liquor license, no permit--you get my drift."

"Penny, I'm a police officer."

"Oh. Yeah. Dammit." There was another pause from Penny, and then, "Could you just not be one for one night?"

"That's not how it works."

"Okay, let me work on things you two can do. Legally. But you understand what I'm saying, right? Make her fall in love with you all over again."

"What if she doesn't want to date me? What if she doesn't want to be married to me anymore?"

"Tess, let's not talk about that, and let's just not even think about divorce, it's too early. First things first. Start with going back to work. Give Baxter some breathing room."

56

Hatch was setting out plates and silverware, Baxter was still sitting on the loveseat but now she was looking through an album of photos from the past two years. Penny rejoined them, carrying a bottle of red from the rack in the hall closet.

"I thought that would help," Hatch remarked, regarding Baxter and the pictures, nodding as Penny showed her the bottle label before Penny set to work opening it.

Hatch called Baxter over to the bar, and she joined Penny already there, both of them sipping their wine while Hatch served the now-filled plates.

"Smells delicious." Baxter leaned over her dish, softly inhaling the warm aromas wafting up from the steaming meat and vegetables.

"I think you'll like it." Penny smiled at her. Hatch pulled a stool up on the other side of the bar and sat opposite them. "You always have before."

Baxter gave a slight nod acknowledging the comment as she took a bite.

Penny smiled at Hatch. "This is excellent, babe."

"Why, thank you, ma'am." Hatch returned her smile with a look of love that Baxter couldn't miss.

"So, how did you two meet?"

"Well, hah, that's...ah...it's kind of a long story," Hatch looked at Penny, not quite sure of how to explain how it had started with Tess and their relationship in Richmond. Would Baxter be as receptive to the truth as she had been nearly a year ago?

"Just tell it, Hatch." Penny knew that there was no point in avoiding the truth.

With Baxter as disconnected as she was from Tess and her life in Tenley, she knew it wouldn't cause her any pain.

57

Over the course of our dinner, Hatch told of how she met
Tess and how we'd all ended up in Tenley on the stake-outs,
then our getting caught, and the rescue in Richmond.

She had my attention, her telling was not just fact-filled but
entertaining, especially when she described seeing Penny for
the very first time, her words leaving Penny blushing a bit
and smiling.

She took on a serious tone, though, when she got to our being
caught and kidnapped, and how Tess, Penny, and her former
partner, along with the officers of the Fourteenth Precinct had
stormed the warehouse, busting the interstate smuggling ring
Hatch and her partner had been tailing for months.

She seemed particularly pleased to tell of how Penny had
noticed a difference between the inside of the truck box and
its exterior, the interior coming up about three feet short. The
DEA CSIs examined the truck, found the false wall, and
informed their officers and investigators down the line,
pulling three trucks that first night, all full of cocaine, heroin,
and bricks of cash wrapped in cellophane.

Lastly, she told of how her career with the DEA had ended,
pulling up her pant leg and showing me the scars left behind
from the surgery on her ankle.

Hatch could have taken a desk job with the Department in
Baltimore, but she had opted instead to come home to Penny.

The two women were smiling at each other over their happy ending, but my ears had pricked up at the mention of Baltimore.

"Did you live there?" I was curious as to whether we'd ever encountered each other, not necessarily in our jobs, but wondering if our circles might have overlapped.

Baltimore is big, no doubt, but women who love women generally have limited social outlets in any city, so it wouldn't have been impossible for us to have been in the same place at the same time.

"It was my base ops, but I was in the field a lot," she replied. "I'd be home for only a week or two at a time in a three month period, and I didn't know a lot of women outside of work. There was one holiday, though, I went with one of the girls to a party on Cody Halstead's Big Damn Boat."

"Oh my god, Cody Halstead! Yes! She's a friend of mine! We go out on week-long floats on the Big Damn Boat once a year in the summer--it's a blast!"

And I cannot tell you the feeling of relief that common link gave me.

It was the first time in a week I'd connected with anything in my past. Granted, it was in Baltimore, but I was happy with it. It gave me the reassurance I needed, to know that I had memories.

And that they were real.

58

Penny looked at Baxter over the rim of her wine glass, saw the light in her eyes, color flooding her cheeks with the revelation that Hatch knew a friend of hers.

"Maybe this will give her a jump-start," she thought as she sipped, aware that Baxter looked more like herself in this moment than she had in the past five days.

Hatch saw it too. "A week on the Big Damn Boat? That really is the name of it," she said in an aside to Penny. "Man, I'm jealous!" She laughed at that. "I can only imagine."

"No, you can't, not in your wildest dreams," Baxter chuckled. "Penny, it isn't just a boat, it's a yacht, sleeps ten, full kitchen, a launch to make runs back to shore. We lack for nothing the whole week." She sighed with delight at the memories. "And I'm getting too old to party like that anymore," she confessed.

"Oh, I don't know, you kept up pretty good with the parties we threw here," Penny offered, smiling slyly at Baxter.

Baxter looked at her, and then Penny saw her lock in and really study her. She held still, felt Baxter's eyes on her.

She was Baxter's first connection to her new life in Tenley-- her first friend here, her first lover. Tess may have been there from the beginning, but Penny was there at the end, had picked up the pieces when Baxter was left devastated by Tess, and not just once, but twice.

If she could will Baxter to remember anything, she wanted her to remember her.

To remember them.

Because they had meant so much to each other, settling in together, both finding a certain comfortable satisfaction in sharing their lives when neither had been so inclined before.

Hatch looked on as Baxter studied Penny. She wasn't threatened by the love Penny had for Baxter, she knew of Penny and Baxter's year together, and she certainly had a history of her own.

She and Penny have that once-in-a-lifetime pairing, perfectly matched and undeniable.

She also knew Penny would do whatever it took to help Baxter get her life back.

Anything less wouldn't be Penny.

59

"I hadn't played with the Pride before, but I saw you sitting in the dugout and I decided, standing on the steps that night, that we were going to be friends."

I laughed. "Really."

"Yes." The word was emphatic.

"And were we?"

"Oh, Baxter, we were so much more."

I looked at Hatch. She just smiled and nodded. There was no jealousy or animosity coming from her.

"But I knew you loved Tess." She got up and fetched one of the photo albums from the book case, flipping through the pages. "Here," she said, holding the book in front of me.

I had seen that picture before, it was a duplicate of the one in my wallet. I nodded, and she flipped the page.

There were two more on the next page, we were still standing close but the look on my face was one of wonder, as Tess held my hands and looked up at me with such plain dispair.

"She thought we were getting married and she'd come to stop you."

"We were getting married? You and me?"

I did not know what to do with that information, and I couldn't believe that I had asked not one, but two women to marry me since I'd moved to Tenley.

Damn, this Lisa Baxter character must have been a real poster child for domestic bliss.

"Not us," she shook her head. "Tess disrupted Dr. Biggs' and Carole Dailey's wedding, you were standing up for Biggs."

I just blinked at that. "So these weren't taken at Tess's and mine."

"No, this was at Biggs' and Carole's, and it was the first you'd seen of each other in a year. You both carry copies of this picture because...look at your faces, Baxter. Do you see it?"

In the photo, I'm looking down at Tess, a soft smile on my lips and in my eyes, Tess is looking up at me as well, holding my hands wrapped in hers, held tight over her heart. She is speaking to me not just with words, her body is compelling me to listen.

I shivered, it came from deep inside, and I closed my eyes.

It was then I could see her. I was looking down into Tess's beautiful green eyes, and once again that odd warmth ignited, leaving me overcome with the realization that Tess Hayes was deeply embedded in my heart, that she was as fixed in the firmament of my world as the stars in the night sky.

I was nodding my head as I wiped my hand over my face, exhaling a little louder than I'd intended. "I see it."

"Okay, maybe that's enough for tonight," Penny patted my thigh as she closed the album and took it from me, handing it to Hatch. "It's getting late. Are you ready to go home or do you have someplace else you need to be?"

I smiled a little weakly at her snark, but was not at all surprised that she could tell I was tired and emotionally drained. "I'm going home."

"Want me to draw you a map?"

I chuckled. "I think I'm good. If I have any problems, I'll flag down a cop."

We all laughed at that.

They both walked me to the door and I shrugged into my coat. Hatch said goodnight, but Penny followed me out onto the porch, her arms crossed against the cold.

I had started down the steps when she called my name. I turned, she was at the top of the steps, and I looked up at her.

"Ma'am?"

"Please be careful."

This wasn't just a mild caution, she was sincere in her warning.

Did she know that I was going back to Baltimore?

"I will."

She leaned down, took my face in her hands and kissed me. It was light and sweet and it made me a little sad.

"I'm sorry, Penny."

I don't know why I said that. Maybe I was apologizing for everything I didn't know. Or maybe it was just...

For everything.

"I know, Baxter. Me too."

I nodded at that and left her there on the step, watching me go.

I think she's always watched me go.

60

When I pulled in behind Tess's Crown Vic, I sat for a minute and looked at the little house. It was dark except for the porch light and the small lamp in the kitchen casting a soft yellow glow through the bay window.

Tess and my girls must have gone to bed.

I crept in as quietly as I could, was met by Sophie and Rosie, giving them the hand signal to be quiet. I petted them and fed them dog cookies and they followed me into the bedroom. It wasn't terribly late, but I was suddenly bone-tired.

Apparently, so was Tess, I could see the outline of her form turned away from me on her side of the bed.

I changed in the bathroom and then I slid between the covers. Once settled, I listened to Tess breathing. She was awake but silent.

I was still carrying that sadness from Penny's. I felt wrapped in it.

"Tess." It came out as a whisper.

"Hm."

"I'm sorry."

She turned over, her head on her pillow, close to mine.

"It's okay."

"No, it's not. I don't know what you see in me, Tess, I don't, but I must have done something right somewhere along the way for you to be here now."

She was quiet, then "Nah, you're a total asshole, Bishop, I knew that when I married you, but you're my asshole, and I will always love you."

I couldn't help but laugh at that.

"Bishop?"

"Hm."

"Hold me."

I was surprised by that, I don't think that was something she was used to asking for.

How could I say no?

I put out my arm, inviting her in. She closed the gap between us and put her head on my shoulder, sighing.

Holding her wrapped in my arm, I listened as she quickly fell asleep.

I followed right behind her.

61

The next morning, I opened my eyes to Tess standing in front of her bureau, and I gawked a bit, I think.

She was a dream in that crisp white linen shirt and panties and I marvelled at her legs, beautifully muscled and smooth, my eyes travelling upward to where they disappeared under the curve of her shirttail.

She looked back at me in the mirror and I'd swear she blushed a bit but not before narrowing her eyes and smiling.

"What are you looking at?"

"I...uh, just...you know...you've got great legs. Do you run?"

"Do I run." She repeated that back to me and the tone of it made me laugh.

"So, yes?"

"Yes."

The feeling of déjà vu washed over me and made my head swim. I let it drop back down on the pillow. "Have we had this conversation before? Because I feel like we have."

She turned and looked at me, then came over and sat on the edge of the bed, lightly brushing my hair off my forehead. "We've had this conversation, or one like it, nearly every day for the past six months," she smiled, but that quickly disappeared. "You're pale."

I laid very still as the dizziness receded. "I'm okay. I just got a little...it felt very strange, like being on a rollercoaster."

She nodded. "I was going to go to work, but if you need me to stay..."

Where I should have been upset that she was leaving me, I can only confirm that I was more than relieved at being left on my own for the first time in days.

And that must have been written all over my face, considering how quickly she got up from the bed.

Her back turned, she stepped into her slacks and tucked in her shirt, then sat down at the foot of the bed while she slipped on her shoes.

"Okay," she said, springing up and brushing the front of her slacks. She disappeared into the closet and came out seconds later with her badge clipped at her waist, her service revolver on her hip as she pulled on her suit jacket. "If you need me, call me. I'll be home this evening."

And then she was gone.

62

I had the whole day ahead of me. The question was where to start.

I pulled out my phone and scrolled through the numbers until I found Justine's. It was a matter of trial and error to send her a text asking if she was free for lunch, and I wasn't sure it had gone through until I heard a chime announcing her answer in return.

We had a date.

It was a bit chilly even in the sun when I met Miz Maggie in the garden later that morning and she took her scissors to me, making quick work in putting right the mess that my hair had become. As she cut, she let the hair fall away so that it would catch on the light wind, sending it spinning through the air to be picked up by the birds nesting in the trees surrounding the property.

The girls wandered the yard while Miz Maggie and I took care of the business at hand. We didn't talk much, and I had the uncomfortable feeling that was really unusual for the two of us. When she was done, she leaned down and kissed the top of my head, patting me on the shoulder before letting me up.

Without thinking, I turned and hugged her and she hugged me back.

"Thank you."

"You're welcome, sweetie."

We smiled at each other, and I wasn't sure if I was supposed to pay her.

"What do I owe you?"

She shook her head. "All I've ever asked from you is to take care of Tess, and you've done that. Beautifully."

I didn't know what to say to that. I was glad to hear that I'd done right by Tess, that I hadn't stayed true to form with her, leaving her frustrated and crying.

Well, at least until recently.

I nodded at that, and we parted ways. I walked back into the carriage house wondering if she'd think as highly of me if she knew who I was about to take to lunch.

Justine was working in a shop on Tenley Square and I had to look up that location online. It was downtown, just off Main. I gathered up my phone and keys and headed out.

63

We met at Justine's store in the square and we walked around the corner to Morton's, just off Main, a busy little place with a fast-food menu for nearby workers to get a quick bite without having to leave the one-mile radius of downtown Tenley.

We were early and able to claim the table at the back corner, away from the crush of folks sure to pack the place during the lunch hour.

I made a space for ketchup in the cardboard tray of french fries, then added salt to the fairly thick red clot. "Thanks for meeting me," I started, looking up at Justine. "I have some questions and I think you're the only one that can answer them."

She smiled at me, her blue eyes twinkling a bit. "Why, sure, sugar, I'm glad you asked. Now, what would you like to know?"

"Well, first, where were we? The night I disappeared."

"You really don't remember?"

"No, I really don't. So how about you tell me about that night from the beginning."

"Well..."

And she paused and looked at me, and I had the sensation this witness was about to try to lie to me. "Just the facts, okay? Things I can verify."

She smirked a bit at that. "Okay, well, it was Thursday evening. We were in Whitmore to pick up crates for the rabies clinic that Dr. Biggs was having that weekend. We had stopped at the Baljean's store there, it's owned by the same people who own the Ferranté store I'm working in today, because I wanted to pick up my pay.

"You came in with me while we waited for Vivian, my boss, to get back from dinner. You were looking at the leather weekend bags when she came back. She cashed me out and then we came home."

"That's it?"

"Well, we dropped off the crates and pads at the hospital, and you got back in your Jeep and left. That's it."

"My Jeep was found in Whitmore."

"Yeah, outside Baljean's. Why did you go back?"

Good question.

"Was anyone else in the store when we were there?"

"Okay, wait a minute." She took a sip of her soda, closing her eyes while she thought. "Sherry and a new girl she was training. A couple of customers. I assisted one while we were waiting because the woman had absolutely no idea what she was doing putting a belt on that dress. Oh, yeah, and the guy in the suit. I don't know his name."

"You don't know his name?"

"Well, gee, Baxter, we've never been formally introduced, and since I don't have to deal with him, I don't pay attention."

"You've seen him before?"

"Yeah. A few times."

"Hm. So, is he an owner? How is he connected to the store?"

"Look, I said I don't know." She was beginning to sound a little perturbed.

"How many stores does this company own?"

"Gawd, what is the deal? Just the two. And the pop-ups."

Pop-ups. Why did that word mean something to me? And there was something else.

"Wait, your boss pay you in cash?"

"Every week."

"All the employees?"

"Yes."

Well.

Huh.

Bingo.

64

I walked Justine back to Ferranté, then headed home to make some notes and chew a bit on the things I learned from my investigation so far.

It was warm in the sun, and I sat down at the table on the porch to ponder the various questions and ideas I was considering while the girls played with their soccer ball.

After an unsuccessful search through the house for a notepad, I had grabbed the WITSEC binder to scribble my thoughts on the back of one of its pages.

Now, then. What could possibly be going on in this sleepy little backwater town that could be even remotely tied to the massively corrupt activities in Baltimore?

Was there a connection, though? Or was I stuck on Baltimore because that's the last thing I remember? What had I seen in that store that made me go back?

Had I been caught snooping? Did someone I can't remember recognize me? Someone had certainly tried to kill me, managing to come very close to pulling that off by dumping me into a culvert thirty feet below the road.

But what were they hiding?

I knew that drugs would naturally be at the top of that list of Things That Could Get Me Killed, and I wrote that down first.

Next was money laundering.

Even an inexperienced criminal could hide thousands of dollars a week in the average day-to-day dealings of a small town and the surrounding communities. Real estate, restaurants, and check-cashing services are everywhere, and that's just to start.

Any business operating with a high rate of cash exchanges could be used to clean money illegally obtained in the selling of drugs, guns, gambling, prostitution--you name it.

I was deep in thought when the dogs suddenly began barking, running toward the gate.

The barks were their happy kind, and I saw why when Tess rounded the corner of the house, smiling at the girls' bouncing and noisy welcomes as she made her way towards the steps. I watched the three of them and it struck me that my animals were as much Tess's as they were ever mine.

I had to take that to heart, really, because it was obvious that they loved her, too.

"Hi," she said, as she gave the soccer ball a whacking kick, sending it nearly to the other side of the yard, the dogs yelping and racing after it. She stepped up onto the porch, smiling when she saw the notebook on my lap. "You're studying," she noted in a pleased tone.

"Oh, hah, yeah," I agreed, flipping over the page I'd been writing on in case she wanted to take a closer look. "That's what I've been doing," I added.

I am such a liar.

I have to think that Lisa Baxter did not keep secrets from Tess, and yet, here I am, sloshing knee-deep into an investigation of sorts, and I'm keeping all of that to myself.

Tess was right. I am an asshole.

"So, are you home for the day?" It was barely three o'clock. I thought I'd be on my own until at least five or so. I tried not to show any disappointment.

"Yeah, I'm taking call for Whyte tomorrow and I need some things from the store. Want to go with me?"

I could have said "no," but the look on her face was obvious, she wanted me to go with her, and I just couldn't hurt her feelings. "Yeah, okay, sure."

The moment I agreed and saw her relief and her happiness, something inside my chest panged, followed by that familiar heat that only she seemed to bring upon me, spreading outwards, and it grew so much warmer that I could feel it under my skin and on my cheeks.

"Give me a minute to change," she said as she opened the door, still smiling.

I was smiling too, now, and I nodded at that.

The door closed behind her and I blew a breath.

Wow.

Well.

So just who am I really lying to?

65

We had picked up the items on Tess's list and I thought we were heading back to the carriage house, so I was thrown a bit when she didn't make our turn off Main, but went on past.

"Where are we going?"

She just smiled. "You'll see."

We ended up at a wide, squat warehouse just outside of Tenley, the sign above the door reading 'Full Count.' Walking into the business, I was immediately taken with the rich, familiar smell of leather and I looked at the variety of baseball and softball gloves hanging on the walls, white spotlights in the ceilings highlighting the collections.

Along with the gloves, there were carousels of baseball and softball bats, batting gloves and helmets, elbow and forearm protectors, facemasks, you name it. Local and national team jerseys and recreational clothing in team colors took up wall and floor space on the far side of the showroom, the high school apparel prominently displayed from rafter beams with school banners and pennants.

I picked out a softball glove and slid my hand into it, naturally burying my nose in the pocket and taking in the rich scent before testing the feel by popping my fist against the palm surface.

Tess just smiled as we wandered through the collections, smiling and shaking her head at the young woman who asked if we needed any help. We made our way around the showroom and then she said, "follow me," pushing through the swinging double doors opposite the store entrance.

Batting cages. Four across the length of the room. Bats were laid out in racks like pool cues, each group defined by length and weight.

"Would you like to hit a few?" Tess smiled.

"I don't know, it's been years," I replied.

"It's only been since September," Tess informed me. "You've been playing for Dr. Biggs' team for the past two years, you're good. You usually play right field and your batting average at the end of the season was .317, up from .300 but that wasn't a full season because of your broken ribs."

"Broken ribs."

"When Krieger shot you. The vest. Remember?"

"Uhm, no, but that would explain why I ache sometimes." I rubbed the heel of my hand on my chest, over the left side of my sternum. "Guess that's a good thing to forget, though, huh?"

"I suppose."

I wasn't quite sure how to take Tess being a bit indifferent to my not remembering getting shot. Maybe she thought it had been a good deterrent to getting shot again.

You know, the old 'aversion therapy' way of thinking.

She went back to her first question. "So, do you want to hit some balls?"

66

I nodded. I actually did want to take some swings.

As I selected a bat, she pushed a five-dollar bill into the change machine and got a handful of quarters back, passing some of them to me in turn. I walked into the center cage and fed the coins into the machine, leaving the remainder on the top of the control box. I made my selections for type of ball and speed then hit the red start button.

I wasn't ready for the first ball, it sped past and left me looking. I swung and missed the second and third, but got a piece of the fourth, flipping it backwards off the bat in what would have been a foul tip in a real game.

I was shaking my head at the fifth and sixth, still unable to connect for a hit of any kind.

I managed to ding the eighth and the ninth balls, they'd have been grounders for sure, but I hit the tenth solid and sent it in a line drive into the center of the net at the back of the cage.

The eleventh and twelfth pitches were line drives out to center as well.

"Stay there," Tess directed as she came into the cage and fed more quarters into the machine, hitting the start and exiting before the ball was launched. I connected with the next four, feeling my body relax into a batting stance with a more fluid swing and finish.

"There ya go!" Tess laughed, clapping her hands. "That's my girl!"

That made me laugh and I missed the next one. "Alright now," I cautioned. "You make me laugh and I'm gonna miss them all."

"Well, you're too easy if that's all it takes to distract you," she replied.

"I may be easy," I grinned at her, "but I'm not cheap."

"Oh, I don't know about that. You've only cost me five bucks so far. That's pretty cheap, if you ask me."

I chipped the next ball toward what would be third base, then looked back at her. "The evening is still young," I chuckled. "Don't you want to take a swing or two?"

"Actually, I do, but you have to promise not to laugh," she admitted. She picked a bat from the rack before striding into the next cage.

I hit my last ball in a line drive straight down the center of the cage, having sent the last four into the nets at the back corners, and I took a minute to watch Tess, leaning on my bat as I stood at the fencing between us.

Like me, she whiffed the first three, catching a piece of the fourth to have it dribble away from her, rolling foul across the third base line painted on the concrete floor.

"Raise your left shoulder," I called to her. She turned to me with a definite 'shut up' sort of look on her face, then missed the next two balls.

I left my cage and went into hers, which was a bit brave of me, really, because she had a bat in her hands and didn't seem too pleased with me telling her how to swing it.

Still, though, there I was.

"Let me...just...show you..." and I had maneuvered behind her, pressing in, my left arm under hers, my right over, tipping her shoulders, our hands holding the bat. The machine fired the ball and we swung through, rocking together from knees to shoulders, connecting with the pitch and easily sending it straight out to the back of the center net.

We held the stance and followed through again, hitting that ball right of center but with good speed in a line drive.

We sent the next ball into the outfield.

She was warm against me and I leaned in, aware of the scent of her, I swear I could taste it, I could taste her, she was there on my tongue. I turned my head, grazing her neck, and I pressed my lips against her skin, hearing her sigh as she relaxed into me.

The last ball flew past as I traced upwards, hearing her gasp. She was warm but I was warmer and I opened my mouth, rumbling in my throat as I moved my tongue over her.

Lowering the bat, I pulled her to me, my hips pressing tight against her backside, as my mouth lightly worked her skin.

My eyes were closed as I lost any thoughts I had about getting too close to her. Too involved.

Too much hers.

"Bishop."

It was a whisper, but whether it was a plea to stop, or to never stop, I couldn't say.

Suddenly, she pulled away, breaking my grip on the bat, on her, and was through the cage door, putting the equipment back, never looking my way as she headed for the exit.

I closed my eyes and took a deep breath before following her out.

Damn.

Damn.

Damn.

67

No words were spoken as Tess drove us home, and we had only just parked at the curb when her friend Ginnie pulled up behind us.

She had come to examine me one last time for Dr. Sampson, to clear me for work the following Monday, and she was all smiles as she met us at the gate. She lost that smile with one look at Tess, though, and we were quiet as we walked into the house.

She sent me off to the bedroom, telling me she'd be along in a minute, and I left them there in the kitchen. I was stretched out on the bed, had actually closed my eyes, but not to sleep. I couldn't help but relive that moment between Tess and me, I couldn't stop tasting her, feeling her softness against my lips.

So, maybe I had worked myself up a bit by the time Ginnie entered the room and closed the door behind her. She pulled her penlight and stethoscope from her bag, took my wrist in her hand to count my pulse.

"Well. Huh. It's a little fast." She looked at me, her head tipped, eyes narrowed as she assessed my appearance. She touched my forehead with the back of her hand, then tucked it in the crease at my shoulder, a smug smirk on her lips. "You're a little warm, too."

She said this in an almost accusatory tone, or, it certainly sounded like that to me, and I wasn't quite sure how to answer, if I even needed to give a reason for it.

"Okay, well, at least your blood pressure's normal," she remarked, unwrapping the cuff.

Then she was shining her penlight in my eyes, first one, then the other, quickly moving on to strength testing and reflexes. I could tell from the speed she was performing the exam that she was building up to something and I wasn't surprised when she put away her gear, then sat down on the bed next to me, balancing on one arm as she leaned across my waist.

"Bishop, I'm going to caution you with a little warning. Do not trifle with Tess. She has been through enough in this lifetime and I am telling you, here and now, that whatever you do, you'd best be sincere about it. Do you understand what I'm saying?"

I wasn't exactly sure but I nodded anyway.

"Good. That said, she is your wife, you know."

I looked at her, now fully aware that I truly did not understand what she was getting at, that I might be misinterpreting her words.

She looked back at me and spelled it all out very plainly.

"She misses you, you dope. Take her to bed. And who knows, it may help with your memory, but even if it doesn't, it's sex, it's good for you."

Calling me out like that, I felt my face redden, and that just made her laugh.

"Lawd, Bishop, did I embarrass you? Maybe you should attend a few of my health science classes out at the high school, those kids will help you get past all that."

She stood and picked up her bag from the foot of the bed, stepping to the door before turning back to me, her hand on the knob.

"You're cleared for work." She paused, then, "And sex, if it doesn't give you a headache." She smiled a very sweet smile and was gone.

68

I was still lying on the bed when Tess peeked around the door jamb.

"Hi." She hesitated, then walked in and stood at the edge of the bed. "Ginnie said you can go back to work Monday."

I shifted over, giving the indication for her to sit. "Among other things," I added, wondering if she'd told Tess everything she'd cleared me for.

Tess took Ginnie's spot, not quite meeting my eyes as she pressed against my hip. We both started talking at the same time.

"Tess..."

"Bishop..."

"I didn't mean to upset you."

"Do you want me to move out?"

We couldn't have been further apart and that realization left us both stunned and staring.

"Tess! Is that--do you think I want you to leave?"

"Bishop, I don't know what you want."

"Do you want to leave?" I paused as I considered what I was going to say. "Do you want a divorce?"

That word nearly stuck in my throat, and then, once it was said, I was very aware that I wanted to take that question back.

She shook her head at that. "No, of course not, I love you, and I believe we'll get through this, but I don't want you to be married to me if it's not what you want anymore."

I sighed at that. "Tess, you're right, I don't know what I want. I know that I don't want to hurt you, but...I don't think I'm the person I once was."

I paused and glanced up at her. "Or, actually, I am exactly the person I have always been, but I'm not who you married. I'm Bishop, not Lisa Baxter."

She took on a stern look. "I didn't marry Lisa Baxter, I married you, the Bishop living her best life. You were happy and I wish I had a way to show you that. When you could have left Tenley, you didn't, you stayed here. That has to mean something."

Maybe that was it. Maybe I couldn't believe that my life had taken a turn for the better, that I loved my job, these people, this town, that I had stayed when I could have run back to Baltimore. That I really was happily married to this beautiful, kind, strong, smart woman who loved me in turn.

I had followed Krieger into what was to have been my deathtrap, it was supposed to be my ending, but I'd come out the other side with a brand new life instead, and I didn't know how to process that. In my head, this had all happened within the past two weeks, but it had been two years in the making.

It was like waking up to a wish granted.

I just don't remember making that wish.

69

I was between awake and asleep, that twilight dream state, and I sighed as Tess's lips softly brushed my neck, her arms around me, holding me against her.

She moved her leg across mine, pulling herself on top of me, her knee finding its way between my thighs and I was suddenly wide awake, gasping a bit when I realized how hot I was.

I don't know how long she'd been at me, I didn't think Tess would normally molest me in my sleep, but who knows? I could be completely wrong about that.

Her hand was under my shirt, she was lightly brushing her fingertips across my chest and I felt my nipples harden.

And now I was to the point that I had to seriously consider waking her up versus letting her finish what she'd started, because damn! and I was honestly torn by those choices.

"Tess," I whispered. "Tess."

"Hm?" She responded, her lips still against my neck, her hand making lazy circles on my belly, dipping under the waistband of my shorts and back up again.

"You awake?"

"Hm?"

"Tess. Wake up."

Her mouth was on my neck and her hand was in my shorts, going south and not stopping until she was lightly tickling the folds at my center. I felt them drawing open to her touch and I couldn't help but move with her as she dipped her fingertips against me.

Geezus.

"Tess!"

She snapped awake at that and she pushed up from me, her hand still between my legs.

"What..."

"Uhm, well..."

"Oh, god, Bishop."

She had looked up at me, then down at the tangle we were in.

I was breathing fast and a bit sweaty, and she was immediately aware that this wasn't just a minor transgression.

The question was what to do about it, and that's exactly what she asked.

"Do you want me...to...?" Her fingers shifted the slightest bit.

I gasped.

"Bishop, I'm sorry, I don't want to leave you like this. Please, let me finish what I started." Her fingers curled the slightest bit as she talked and I pushed against them and groaned.

This should not be so hard to decide.

She's my wife, she's been my wife for months, this wasn't our first time.

And yet.

It sort of was.

Oh, gawd. Stll, though, she had me halfway there...

"Okay. Okay."

She leaned down and softly pressed her lips to mine, opening her mouth to me, and I slipped my tongue inside, moaning with the taste of her as she moved with me. Her fingers lightly followed along below and I gave in to her touch.

She was soft and sweet in her approach to me, a bit tentative at first, then she took command, let go of whatever had held her back.

As she began making love to me, I found her to be the source of that deep longing from not so long ago and that constant sadness I seemed to carry with me retreated into the darkness.

Her body on mine, I held her, was moving under her as she imparted deep kisses in turn, then tracked down, finding my nipple, sucking and tonguing it while she fingered me to a rocking orgasm.

She kept her hand in place until the twitching contractions had subsided, holding me in the crook of her arm, her head against mine as I regained my composure.

When she was free, she straightened up and looked at me in the dim light.

"I'm so sorry."

"Don't apologize, I think this was my fault."

"And just how do you come to that conclusion?"

"Because I started it. This afternoon."

She considered that. "No, you don't take responsibility for my molesting you in your sleep. That's on me."

I blew a breath. "So. We have a really hot sex life, huh?"

"'Really hot' doesn't begin to describe it. More like, 'best I've ever had' kind of sex life."

Well, she'd certainly shown me that she knew how to send me over the edge. I nodded at that.

She started to chuckle.

"What? Tell me."

"I should have made the same promise to you when you swore you wouldn't assault me in my sleep. You were so serious and so cute, thinking that you had to promise to behave, when I'm the one who usually wakes you up."

"Really. You thought I was cute."

She giggled again. "I do think you're cute. And so honorable and forthright. And...I just realized I could absolutely fill your head with all kinds of things that you supposedly do and you'd have no reason to doubt me. I could mold you into the most perfect wife and you would never know if anything I tell you is true or not."

"You wouldn't do that. Would you?"

"No. Of course not."

That little chuckle at the end was not very reassuring.

I rolled over and pinned her. "Promise me."

70

Grinning down at her, I could see her looking up at me, the smile in her eyes and on her lips turning to want, written there in her gaze. Fire bloomed in my chest and between my legs and I didn't hesitate when I leaned down and pressed my lips to hers.

She pulled me in.

I kissed her, long and deep, cradling her in my arm, holding her under my mouth, my other hand gliding down and over her hip, skimming the inside of her thigh as she bent her knee and opened herself to my fingers lightly brushing over her.

I could feel her heat and I pressed my palm against her mound, rubbing the heel of my hand against her clit, still cloaked in her swollen folds.

She moaned and pushed back against me, her hips slowly gyrating, following my tongue and hand as I led her in a sensuous dance, our mouths and bodies combining and moving together as I slipped inside, leaving her breathless as I dipped and rolled and brought her to the edge. She bucked and rocked against me.

"Oh, dear god, Bishop," she gasped, grabbing at me, hands pulling, her nails digging in, leaving stinging trails over my back and shoulders. I buried my mouth against her neck, marking her as I rode her through the shuddering spasms.

She was tight against my fingers, stiffening, waves of convulsions rolling over her, her core so hot and wet as she came.

There was no thinking, it was all action and reaction, and I didn't want to stop, I wanted to stay in this space and time, to float here, where there was only the give and take between us, to feel and taste and move to her. I slowed in my touches, waited for her to catch her breath, to catch up as I pressed and stroked her.

She followed, and we were in it again, melting into each other, thrusting and swaying. My thigh was between her legs, my fingers inside, heel on her clit, pushing deep and lifting her with the stroking, the roughness of her g-spot taking the brunt. She was on the crest, and I kept her there, she was nearly growling, gutteral, clawing as she sought release, her noises becoming a howl as she came, a vocal wordless exclamation that lasted as long as her orgasm.

And then she was a limp heap under me and I withdrew and pulled her close. I wrapped us in the cover, still holding tight to her, as we laid together in the quiet.

71

The next morning, we were both a bit sheepish as I inspected the rather savage love bite I had left on Tess's neck, and she assessed the scratches and marks she'd inflicted on my back and shoulders, washing them and then applying a bit of antibiotic ointment to two of the deeper ones.

We spent the weekend in couple-mode, going to an afternoon matinee, followed by dinner on Saturday, falling together into bed only to find ourselves emboldened by the darkness once again, our approach to each other gentler this time, with strokes and touches evoking shudders and soft sighs as we set a slower pace, reaching the peaks with quiet whispers invoking the gods.

On Sunday, we had a late lunch at the Fowlers. Ginnie eyed the deep purple mark on Tess's neck when we walked in, acknowledging it with a knowing smirk. I felt the blush on my own cheeks when she smiled at me for confirmation.

Ginnie Fowler fries the best chicken I have ever eaten.

We went to bed that night, both of us content, Tess under my arm and curled against me as we drifted off to sleep.

72

I started work at the animal hospital that next morning. Dr. Biggs was smiling, warm, and friendly when she met me in the lab and showed me the layout, leaving me in the kennels with Tracey, the groomer, who seemed to be a bit perplexed at having to explain my job duties.

"Baxter, you've been doing this job for the past two years, you really don't remember how this all goes?" We fed and watered the dogs in the kennels after she showed me the clipboard detailing the discharges, surgeries, and boardings.

She pulled towels out of the dryer and dropped them on its top. "Fold these, then put them in the cupboards at my grooming station. Justine will be here shortly and you can follow her."

I nodded at that. What else could I do? I felt like a kid at my first job and Tracey was only too happy to hand me off.

Justine joined us about an hour later and I tagged along behind her for the rest of the day. She seemed to find that amusing, but she took the lead and didn't give me grief over showing me the routines. I told her that she was easy to work with, and she just smiled at that. "I had a good teacher," she informed me.

Tracey cut me loose around four o'clock and I made my way to the front door, the receptionist calling "have a good night, Baxter, see you tomorrow."

I sat in the Jeep in the parking lot for a minute or so after I cranked it, honestly wondering if she really would be seeing me tomorrow.

"Hi, Baxter."

I startled at that, turning to look and noting a rather strikingly-pretty woman standing at the passenger door, peering at me through the window.

"Can I get in? It's a little cold out here."

I think she saw the confusion on my face and she laughed. "I'm sorry," she smiled as she shook her head, "you don't recognize me. I'm Carole, Biggs' wife."

I nodded at that, my eyes a bit wide, but I leaned over and opened the door.

"Brrr. Well, it *is* nearly Christmas, though, isn't it," she remarked as she settled herself into the passenger seat. "So! Baxter! How was your day?"

I was torn between telling her a lie, that it'd been "fine, great," smiling all the while, versus the truth, and I swear I think she knew it.

She tilted her head, a slight frown on her mouth. "Hard day?"

"It was..." and I waved my hand a bit, a nonchalant sort of gesture. I couldn't settle on the next word, so I just left it there.

"Hm. It wasn't for you, then, was it." That was a statement.

It was her wife's practice, her business, I didn't want to say anything that would be taken poorly, or misunderstood.

"It's okay. This is all new to you, I understand that, and I also realize that you're not the same person who walked in here two years ago."

73

Her words struck deep. How did she know? Could she see it? Did I look different to her?

"Look, Baxter, you don't have to do this, you know. There are other jobs out there. You could even go back to school if you'd like. I teach at the college, you should come out and take a look, talk to someone in Admissions. I will tell you that Biggs loves you, she only wants what's best for you and that would be whatever makes you happy."

I stared out the windshield, not really seeing anything beyond it as I worked to explain what I was thinking. "I appreciate everything Dr. Biggs has done for me, I do, even if I can't remember any of it, and I don't want to hurt her. She's softhearted, I can tell, she'll take it personally, and it's not. Personal, that is."

I turned in my seat so that I could look at Carole. "I don't know what I want. Maybe it was easier two years ago because the plans were already made, and I just went along with them. Now, though, I'm trying to make it all fit, but I don't know how to do that."

Carole nodded at that. "At home, too?"

"Oh, god. That's just..." I closed my eyes and shook my head.

"A whole 'nother ball game, huh?"

I nodded. "I don't know this person you all know as Baxter, and I'm having a really hard time with that, because that's who everyone loves, or seems to, and I don't know what made her so different from me. I feel like I'm acting, like I'm playing a role when people think I'm Baxter, it's like...like being undercover."

And those words hit home.

They echoed in my head and I was suddenly wondering if that was how I'd approached my new life from the very start.

Had I seen it as going deep undercover?

Carole saw the realization cross my face, I know she did, the look of surprise she wore told me so, and then she fell into the ruse with me, becoming all business.

"Well, then, Bishop. Where does your roleplaying as Baxter take you now? My offer stands, come out to the school and I'll take you on a tour. I think Biggs will be happy for you no matter what you decide, so long as you play for her softball team next season. The only way you'll break her heart is if you quit her team--and don't even think of playing for anyone else, that would absolutely kill her."

She reached into her purse and pulled out a card, handing it to me before she opened the door and got out. "Call me," she smiled, nodding through the window.

I watched her walk across the lot to the front door, and she stopped to smile and wave before she went into the reception area. I looked down at the card printed with her name and office numbers.

Finally.

I was going to make some decisions of my own.

74

The next morning, I stepped up and took over running the kennel while Tracey did an early grooming job. Justine came in just after nine o'clock and we finished the chores in time for lunch. Dr. Biggs came looking for me, telling me we were going to the Pharmacy and I nodded, smiling, remembering Tess telling me that Biggs and I did that on a regular basis.

We were seated at the short side of the counter, and I took a minute to look over the menu. Biggs chuckled when I gave Bernice my order.

Bernice just pursed her lips and shook her head as she headed back to the grill.

"What?"

"That's your usual order."

"Oh. Huh."

She nodded, her voice low. "Well, at least you and Baxter have the same food preferences." She smiled when she said that.

It left me a bit uncomfortable, wondering if Carole had told her about our discussion in the Jeep. I didn't have to wonder long, Biggs cut right to the chase, leaning close as she whispered.

"Would you prefer I call you Baxter? Or Bishop?"

"Baxter's fine, it's what you're used to." I whispered back. "And it is my legal name under WITSEC, I wouldn't want to piss them off."

"Okay." She nodded, straightening up and taking on a normal tone. "That said, Carole tells me you haven't been able to reclaim any memories."

"Well...no, I haven't." I shook my head, feeling like I'd somehow failed this woman I didn't even know.

She nodded at that. "Look, Baxter, I just want you to be happy. If that means you want to do something else for a living, or go back to school, I'm behind you one hundred percent. If you need anything--anything at all--you just call me. Or, if you're at the school, tell Carole. Okay?"

"Yes, ma'am." I was suddenly so sad, looking at her, giving me her support but so heartbroken at my leaving her practice that she couldn't look me in the eye.

Bernice brought our food and we spent the next few minutes working on our sandwiches.

"I have to bring this up. I really hope you'll still play on my team in the spring."   .

I smiled at that. Something told me that Biggs had three things she loved more than anything else in this world: Carole, her practice, and softball.

And they were not necessarily in that order.

"Absolutely." I crossed my heart.

Within two seconds of doing that, I saw, in my mind, Tess sitting opposite me in our bed, me earnestly crossing my heart, and I closed my eyes, trying to remember what I'd promised her.

"You okay?"

I opened my eyes, blinking. "Yeah, I just...that was weird. Almost like an out-of-body kind of thing."

Biggs was squinting as she looked at me. "Look, I know it's a little crowded in there, but--stay in your body, Baxter."

I burst out laughing.

So did she.

75

I told Dr. Biggs I'd work through New Years because the schedule was heavy on the grooming and boarding side of the practice, and she was happy to hear that.

I wanted to tell Tess I was working out my notice, but I hadn't made any decisions as to what I was going to do next and I didn't want to open that particular discussion without some answers. Carole had sent me the college catalog via Dr. Biggs and I spent down times in the kennels looking at the various courses and degrees offered.

Of course I was drawn to the Law Enforcement curriculum, and I looked up Hatch in the instructors and teachers section, snickering when I learned that her first name was Jolene. Looking at the course schedule, I shook my head at knowing that I was well past what these students were being taught, having already graduated the academy in Maryland.

And that got me to thinking. I flipped open my phone and scrolled through the contacts list. Yep, I had Hatch's number, and I sent off a text to her asking if she was free to talk that afternoon. I got a response back within a couple of minutes telling me that she'd be in her office between four and five-thirty. I answered that I'd tag her when I left work, getting an 'ok' in reply.

I have got to get a new phone.

Justine was in Central Supply and I asked her for directions to the campus. She shook her head.

"No."

Well. Okay. "Why not?"

"Because you can just follow me, I've got to meet some friends there when I get off." She smirked at that.

She must have felt my eyes on her because she glanced up at me, then away, but made sure to jut her hip towards me, pressing against my thigh.

I called her on it, leaning into her, my lips close to her ear. "Think you're cute, don't you?" I whispered.

"You know I am," she whispered in turn, turning her head and leaning towards me with her neck exposed.

I could smell her soap from her shower, I'm pretty sure it had the word 'ocean' in its name. I dropped my head towards her bare neck, she could feel my breath warming her skin, and then I snarled and clicked my teeth, laughing as she screeched and pulled away.

"That'll teach you."

"Yes, that was very educational, thank you. I'll just have to set a trap for that big bad wolf," she smiled. "And I'll make it howl when I catch it."

I laughed at that.

She was grinning, but her eyes were serious.

76

I followed Justine to the campus and pulled into the parking slot next to hers. Waving, I headed toward the Student Center, but she called me back.

Her two girlfriends had gotten out of their car parked on the other side of hers and I joined all three of them at the trunk of Justine's sedan. She popped the lid and I smelled the leather in seconds. The space was loaded with pocketbooks, purses, and satchels, most likely from the store.

I squinted at that. Why was her trunk full of goods from the store? Had she bought it all at a discount and was reselling it to students at a profit? Or had she stolen it?

She reached in and pulled out a small plastic bag. "You forgot this," she said, handing it to me. I pulled out a small, thin brown leather wallet, and I turned it in my hands.

"You bought that for Tess. For Christmas. You left it in the kennels."

I know she saw me trying to remember, and I shook my head and closed my eyes. "I guess I did. Forget about it, that is. Thanks."

She smiled and nodded. "Merry Christmas, Baxter."

She stepped up and kissed me, catching me by surprise, her lips on mine just long enough that the girls waiting for her exchanged looks, and I don't know if she did it more for their reaction or for mine.

It wouldn't be the first time I'd been used by a woman to prove to her friends just how edgy she was.

I stepped back from her, blinking, and something deep inside me flipped upside down. None of this felt right, and I think she knew it.

"I've got to go." I put the bag in the center console of the Jeep then made my way towards the short set of stairs leading up to the building. I could hear the girls quietly squealing a bit at Justine's bravery, though I thought it was more likely her gall.

Inside the Student Center, I stopped at the campus directory posted on a very large free-standing display just inside the atrium. The red tab with 'You Are Here' gave me my bearings, and I laughed when I thought that I could really use one of those for the map in my head.

Crossing through the center, I exited the door on the opposite side. It let me out onto a rather large quad of intersecting sidewalks, green spaces, and concrete picnic tables, and I made my way towards the Public Services building containing the schools for Law Enforcement, Fire and Rescue, and the Wildlife and Forestry Service.

Halfway there, I saw Hatch and a petite African-American woman as they passed through the double doors of the Communications Pavilion on the opposite end of the quad, and I changed course to meet them.

"Hey, Baxter, you made it!" Hatch and I shook hands.

"Thanks for meeting with me, I appreciate it." I looked down at her companion, smiling as I nodded. "Hello."

"Hi, Baxter."

Hatch caught the millisecond of confusion that flickered across my face and understood the cause.

"Baxter, this is Erika Bentley, she's the chairman of the Communications Department."

Erika looked more than a little puzzled as Hatch introduced us. "We've met."

"No, actually, you haven't, not this version of Baxter, but I'll explain it when we have coffee tomorrow," Hatch grinned.

That certainly compounded Erika's bafflement, but she pursed her lips and nodded. "I'll remind you."

"Great. I'll be in touch. See you soon."

We all smiled at each other as we parted ways, Hatch leading me towards her building on the far end of the quad.

"Now, what's up?"

"Well. I've quit my job."

"So I've been told."

"Told! By who?"

"Carole. She didn't think you'd mind, I suppose she knew you'd probably head in my direction, with your work history and all."

I nodded at that. Carole and Dr. Biggs are quite a pair. Both smart but in entirely different ways. A perfect match.

We entered the Public Services building and rode the elevator to the third floor. Hatch walked me down the hall and steered me through the reception area into her office.

77

It was fresh, with new office furniture, the far wall comprised of a row of windows that looked out onto a green space with a fire tower at its center for mock training and drills.

"Nice."

"Yeah, some days it even beats the inside of a surveillance truck."

I caught her slightly sad look, saw it quickly replaced with a smile.

Two overstuffed chairs separated by a low table were set in the inside corner of the room and she took a seat in one, indicating I take the other.

We settled in and she looked at me and smiled. "So, you want to be a cop."

"Hatch, I *am* a cop."

"Well, no, see, I did a little checking and you're really not, Baxter. Not anymore. As far as the Maryland Police and Correctional Trainings Commission is concerned, you're dead."

Well.

Well.

Gaw*damn.*

I was on my feet. "What! How?"

Hatch waved me back down into the chair.

"It was all part of your WITSEC scenario. They killed you off in that fire, the one you think happened a few weeks ago. As far as the Academy and the Commission are concerned, you don't exist. There's nothing left of you except for your name on the Memorial Wall."

"Oh, geezus, Hatch, no..." I rocked back and closed my eyes, tears slipping from the corners and tracking down my face. I couldn't have stopped them.

It really was all gone.

I was gone. My whole life had been erased.

I wiped my eyes, rubbed my sleeve under my nose. "All I ever wanted was to be a cop. And I was good at it, Hatch. I was a good cop.

"Krieger, and the guys he was meeting, talking to, when we were out on patrol, I tracked them down, found out who they were. I learned who was doing what and where, but Krieger, that son of a bitch, that miserable piece of shit, he was the guy I wanted to take down the most. He hated me, he made my training period hell. He did everything he could to make me quit, telling my captain I was a stupid dyke bitch and that the Department didn't need a woman like me. He knew I was too close, that I would figure it out, and he wanted me gone. When he couldn't get me kicked off the force, he wanted me dead. And Tess and Penny tell me I killed him, but I don't remember any of that!

"And now I can't even go back and finish what I started."

Hatch leaned over and patted my knee. "Nope. You can't. And the sooner you come to grips with it, the better off you'll be."

She leaned back in her chair, her arms crossed. "Baxter, you've survived this. It's been two years. You're past being a police officer, you've moved on. You have an awesome life with Tess, and god knows, Dr. Biggs and Carole think the world of you. You have friends who love you, work that makes you happy--you really have a lot to be thankful for."

Maybe her words hit me as smarmy and too slick. Too polished.

Too practiced.

I stared at her, unable to believe that she could just lie to herself like that. "Is that how *you* do it, Hatch? Huh?"

I felt the cold anger growing. "Is that the kind of crap they serve up to you in your therapy sessions? They tell you to smile and count your blessings? Is that how you put your own career behind you?"

I was on my feet, louder now and glaring down at her. "Do you sit here in this office and say to yourself that it's better than being in the back of a surveillance truck? Is that how you've come to grips with *your* damage?"

Hoo boy.

Jolene Hatcher could have gotten angry and thrown me out of her office, she could have punched me in the face--really, I deserved it--but she didn't.

We stared at each other, seconds stretching out in the silent frost between us. And just maybe I wanted her to take a swing at me, maybe I wanted a brawl with her, a physical altercation to let loose my anger at the twist my life has taken.

She didn't say a word, but her jaw was clenched, her own anger brewing just underneath. She opened her mouth as if to set me straight, I could see it coming, then she shook her head. "Damn, Baxter, you really are an asshole, you know that?"

I let my head fall back as I took a breath and dropped down into my seat. Another minute passed and then I made amends. "Sorry, Hatch. I guess I'm just not taking the impact my death has had on my life very well."

She nodded. "I understand. I do. It's a hard adjustment to make, forgetting you don't carry a badge anymore. I had to apologize to Penny a few times when I first got here."

"Oh, man, that poor woman. I imagine she's put up with quite a bit from the two of us."

"She's a fuckin' saint. If she loves you, she loves you."

I nodded, knowing, in my heart, there was no arguing with that.

"So, what do I do now? Could I go through school again? As Lisa Baxter?"

"After all you've been through, you still want to be a police officer?"

"Hatch, I don't know anything else."

"Baxter, you *do*. You know how to take care of animals, and you're good at it. And I could tell that you really, really loved it."

I was looking at the floor while she talked, I just could not make the connection to this person she was describing. I let her finish, then waited a beat or two.

"But...I could go back to school if I wanted. Yes?"

Hatch just sighed.

Christmas came and went. I don't think that, between Tess or me, we were quite prepared for it, the Christmas spirit never seemed to find its way into our little house. It was the twenty-second of December when we realized we hadn't even put up so much as a wreath on the door.

"Do you want to?"

"What--get a tree? Do you have decorations for it?"

"No. I never put one up, it just wasn't something I wanted to do."

"Huh. Me neither. Well, I did one year, but it just seemed silly, having a tree, sitting there looking at it by myself. I took it down Christmas Day, and that was that."

Two days later, on Christmas Eve, I bought a very small mechanical desktop tree from the Pharmacy, about six inches high, it was decorated with little battery-operated lights and played music, and I put that on the bar top in the kitchen on Christmas morning, with Tess's present underneath it.

She smiled when she saw it, made the appropriate oh's and ah's over it, and laughed a bit when she opened her gift.

"Leather seems to be the theme for our first Christmas," she chuckled, as she handed me my present.

I tore off the wrappings and laughed. It was a new softball glove. I buried my face in the pocket and sniffed. "Ah. I love that smell."

She nodded. "Who doesn't?"

I kept the glove to my face. It was there, I could feel it, that elusive memory lingering just on the edge of recall.

79

Winter quarter was to start the first week of January and I was blindsided by the fact that none of my college credits would transfer.

Because I was dead.

You'd think I'd learned to anticipate that by now.

Hatch pulled some very long strings and had high school records fudged within a week by a friend in the DEA, so I didn't have to take the GED (thank god), but I did have to enroll as a freshman and take every last damn general education class that all new students have to take before they could transfer into their respective majors.

It was afternoon, the thirtieth of December, we were in Carole's office, and she was very sympathetic, so was Hatch, but there was nothing to be done.

I wanted to throw up.

"There's still time, you could switch to evening courses, there are more people your age in those," Hatch advised.

"Tess would kill me. Literally. In my sleep. To be going back to school to be a cop again, and then be gone every evening on top of that? She'd be livid. She will be anyway, but I shouldn't actively antagonize her."

"She doesn't know about this yet?"

"No, I want everything firmly locked in place before I tell her. So, I'm asking that neither of you say a word about it when you see her tonight. Okay?"

"If you think that's best, Baxter," Carole, sitting at her desk, looked at me over the top of her reading glasses. "Personally, I think you should tell her, and the sooner the better, because if she finds out from someone else that you've been keeping secrets..."

She didn't have to finish that sentence.

"I know."

Carole clicked some keys on her keyboard, hitting the last two like a maestro conducting the final notes of a long piece, arms rising up and then falling to her side. "Done. You're in. I've emailed your course schedule, so check it against your hard copy, though I don't see anything wrong from this end."

"And again," she said, swinging her chair around to face me, dropping her glasses onto the desk, "as your academic advisor, I am hereby advising you to tell your wife that you are a full-time student enrolled in Whitmore Community College, and that you are pursuing a degree in law enforcement before she finds out on her own."

80

We were gathering together at Biggs' and Carole's house that night, an annual end-of-the-year get-together as their way of showing how much they loved us. It was the usual group of women, but they would all be new to me, and I told Tess that I wanted to pass out name tags. She laughed at that and told me she'd give me their names as we mingled.

"What if you forget?"

"Bishop, I've known these women for over a year myself, and some of them my whole life, I really don't think it's going to be a problem."

Okay, maybe I was having a little social anxiety. I blew out a breath. Loudly.

I was driving her sedan and she smiled, leaning across the console and kissing me on my temple. "You're adorable."

"Yeah, that's me." I smiled at her comment and her kiss, both an easy exchange between us.

The night air was brisk. If it was any colder, it could snow, and we quickened our pace up the stone walkway to the front door. It opened as we reached it and Biggs stood there smiling, dressed in a very natty tux.

"Damn, Dr. Biggs." I was in black dress pants and a dark red, short-waisted jacket with a white linen buttondown underneath, but I felt dressed like a waiter. Or a matador. I couldn't decide. "I didn't know it was formal."

"You look great, Baxter, I'm so glad you're here. Tess, you are gorgeous, as always. Come in, please." Her happiness could only be gauged by the wattage she generated.

"Wait for us!" Hatch and Penny both hurried in behind us and we all stood in a cluster there in the foyer as we appraised everyone's appearance.

"Wow, Coach, you clean up nice!" Penny gave Dr. Biggs' the side-eye as she looked her up and down.

"Penny, you're lovely," Dr. Biggs gave a half-bow, smiling in appreciation. "Hatch, good to see you."

"You, too, Dr. Biggs."

Carole swept in, her hair in an updo, her floor-length dress a work of art in a beautiful rich red-and-gold tapestry. "Hello all," she smiled.

"Stunning," Penny declared. "I'm too short to pull off that dress."

Biggs laughed. "I'm not," she said, smirking as she gathered our coats.

Carole just smiled at her wife's joke and shook her head. "This way, if you please."

"Here we go," I whispered to Tess.

She leaned into me as she took my arm and we followed the others into the living room.

81

Tess and I spent the next hour talking with the women in attendance, an even dozen in total. Some were paired by marriage, or engagement, or longevity, to be honest, but there were a few single women and their plus-ones. I had quickly surveyed the room when we walked in--it's a habit, part of being a cop, I suppose, though I've always done it, even as a kid.

Growing up in the system as a foster kid meant that I could end up in some rather questionable living arrangements and I took the appropriate precautions to stay out of the reach of anyone looking to harm me, or have a bit of fun at my expense. I'd had to fight my way out of more than a few living rooms and kitchens before I'd learned to scan any room I was entering, hanging back at the door for a beat or two while I assessed the environment.

That habit kept me out of trouble and may have actually saved my life when I'd hesitated before going into that warehouse basement behind Krieger.

Anyway, in this instance, I was looking for anyone who might have been even remotely familiar.

And Justine.

Because...she's Justine.

And because I had so recently learned that I couldn't trust her.

Over time, we made our way around the room, joining Hatch and Penny talking with Erika and her date, a handsome African-American woman in a suit and tie. Penny introduced me to "Jacks," and we shook hands, with Jacks smiling hello, then saying, "You really don't remember a thing."

"Jacks..." Penny cautioned.

"Look, I'm sorry, it's just...you read about shit like this, I'd never believe it if I didn't see it for myself. No disrespect, my new friend, it's just that we've played ball for the past two years, had cookouts and parties when you were with Penny, you were my best bud, aside from our girl here," she put her arm around Penny's shoulder and pulled her close. "If you really want to know, it kinda hurts that you'd forget me."

And in that moment, I think Jacks put into words the one thing that those women had thought when this all started in that hospital room a month ago--that I could so easily forget them.

The 'how could you?' evoked a visceral response and I needed air. "Anyone else need anything from the kitchen?" I smiled a little weakly, looked around the group. "Excuse me."

I made my way back to the foyer and crossed into the dining room. The long table was beautifully dressed with a white linen tablecloth and place settings of crystal and china, the candled centerpieces of red and green halving the wide expanse.

Carole entered from a doorway on the other side of the room and stood looking, assessing the details for anything missing or out of place, smiling when she saw me.

"Hello, Baxter. Do you need something?"

"The kitchen?" It was more a question than an answer, and she tilted her head.

"What about it?"

"Where is it?"

"Oh, dear lord, yes, okay, now I'm with you. Through here."

She turned and I followed her down a short hall, likely the former servers' pantry, to the kitchen proper. It was a stunningly beautiful piece of work in itself, well-lit with a center island, the functional workspaces flanking the commercial stainless steel appliances. An open chef's stove with a double oven took up the center of the outer wall, the large exhaust hood above it vented to the outside.

Honestly, it was breathtaking.

"Who cooks?" I asked.

"Oh. Ah, well, I do. Biggs, on occasion, but she does more of the grilling. I find it very relaxing."

"Any particular cuisine?"

"I think I've tried nearly everything. I like the complexity of a French menu, Italian is comforting with its marinaras and soups, but I probably cook Chinese and Thai more than anything else, especially when we're busy. You've enjoyed quite a few meals here yourself."

I nodded at that. Of course I had.

"Can I get you something?"

"No, thank you, I just need a minute."

"A little overwhelmed?"

"It's always stressful meeting new people."

Her forehead knotted a bit as she considered that. "Yes, I suppose that's exactly how it is for you tonight."

She reached and took the empty wine glass from my hand, pouring from the bottle on the counter.

"Biggs and I opened this earlier, it's a very nice Pinot Grigio, I think you'll like it."

I took a sip. "It's got a bit of fizz to it, doesn't it."

"Yes, very refreshing."

I nodded and took another sip.

"So, aside from being stressed with the gathering, how are you? Have you talked to Tess yet?"

I pursed my lips at that, and dropped my eyes.

"Baxter...she's going to hear about it sooner or later, you have to tell her."

"Tell who what?"

Biggs came into the kitchen through the main hallway door, carrying two empty wine bottles. She walked over to the sink and deposited them in the container behind the cabinet door underneath.

Carole looked at me, asking with her eyes if Biggs knew of my plans. I shook my head, then took a deep breath before answering her question.

"Carole is saying I need to tell Tess that I'm going back to school. To be a police officer again."

Biggs frowned a bit and her chin fell to her chest as she shook her head. "Baxter..." And then she stopped. Took a deep breath. "If that's what you really want."

She stepped across the space between us and reached out for my hand. "I wish you the best of luck in your schooling, then." Our hands firmly clasped and she was smiling, but there was a sadness there, I could see it.

I could feel it.

"Schooling--what schooling?"

We all turned.

Tess stood behind us in the pantry doorway.

Oh.

Well.

Damn.

82

She stepped into the kitchen, the question still hanging in the air.

"Tess, your glass is empty, let me take care of that." Carole took the glass from Tess's hand and poured.

She set it down on the counter, then turned to me, one eyebrow raised.

"Come along, dear, we'll leave them to it." She wrapped her arm through Biggs' and walked her out of the kitchen.

I stood there, biting my lip and unable to look at Tess. The silence between us was thick and I was desperate to break it. "Here, try this. It's nice. And fizzy." I passed her the glass and took a big swallow from my own.

"What schooling, Bishop? What's going on?"

"Okay, so..." and I proceeded to tell her what I'd been doing behind the scenes (behind her back) about returning to school and how I would be starting classes at the end of the following week. I wish I could tell you that she took it well, but the undercurrent flowing from her was disappointment laced with maybe just a touch of anger. When I finished, I waited for a response of some kind, but it didn't come.

In fact, she didn't say a word, just picked up her glass and walked out the way she came.

83

I was still standing at the bar when Carole came back in, smiling but moving quickly as she opened the double ovens and removed the pans and trays, placing them into the warmers above.

"Another minute and this roast would have been overdone." She inserted a large fork in each end of the roast, lifting it out of the pan and setting it on a carving board on the island.

"I'm sorry, Carole, I feel like I've put you in a spot."

"I don't think Tess will hold this against me. I think she'll come around to the idea that she just wants you to be happy, no matter how it works out. You've hurt her, though, keeping secrets, and you know it, but at least it came from you and not through the grapevine."

I nodded, my mouth pulled sideways as I considered that.

"Now, if you would go find Biggs and tell her I need her, please? Dinner will be in ten minutes or so."

"Sure," I replied, exiting the main door to the hallway. Biggs was in the living room, talking with a couple from Whitmore, and I communicated Carole's want to her with a hand signal before rejoining Hatch and Penny, holding our place in the corner along with Erika and Jacks.

"Where's Tess?"

"She's not with you?"

"No." I dragged out that word and Hatch tipped her head when I looked at her. She took me by the arm and steered me to the unoccupied corner across the room.

"I don't like the sound of that."

"She just found out I'm going back to school."

"Oh. Shit. Really. Bad timing."

"Yeah, I know."

"How'd she take it?"

"I don't know, she didn't say anything, she just walked out."

Tess entered the living room as I said those words, was moving towards our little group. Hatch and I made our way back as well, Tess smiling at me as she wrapped her arm in mine and pulled me close.

I wasn't exactly sure how to interpret that.

Carole arrived at the hallway door and invited us all into the dining room. Tess had not let go of my arm and as our little cluster brought up the rear, she leaned into me, still smiling, her lips at my ear.

"We'll talk later."

84

Dinner was lovely but over with far too quickly to my way of thinking, though I was probably just trying to postpone the discussion Tess had promised we were going to have.

We were on our way home, nearly there, and I don't think she thought me as adorable as I'd been on our way to the dinner party.

I had tapped the steering wheel buttons through the radio stations for something nice to listen to, settling for a 'best of' collection of music requests being played by the college station when Tess reached over and turned it down at the panel.

I knew why. I glanced over at her, she was sitting with her arms crossed over her lap, her legs crossed at the ankles. No one needed to tell me she was protecting herself, that she was closing herself off to being hurt.

To my hurting her.

"Tess, I was going to tell you."

"When? In time to be at your graduation?"

She caught me by surprise with that and I choke-laughed. "I'm sorry."

She was shaking her head. "I don't understand, Bishop. What else aren't you telling me?"

Was I keeping any more secrets from her?

I didn't want to answer that, so I turned the tables on her. "Do you want to change anything, Tess?"

She didn't move. "I don't want to but you're not giving me any choice."

Well, I asked for it. My blood ran cold hearing her words.

She shifted in her seat, turning her body towards me but still closed in the way she held herself, "I love you, I do, I married you, you're my wife, but if this isn't the life you want for yourself, I will give you a divorce."

My mouth was dry.

Her words scared me. I was going to lose her and I didn't even know her.

She was just getting warmed up.

"I also have to remind you that you are still under the protection of the Witness Security Service and there are limits to what you're permitted to do as part of your agreement with WITSEC. Most particularly, you are not to return to the Baltimore area without forfeiting your protection, your new identity, and your safety."

Our eyes were locked on each other.

I'd swear she knew.

85

"Bishop, you were meant to be kept safe, WITSEC hid you for a reason, one that I don't know. If you have any ideas about returning to Baltimore, just know that I will not stand in your way, but you are on your own because that is a suicide mission and I cannot watch you die. Not again."

We'd been parked behind the Jeep nearly since she started talking, and now I turned off the engine and handed her the keys.

She got out of the car first and I followed, stopping at the driver's side, watching as she made her way through the gate, the girls meeting her as she reached the porch and went inside.

I stood there looking at the carriage house, then walked to the Jeep, pulling out from the curb seconds later.

86

"Well, hey, sugar, what can I get'cha?"

I had started down the bypass, heading to Richmond and the northbound lane of the interstate, but took the last available exit about ten miles out of Tenley. I realized that until I could remember what I'd seen or heard that night in Baljean's, the whole trip would be a useless, dangerous waste of time, so I was aimlessly wandering the two-lane backroads as I pondered on the current state of my new life and Tess's words.

I can't tell you how long I'd been driving before I was parked in that gravel lot. The honky tonk, or roadhouse, or whatever you want to call it, was practically empty--just me, the frizzy-haired, middle-aged, take-no-shit woman tending the bar, and two fellas playing pool on one of the tables at the back. A love song was playing low from the old boombox on the shelf over the bar while the tv next to it was tuned to the highlights of the past football season, the sound muted.

I gave her a weak smile and gestured toward the beer taps. "Draft, please."

She picked a red plastic cup off the top of the stack and pulled the beer, expertly drawing it with a thin head of foam nearly reaching the top. I laid a five-dollar bill on the bar and she traded that for a bowl of roasted peanuts still in their shells.

"Those are fresh, ain't nobody else had their fingers in 'em if you're wonderin'." She smiled at that and I had to laugh.

"And there ya go," she said, laying my dollars and change on the bar.

I sipped my beer and looked around. I'd been in more than one bar like this and I made sure not to make too much eye contact with the men in the place. Some would consider it an invitation and others would think it was a threat.

The place was oddly quiet. It was late, though, and just past the middle of the week. Maybe the regulars were saving up their money and strength for the New Year's Eve celebration, advertised in flyers posted around the room, promising live music for a five dollar-per-person cover charge.

A few more sips and I picked a peanut from the bowl, cracking it open and popping the nuts from the half shell into my mouth. They were good, perfect. I nodded to the woman and smiled. She smiled back.

"My mama roasts those. Good, ain't they?"

One of the men called from the back. "Jean, can you bring us two more?"

"Be right there, Jerry," she hollered back, turning to pull two bottles from the chest cooler behind her, popping the tops before she set them on a round serving tray, taking a fresh ashtray from the stack at the end of the bar as she made her way to Jerry and his friend.

I sipped from my cup, then picked another peanut from the bowl. The song on the radio ended and the softest, sexiest voice I'd ever heard was coming from the speakers.

"The next caller is Mack from Elmwood, requesting this song for his wife, June. Tonight is their thirtieth anniversary and this is the song that was playing when they met. It was the first song they'd ever danced to, it was their first dance at their wedding, and June, Mack wants you to know that he thanks the good Lord every day that you said yes when he asked you to marry him. Happy Anniversary."

The acoustic guitar chords opening the rather obscure country love song had begun playing as the woman was talking. If I'd heard it before, I couldn't recall, but I was having trouble remembering a lot of things anyway, it would just be one more thing to add to the list.

I had my eyes on the TV, but I was listening to the music as I worked my way through the bowl of nuts, and I thought about Mack and June, two young people finding each other at a dance and taking that chance down the line that they were made for each other, like the lyrics in the song.

Did they think it was a sign that they were meant to be? Did they begin their lives together because a song on the radio told them to? Or was it a reflection of their attraction to each other and it just added fuel to their fire?

Did Tess and I have a song?

"You look pensive."

Jean had returned and was sitting on an old metal, red leather-topped stool, leaning back against the wall and playing a match-three game on her phone to kill time while she waited for her customers to need something from her.

I looked at her, surprised by her words.

"What, you think I don't know what 'pensive' means?"

"No, no, of course not."

"Yeah, right," she chuckled. "I have the 'Word-A-Day' app, my daughter thought she was bein' funny downloadin' it on my phone, but it's been kinda fun. I've used a lot of the words but that was the first time I've used 'pensive.' I was right, though, wasn't I?"

I smiled and ducked my head a bit. "Yes, ma'am, you were right."

"So, what're you puzzlin' over?"

Oh, where to start. I was shaking my head as I sorted through all the things I had been thinking, it was a steady stream of consciousness touched off by that love song.

"That much, huh?" Jean laughed, watching me cycle through my thoughts.

How do I even begin?

"Okay." I cracked open another peanut shell. "What if I told you that I woke up one day and my entire life was a lie?" I popped the nuts into my mouth.

"Oh! You mean like you're a--what do they call it? An imposter? That everything you have is because you're a liar?"

I laughed and nodded. "Okay. Yeah. That's it."

"Well, let's see. I think that's somethin' everyone goes through at some point in their lives, that they're not the person everyone thinks they are, it's all an act. That they got to where they are by hook or by crook, or by pure dumb luck. They're afraid they're gonna be found out and they'll lose everything they have, from their house and family and friends to their job."

I smiled and nodded at that. "Okay, but what if I told you my problem is just the opposite, that I woke up and everyone knows I'm a liar, I have a house and a wife and friends, but I don't know how I got them. And if I stop lying, if I go back to my old life, I lose everything."

"Wait, hon, back up a minute. What do you mean 'woke up?' Like you just realized it?"

"No, I really mean 'woke up.' I was sort of unconscious, they say I was only out a day or so, but I've lost two years."

"So it's really more like you came-to in a--what do they call it? An alternate universe? I saw a movie like that once, freaked me out."

Now that made me laugh, but the truth of it resonated with me.

Jean stood up and stepped across the space to settle her elbows on the wooden bar, leaning toward me with her head tipped in thought. "You know what? Maybe you're just lookin' at this from the wrong direction."

She took my nearly empty cup and filled it midway with more beer. "On the house."

She set it down in front of me then pointed at it as she sat back down on her stool. "Half empty or half full."

She didn't really want an answer.

Another love song was playing on the radio, it was a song about loving someone from a distance and asking for a chance. There was something about this one, something that made me want to laugh and cry at the same time, but I can't tell you why.

"Are you all right?"

"This song..."

"Oh, I love this song, that's Jessie Melton, she's from Bell City, jus' up the road, you know. It's her first hit and it's a good one, really, but I think I would have liked it more if it had a better ending. Folks need that 'Happily Ever After,' you know."

I nodded.

She smiled. "Like you. Sounds to me like maybe you woke up to a happier life than the one you went to sleep on. People who love you, a place to call home...those aren't problems, sugar, those are blessin's"

She was preaching the same sermon as Hatch that day in her office.

Maybe there is something to the idea that when the Universe is speaking to you, you need to pay attention and you should go in the direction that it's leading you.

And then she was picking up my cup and pouring the beer into the spillway under the taps. "I shouldn't do this, it's bad for business, but--go home."

I nodded and slid off the barstool, headed for the door.

"Wait. How do I get back to Tenley?"

"Turn left outta the parkin' lot, then follow the signs."

Follow the signs.

Yep. Really can't ignore that.

"Hey, Jean," I called back as I crossed the threshold. "Thanks."

"You're welcome, hon, any time. Drive safe! And have a Happy New Year!"

88

It was cold, and I was surprised to find Tess sitting on the steps, my girls running back to her after meeting me at the gate. She'd been crying and she tried to hide that from me.

I sat down, closer than I would have nearly two hours ago, my shoulder brushing against hers.

"Bishop, I'm sorry. I've been micromanaging your life since I brought you home and I should have known better. You may not know me, but I know you and the last thing you'll tolerate is feeling pinned down."

I nodded at that. She was right.

"I've been wondering...do you think about me, Bishop? Would you even miss me? If I wasn't here?" Her voice was suffused with sadness. "Everything I feel for you is so intense, it's almost painful. It hurts to love you, Bishop, but I understand--I do--if you want me to leave."

All this time, she was afraid I'd leave her, and now, suddenly, I was the one who was afraid.

Had it taken me too long to get here, to admit that even though my head didn't remember her, my heart did?

I had to gather my strength to get the words out, the pain in my chest was so deep. "Is that what you want?"

Silence hung between us and as it grew, the beat of my heart began pounding in my ears.

Don't go, don't go, don't go...

Her answer came as a whisper.

"I want you."

I nodded, relief flooding through me, and I slipped my arm through hers, pulling her up against me and resting my hand on her thigh.

"I want you, too."

The red cup was half full.

89

I was looking at her, studying her profile as she watched the dogs wandering through the yard. When she felt my gaze on her, she dropped her eyes, a shy smile on her lips as she looked down at her hands in her lap.

And then she straightened up and turned to me, meeting my eyes and gazing upon my face much the same way I'd looked at hers. She walked a tightrope of shyness and confidence, she knew me and yet she didn't, and it must have been odd for her to have such opposing feelings.

I was taken with the shine of her eyes as she leaned in, I doubt she had even considered it, and she touched her mouth to mine--lightly, barely joined, and holding us there. I could feel her breath, her air brushing over my lips like the tips of feathers.

I didn't move. Neither did she.

If there is such a thing as a tantric kiss, this was it.

And then she ever so slowly leaned into me, closing the tiny spaces between us and I wrapped my arms around her, pulled her against me. She flicked just inside my mouth, taking a taste, her sweetness mixing with the beer and the saltiness of the peanuts that remained in mine, the delicate sway of her tongue teasing as I chased it with my own.

It was heady and hot and I wanted this woman, wanted her like I'd wanted no other before her. The scent of her skin, her taste was maddening, and I could have pushed her down on the porch and devoured her there if I'd had an ounce less restraint.

She pulled away, then nuzzled her mouth against my neck. "Bishop, take me to bed."

"I'm sorry, Tess," I replied, shaking my head. "I...I can't."

The look on her face was stark disbelief, and I regretted my words immediately. I hadn't meant to hurt her.

"It's just...I don't sleep with married women."

I followed that with a grin, laughing out loud, and then--oh, shit.

It was on.

She had me up and on my feet in an instant, my arm in a hold I wasn't familiar with, designed to subdue subjects in custody before the cuffs could be applied and I can tell you that she had full control of me then.

And she knew it.

She leaned close, smiling wickedly. "Do you remember what we just talked about, you and your not liking feeling pinned down? Being told what to do?"

I nodded, my eyes wide.

"Well, we're just going to disregard those little issues of yours for tonight."

With that, she steered me into the house.

90

Pushing me along, she maneuvered us into the hallway, crashing us against the wall. Releasing her hold, she stripped off my jacket, pulling my shirt open, buttons scattering over the floor as she leaned against me, dropping hungry kisses on my neck and along my collarbone. Rubbing her hands over my bare skin, tracking down to the top of my pants, she unsnapped them, pushing them down to my hips as she kissed and licked at the skin of my belly, leading down to my center.

I inhaled sharply as she got closer, and she heard that. She stood up to her full height, turning and shoving me face-first against the wall, kicking my feet apart in the search position and pressing me flat with her body. Her hands, now inside my pants, roved across the top of my buttocks, then followed the lines of my hips around to the creases of my thighs, each hand taking turns dipping and skimming my center, fingers stroking just inside the folds, and I groaned and thrust against the wall each time she touched the center, hoping to trap her hand there.

"You okay, baby?" I could hear the smile in her voice and her tone was deliciously, playfully evil. She didn't sound like she cared if I was or not, frankly, and she didn't stop, her hands still moving, stroking.

Honestly, I'd never been handled like this before, or that I could remember, and I wondered if this was a routine feature of our marriage. I swallowed, nodded. "Yes."

"Is 'waffles' still your safe word?"

"I'm gonna need a safe word? I mean, yes, it is, and I'm oddly excited that you would know it..."

"Hush."

She grabbed my wrist and the back of my pants and marched me into the bedroom, shoving me onto the bed. She shucked off my shoes and pants, pitching them into the corner of the room.

This woman had me stripped and spread-eagled and then she began to take off her clothes.

In the light of the small lamp next to the bed, I was stunned by her beauty. She was a sculptor's delight, muscles defined and symmetrical, her form was perfect. She was smooth and beautifully made, fluid in her movements as she straddled me on the bed, leaning down and delivering light kisses over my chest and along my shoulders.

I ran my hands along her flanks, stroking down to the cheeks of her buttocks and squeezing, pulling her down. She backed off, my hands now at her waist as she shook her head.

"No. This is mine."

I smiled at that, and then I gave myself over to Tess.

I was in really good hands.

Her mouth on mine, her hands were grasping, pulling through my hair, and then she was turning my head to nip, to suck, moving over my body, leaving me moaning and writhing at the pleasures she was bestowing upon me. She turned me to-and-fro, hitting sweet-spot erogenous zones I didn't know I had.

And when she had touched every part of me, had me sweating and saying her name, she took to her knees, bowing before me, blessing me with her mouth.

Dear gawd.

We may have been married for months, but that night was honeymoon sex as Tess sealed her love for me.

As she claimed me.

And I surrendered to her, fully and completely.

She set the pace and I met her there, and when I was giving back, thrilling to her moans and her hoarse calling of my name, I finally silenced that voice in my head telling me to run.

91

We spent the whole of New Year's Eve and New Year's Day in the warm cocoon of our carriage house, mostly naked and horizontal. The fireworks sounding off at midnight lead to laughter about starting the new year off with lots of bangs and booms.

All things considered, ours was not unlike an arranged marriage, one of two strangers coming together. I knew that she was special to me, I could not deny the deeply emotional connection between us, and I shared that thought with her, telling her I was saddened by the fact that I could not remember how she'd found her way into my heart.

"Then I will remind you," she replied, kissing me gently. "Or we'll make new memories."

I shook my head as I leaned up, looking into her eyes, and then I kissed her, softly, smiling as I broke away.

"Maybe the best thing to happen in all of this is that I get to fall in love with you all over again," I whispered.

"Well, now, that's seeing the glass half-full."

Uhm. Yes.

92

I was intent in learning everything I could about Tess, and I initiated a crash course in her likes and dislikes, though there seemed to be only a few of those and mostly pertaining to food.

"Favorite color."

"Blue."

"Go-to comfort food."

"Chinese."

I nodded at that, chuckling. "I think mine is Ginnie's chicken. You take your coffee black with two sugars. What donut goes with that?"

"Boston creme."

"Good choice. Best day?"

"The day we got married. That was the best day."

She was smiling as she kissed me, adding to her answer. "The best week..."

Another kiss. "...the best year..."

93

I found her life story heartbreakingly painful and extraordinarily brave.

I think there are few others who actually know that she holds everyone at arm's length because she can't bear the pain of losing them too soon, and the fear that she will is always there, buried in the deepest part of her.

I am the one who lived, though, even when she'd watched me take those two bullets on that airport tarmac.

And maybe she didn't trust herself enough to bet her life on love alone, so she'd left me and gone to Richmond, returning months later to take me back.

Oh, Tess.

To put your faith in me.

I think that's the scariest part of all.

94

The holidays were done, Tess was working, and I had started back to school.

The morning I was to attend my first classes, Tess surprised me with a present to start me off right. Inside the package was a very nice pen, a three-sectioned notebook, and a small leather backpack to carry it all.

Oh, and a peanut butter sandwich with the crusts cut off, sealed in an evidence bag with my name on it.

I laughed, holding up the bagged goodie. "No one's ever done that for me before."

She hugged me and smiled back. "I hope you have a good day," she remarked before kissing me and picking her car keys off the hook by the door to the mudroom.

I had the feeling that she was not quite there yet with accepting my new former-life choices, so I really think that could have translated to "I wish you'd reconsider and go back to your job with Dr. Biggs."

But maybe that was just me.

"You, too," I called to her as she went out the door.

An hour later, I was parked outside Whitmore Community College.

I was a student once again.

95

Checking my schedule against the campus map in my orientation packet had me running for my last class in the Communications building on the other side of the quad, up the stairs to the second floor, skidding into the classroom as the instructor was closing the door.

"Well, hello, Baxter, you almost missed the first class," Erika Bentley smiled.

"Sorry." I smiled back at her before finding a seat near the rear of the room and settling in. It was my last class of the day, it was nearly two o'clock and I was hoping the class would adjourn ahead of schedule like the two others I'd had earlier that day.

I scanned the other students in the classroom, wondering if I was, once again, the oldest person there aside from the instructor, when my eyes fell on long blonde hair near the far wall by the windows.

Justine turned and looked at me, smiling as she gathered her things and made her way towards my section of seats.

"Hi." She hung her bag over the back of the chair next to mine and sat down.

"Hello."

"So, are you just hanging out, or are you a student?" She saw my folded class schedule sitting on my desk and reached over, picking it up. "Ah, you're a student." She perused my list of classes. "Ew. Really?"

"What?"

"Just the thought of having to take first-year English again makes me shudder."

I laughed. "Yeah, me too."

"At least you got Hailey as an instructor, she's interesting-- nice to look at, too."

Having already had her class, I nodded, because I really couldn't disagree with Justine's assessment.

Erika started at the top of the hour with a ten-minute informational lecture about her Communications class and what was expected of us as her students before dismissing us for the day, saying that she would be using the entire session after Drop/Add was finished and not to get too comfortable with early dismissal.

As I waited behind the other students to make their way out of the classroom, Justine fell in next to me.

"I'm hungry," she grinned.

Tess's peanut butter sandwich was long gone. "Me too," I nodded.

"Are you hungry for what I'm hungry for?"

I looked at her. That smile was just a little too engaging. "If it's food."

"Alright, alright. I'm going to Lin's, I feel like Chinese. Do you want to go with me?"

"Is it good?"

"Best you'll ever have. You haven't eaten there?"

I shrugged and shook my head. "Not that I remember."

"Oh, then c'mon, let me take you there for your first time!"

I laughed at that, she'd caught me by surprise. "Okay, well, if it's that good, how can I pass it up?"

She slipped her arm through mine, then squeezed a bit as she leaned against me, taking on a seductive tone. "It's so good, Baxter. You won't regret it, I promise."

We passed by Erika, and I noted the puzzled look on her face as she watched the two of us, arm-in-arm and smiling as we moved through the doorway with the rest of the class.

96

The girl was not wrong. Lin's Buffet has the best Chinese food I've ever eaten.

"Auugh," I moaned, pushing away my third plate from the steam tables. "Make me stop."

"I'd never make you stop," Justine smirked, licking the barbeque pork sauce from her fingers.

"Okay, now, you stop."

She laughed at that. "Good, right?"

"Yeah, you were right. Thanks for telling me about it. I'm gonna have to bring a bigger snack if I'm that hungry every day." She smiled when she saw the cautionary look I was giving her, the one that said "don't go there."

"You're no fun."

"Nope. Not one bit."

The waitress stopped by and filled our glasses with tea, smiling at me. "Good to see you, it's been a while."

My eyes went wide at that, and I smiled at her. "Thanks. You, too." I scowled and dropped my eyes as soon as she moved past me to the next table. Justine was watching.

"You okay?"

"I've been here before and I don't remember."

"Yeah, well, that's kinda the way you've been operating for the past month or so, you know. Every day, you go new places and meet new people."

"That's..."and I nodded, considering her words. "Yeah, that's my life."

"So," she leaned forward, lowering her voice. "You really don't remember us?"

I looked at her, and I tried not to get rattled by that, but I felt my heartbeat pick up--my breathing, too.

I didn't know the truth, but she did.

Her eyes narrowed with her smile, the edges of her mouth pulling upward. "Geez, Baxter, don't panic. It's not that big a deal."

Maybe not to her. "It's just not something I've done before, it's not something I would do."

"That's what you kept saying the first time," she smiled, shaking her head. "Afterwards, that really didn't seem to be an issue anymore." She looked very pleased with herself.

Damn.

I hated this.

I hated not knowing the truth.

I stood up and picked up the check, laid some dollars on the table to cover the tip. "Okay, I'm done. Thanks."

"Baxter, wait." She reached up and grabbed my arm. "I'm sorry, please don't go. Come to Baljean's with me, I've got the place to myself until six."

Well.

Shit.

She's just made it interesting. If I go with her, I can look around, search the place. Try to figure out why I'd gone back, what I might have seen that got me into trouble.

I sat back down.

"Let me finish this, then we'll go," she said, eyeing me as she licked the sauce from her fingers.

On our way out, I felt like I was being watched. When I looked over my shoulder, I noticed a man standing at the kitchen door with our waitress and I wondered who he was.

I got my answer walking to the Jeep, when I saw the billboard advertising the Tri-County Real Estate and Home Sales Company. He and his team of agents were smiling down at me, ready to assist me with all my real estate needs.

So it seems that Lin is also in the real estate business.

97

It was three-fifteen and I had parked my Jeep next to Justine's sedan in the lot across from Baljean's. She went in and I waited about ten minutes before the other salesperson left, watching her drive out of the parking lot and onto the highway. Justine waved to me from the window, then I crossed the parking lot and went into the store.

Ah, leather. I looked around, with absolutely no recollection whatsoever of having been here before.

New places every day, just like the girl said.

She was going through her duties, checking displays, looking for anything out of place as she walked around the store.

"Are there security cameras in here?"

"Yeah, at the cash register and at the entrance to the dressing room."

"Can they be accessed from the web? Can anyone outside of the store see us?"

"Not that I know of, but I've never thought of that. Maybe."

I had been keeping my head down, avoiding a full facial view. "Where's the storeroom?"

"At the end of the dressing rooms."

Well, now, that made things easier.

I wandered over to a collection of bowling and Hawaiian shirts and picked two from the rack.

"Whoa, those are nice." She admired my choices.

"Yeah, this one looks vintage." I held it out and took a closer look. There was a price tag but no manufacturer label in the collar.

I made my way to the dressing rooms and through the louvered doorway, noting the office door directly across from the entrance, the curtained dressing rooms to my left. I dropped the shirt hanger over the hook outside the middle dressing room and walked on toward the door marked 'Employees Only.' Turning the knob, I opened the door and stepped into the grey-walled storage area.

There were boxes stacked floor to ceiling across the entire back wall. To my right was another metal door under the illuminated exit sign, an 'Alarm will sound' decal posted above the panic bar.

I lifted the flaps of the box on top of a short stack.

Pocketbooks.

The next box held more of the same.

Why would this merchandise be boxed with no special care but for the tissue paper they were wrapped in, no real steps taken to keep them pristine if they were real.

More boxes filled with scarves, shirts, light jackets.

Jewelry, pins, earrings.

None with packing slips, shipping labels, nothing to identify the origins of the goods.

And then I heard a voice in my head saying, "These are really good knock-offs."

I froze at that, my eyes closed as I tried to capture the time and the place, who said it, but the thought was just a whisper and it disappeared like blown dust.

I shook my head and turned to make my way out, running into Justine. "These are knock-offs."

"Yes, we've talked about this," she agreed, "and we have company." She grabbed my arm and pulled me back through the doorway, shoving me into the nearest dressing room and pulling the curtain.

98

"Justine."

The voice was an older woman's and the tone of it was more than a little perturbed.

"I'm coming, ma'am," Justine called, passing me one of the Hawaiian shirts through the curtain. I heard the louvered doors swing on their hinges as she passed through. I stood listening.

"I was assisting a customer, Mrs. Bennett."

"You know that I don't like the showroom left unattended," Mrs. Bennett scolded.

"Yes, ma'am."

I heard the front door open.

"Cecelia, hello," Mrs. Bennett called to the visitor. "Is Lin with you?"

"He said to start without him, he'd be in soon."

"Fine."

For some unexplained reason, I had the feeling I needed to get out before I ran into Lin.

I heard the squeak of the louvered doors as they entered the dressing rooms and I sneaked a peek as the two women passed, crossing into the office, the door shutting behind them.

I had seen one of the women before, I would swear it, but I couldn't remember where.

I paused to consider that but only for a second, then hightailed it out of the dressing rooms and into the store. I spotted Justine as I made my way to the door.

"See ya," I whispered as I passed by, keeping my head down until I was on the other side of the glass front door.

I straightened up as I reached the parking lot and went right to the Jeep. I didn't waste any time getting out of there.

99

Driving down the four-lane highway, nearly to Tenley, I came upon another billboard for the Tri-County Real Estate and Home Sales company, and I pulled to a stop on the shoulder to take a closer look. It was the same group photo with the associates and Lin, and I shook my head at that.

So far, he was two-for-three on my money-laundering list.

One of the blondes also caught my eye. Was that Cecelia, the woman I'd just seen in Baljean's?

I wondered about the rest of that group, if they had any idea of what was going on right under their noses.

And then I had to laugh because, with my amnesia, I had absolutely no idea what was going on either, no real evidence of wrongdoing on Lin's part, or anyone's for that matter, just wild speculation at this point.

The only exception was the counterfeit goods in Baljean's.

What happened the night I ended up in that culvert? How do I pull all of this together into a cohesive case?

Maybe it's a good thing I'm going back to school.

I'd forgotten how to be a cop.

I have to start at the end and work backwards.

100

That night, I woke up to a still-dark room, Tess wrapped against me. I blinked several times, as if that would bring the dream into focus, like tuning my brain into the station I was trying so hard to receive. I still heard snatches of conversation, and I had felt the presence of others, I just couldn't see their faces, or hear many of the words fading in and out.

It had been happening more and more over the course of the past month, and I knew that a lot of it was my memory refilling the gaps and whole portions of spaces left blank from my fall. I hadn't told Tess, I didn't want to get her hopes up, but my dreams included more and more people and places from the past two years, Dr. Biggs being a good part of that.

More than once, I had dreamed of standing in the lab of the animal hospital, talking and laughing with Biggs, Meg, Tracey, and Madge. Or on a field of green, the warm sun and the smell of grass and dirt so real I could taste it.

And Tess, from a time and a place I didn't remember but knew to be true. Little more than a presence, always on the edges, just there and tending to me.

It was coming back.

I just needed more time.

101

I made my way to Hatch's office, going against flow of students making their way to the stairwells and elevators in the period between classes. I entered the reception area of the instructors' offices and stood in front of the desk manned by the student gatekeeper fulfilling his work-study program requirements for the department.

"Is Hatch in?"

He looked at me as if I'd spoken in a foreign language.

"Hatcher," I clarified. "Is she in?"

He squinted and I had the distinct impression that he was being deliberately obtuse, a common response from a male who resented females in general and butch women in particular. He seemed to revel in his passive-aggressive position of authority, but I was older, wiser.

And faster.

I blew an exasperated breath and skirted past his desk, heading for Hatch's office.

"Hey! You can't..."

I was at her door, tapping twice and opening it before the kid caught up with me. Hatch was behind her desk, reading from a set of papers in her hand, standing up in surprise as we burst through the door.

"What the hell?"

"Hatch, I just need a minute..."

"No, wait, I didn't say you could..." The kid was way beyond being on my last nerve now, and I took his meaty paw from my shoulder and applied the hold Tess had used on me to render him frozen to the spot.

"I don't need your permission, boy. Not now, not ever. I asked you a question that you didn't seem inclined to answer, and now here we are. If you're thinking of graduating in law enforcement or firefighting or as an EMT, you'd best get used to dealing with women from here on, because they'll have your back out there, so you'd better have theirs. Do you read me?"

"Yes."

I leaned closer. "Yes, what?"

"Yes, ma'am."

"That's better." I maneuvered him back over the threshold, releasing my hold as he crossed it, closing the door behind him.

Hatch stood looking at me as I turned back to her. "Damn, Baxter, have you ever seen anyone about those anger issues of yours?" She was smiling, though, and shaking her head. "You just shortened my lecture on professional relationships to less than five minutes. Ah, well, it comes at mid-terms, the class will appreciate being let out early."

She sat back down and rolled up to her desk, crossing her arms on its surface. "Now, what can I do for you?"

"Hatch, I need your help. I want to retrace my steps the night I went missing."

Her face registered surprise at that. "Why?"

"I want to know how I ended up in that ditch."

102

We stood at the top of the embankment, looking down.

"Geezus."

"Yeah, it's steep. The EMTs pulled you out on a backboard with a tow line. You'd have had a helluva time getting up and out of there on your own."

We stood on the streetside of the guardrail and we'd both been leaning over the thick metal to see over the edge. Now, I crossed the barrier and peered down into the culvert.

"How the hell did anyone know I was down there?"

"A woman walking her dog on the other side saw you and called it in."

As I turned to see where Hatch was pointing, I slipped, and Hatch grabbed me to stop my going over the edge along with the small pieces of loose gravel and sand under my feet.

"Well, huh. I think that explains that."

The fear on Hatch's face was replaced with a quizzical look, but she still had a death grip on my forearm. "What?"

"I don't think I was thrown." I crossed back over the rail and I heard her breathe a sigh of relief.

"I think I fell."

103

The cloudy conditions of the winter evening triggered the old mercury vapor streetlight on the far side of the faded blacktop and it buzzed to life. In the twilight, I could see that the wide metal guardrail was now casting a significant shadow on the space behind it, leaving all but the narrow edge of the culvert in darkness.

"How did I end up here? Why?"

Hatch was looking down at her phone. I shook my head. "Dude, really? This is no time to check your messages."

"What?" She shook her head. "No, I'm looking at a map. I couldn't figure out why you left your Jeep in the parking lot of the mall, but now..." She turned so that we could both see the phone screen. "We know you'd been at Baljean's earlier with Justine, and that you went back after finishing your errand for Dr. Biggs. The mall is a little over a quarter-mile away, I can see the top of the mall sign, but we're on the road behind it."

She scowled as she considered her thinking. "Baxter, I think someone was chasing you."

104

We were sitting in Hatch's truck, now idling in the space next to my Jeep in the empty college parking lot, and I shared my thoughts regarding the money-laundering and the real estate company in addition to the fake goods. Hatch nodded as I laid out my findings, then we both went quiet while we considered it all.

After a few minutes, Hatch spoke up.

"I have an idea."

Her tone was tentative and I looked at her, both eyebrows raised to encourage her to continue.

"Promise not to laugh or blow me off."

"Okay." I drew the word out because now it was my turn to be tentative.

"Have you ever been hypnotized?"

"Oh, wow, Hatch. Really?"

"You promised."

"Yeah, but seriously. I had no idea you were going to suggest that."

"Look, I have a friend, Elsbeth McKay, she's very good at it and it goes without saying that she's a real trip at parties, but what if it could work? What if it brings your memory back?"

"Hatch, I'm a skeptic, it wouldn't work on me, we're the worst for being placed into a hypnotic state. We fight it every step of the way."

"Baxter, c'mon, she's in Richmond, we could have all the answers by the end of the week. Elsbeth could put you under and then maybe we can extract any info you got that night. Look, I agree with you, I think there's a helluva lot going on under the radar with these businesses, and maybe the local law enforcement is in on it, just like what you found in Baltimore, but you can't go back to the store if anyone is watching for you. And you never know who you may run into that recognizes you, it's not safe."

I thought about that, and I suddenly remembered Lin standing in his restaurant kitchen door looking at me. I shuddered a bit, recalling his cold gaze.

"Look, let me make a call, set it up. Baxter, what if you could be back to your old self by Monday morning? How can you turn that down? Why the hell would you?"

I was nodding. Hatch was right.

What if I had everything we needed to know about the counterfeit goods and the money laundering all boxed up and tied with a pretty little bow locked inside my thick skull?

And Hatch made a very good point--what if I could get my all of my memory back?

"Okay. Make the call."

"Would you like to go to Richmond this weekend?"

Tess was sitting in her chaise with a book on her lap, Smokey cuddled with her on the blanket over her legs. I crossed the room and sat down on the edge of the seat by her knees. The grey cat grumbled a bit but didn't give up an inch of space.

"Richmond? Why?"

"Well..." and so I told her about Hatch's idea, that Elsbeth McKay was available and that she was frankly excited by the premise that she could help me regain my memory, looking at it from a psychologist's point of view. She was curious to know if she could access my memories that, while not repressed, like most of her patients, I simply couldn't recall because I had lost the connection from physical trauma.

She believed they were there, she just had to get at them from another direction.

"Hypnosis."

"Yes."

Her forehead creased and her lips pursed while she considered the idea. It didn't take long.

"She thinks she can help you? Well, then, why not? It can't hurt, right?"

"Ohhhh, Hatch, it is so good to see you, darlin'!"

Her deep-south twang was a bit of a surprise.

Elsbeth McKay might have been in her mid-thirties but it was hard to tell, she was dressed in a ball cap, her red hair a color not normally found in nature pulled into a ponytail through the hole in the back, and she was wearing a letterman's jacket from Covington High over a black sweater, jeans, and Chuck Taylors.

She was a little taller than Penny, and thin, with a heart-shaped face, her eyes aquamarine in color. Hatch blushed at her words, but she stepped into the woman's outstretched arms, leaning down and chuckling a bit when the woman pulled her tight against her, rocking them to-and-fro before releasing her.

"That's just as lovely as it ever was, Hatch, thank you!" That 'yew' rang out and Hatch smiled wide, blushing again, with a nod and a "You're welcome, ma'am."

Elsbeth turned quickly to the group of women with her, smiling at them all as Hatch made the introductions.

"Hello, oh, Tess, I just love your hair! And your eyes." She practically sighed at that. "Wow."

She turned to Penny, her mouth pursed a bit as she considered her. "So you're the one." Her tone was almost accusatory.

Penny's eyes narrowed, cocking her head as she appeared to size up Elsbeth in turn. "The one?"

Elsbeth laughed a warm, low laugh.

"The one who caught this big lug," she said, wrapping her arm around Hatch's waist and pulling her tight against her, Hatch shaking her head at that.

Penny and Tess both raised singular brows at Elsbeth, who moved on to Bishop, having saved her for last.

"So, Bishop, you're my subject." Elsbeth was smiling up at her, looking straight into her eyes, lightly running her hand up and down the length of Bishop's arm. "I'm going to use your real name during the session, hon, I want your full attention. So now, don't you be nervous, there's nothing to worry about. Just like I told you on the phone when y'all called, you're just going to take a nap and have the best sleep you've ever had while you tell us everything that you don't know you know."

She chuckled a bit at that. "And then you'll wake up to me tapping the back of your hand, all happy and refreshed, okay?" Her eyes sparkled and her smile was genuine as she tipped her head at Bishop, who was nodding and smiling, though a bit weakly, at her reassurance.

She nodded to the other women as she wrapped her arm through Bishop's, walking her through the door and leading them all into her office.

107

It was a large room, a row of windows with a southern exposure catching the golden rays of the winter sun as it sank into the late afternoon. The natural lighting enhanced the pale yellow walls, the furniture upholstered in deep reds and golds adding to the soothing warmth of it all.

The sofa was flanked by walnut end tables, the coffee table and wing-back chairs forming a tableau in front of the sofa.

Elsbeth's desk, its polished mahogany top as wide as a full-sized bed, suited the small desk chair upholstered in pearl behind it, the pair set at an angle in the far corner near the windows, with a pedaling exerciser visible underneath.

In the other corner was a wet bar and a rather complex-looking coffee maker in a recessed area usually hidden behind wooden pocket doors.

"Pretty sweet for an FBI agent, huh, Tess?" Elsbeth smiled at her, nodding her head as she took off her jacket and cap and threw it onto the chair behind her desk. Tess returned her nod, a little rattled that a woman she'd just met was reading her mind.

Elsbeth continued on in a far more serious tone.

"I work with officers and agents who have gone through a traumatic encounter or event, they've been physically wounded, or they've had to kill someone in self-defense, or at the defense of others, or someone died because they couldn't save them.

"They've seen the brutality humans can inflict upon one another and it haunts them. The last thing I want to do is stress them in the aftermath, so I try to make this room as comfortable as possible."

She walked over to the wet bar and poured five glasses from an open bottle of white wine, then carried them on a serving tray to her company. "Now, though, this isn't work, this is a favor for a very old friend, and it's Saturday afternoon--let's drink!"

108

They all sat down and relaxed, the wine was good, and plentiful, Elsbeth refilling their glasses as they talked and laughed, Hatch and Elsbeth catching up, Elsbeth sharing pictures of her with her husband, their three-year-old son, and one-year-old baby daughter, before they settled down to the business at hand.

Bishop was sitting in the wingback with the glow of the afternoon light from the windows behind her. Elsbeth smiled at her, then leaned forward and stroked her hand down the length of her arm.

"Bishop, are you having a good time?"

Bishop smiled back. "Yes, of course."

Looking directly into her eyes, Elsbeth kept her hand on Bishop. "Bishop, hey, listen, hon, I told you how I would do this, remember?" She was lightly stroking Bishop's arm as she talked, leading Bishop along as she had her focus on relaxing and breathing, her voice soft as she conveyed calmness and tranquility.

The others looked on, the whole room caught up in the quiet as Elsbeth spoke only to Bishop. "I'm going to count backwards from fifteen and when I reach 'eight,' I want you to feel sleepy, and when I reach 'four,' you'll fall asleep."

Bishop had settled back in her chair, looking skeptical when they'd started, but when Elsbeth whispered 'four,' Bishop's eyes closed and her chin fell to her chest.

"Wow." Penny whispered.

"When Hatch called, I had her put Bishop on the phone. She told me she couldn't be hypnotised, but everyone's a skeptic, you know. It's a control issue, really. I gave her some pre-hypnotic suggestions, some thoughts that would put her at ease to prepare her for this, and I just reminded her of all that. Okay, so, let's get to work."

She turned to Hatch, taking a swallow of her wine as Hatch handed her a folded piece of paper--a list of questions to ask--nodding to Elsbeth as she set her phone on the coffee table with the voice recorder app running.

"Hi, Bishop. Are you comfortable?"

"Yes."

"Okay. Now, I'm going to ask you some questions, and I want you to answer with as much information as you can. I want you to tell me what you see, what you hear, even what you smell. Nod your head if you understand."

Bishop nodded.

"Good. Tell me what happened at Baljean's."

109

Walking into the store, I smell the leather, I see the sales women behind the counter. They look up as I come in and I see their frowns--the store is near closing and they don't want to be late getting out. I take a shirt from the rack, it's one I'd looked at when I was there earlier, and I take it to the dressing room.

"I won't be but a minute," I tell them as I pass the register. I'm looking for the two women I'd seen earlier, Vivian, the store owner, and Cecelia, who I'd recognized as Tess's real estate agent. When they'd passed by me earlier, Joan was talking about the sale of some commercial property to the Tri-County Real Estate company, saying Lin had agreed that its price could be easily inflated in the resales.

Entering the dressing rooms, I notice that the door to the office is open the slightest bit, and I hear talking. I'm hoping that it's the women I'd seen earlier, but the voices include a man's. All are speaking in hushed tones. I take the dressing room closest to the office, but I still can't hear the conversation, so I move into the space leading to the office door.

"...okay, so with your purchase from Tri-County for one hundred thirty-five thousand, I buy it from you for one hundred and sixty thousand, that clears another twenty-five thousand. How much have we moved so far, Cecelia?"

"Three hundred and seventy-six thousand dollars in real estate alone this week, including the three residential properties in Elmwood and Tenley. Buying that run-down strip mall in Bell City helped, but we've still got another quarter-million or so to go."

A man's voice cuts in. "I've fluffed the bid from Tri-County Construction for the renovations, that should take care of the remainder."

So now I'm pretty sure they're laundering money. They're buying and selling properties to each other, inflating the price each time the deed goes around the table, using the dirty money in the transactions, and Tri-County Real Estate apparently owns the construction company as well.

The voices have become muddled, the store's heating unit has come on, the flow of the forced air pushes the door nearly closed.

I move to just outside the doorway, leaning close and straining to hear.

"Castile wants to open another real estate office in the Virginia Beach area, I'm meeting with Carrie Jenkins of Wayside Properties over there next week."

Castile.

My blood runs cold.

Castile.

There can't be two of them.

But it would make perfect sense, wouldn't it? Castile heads the biggest drug-running operation from the East Coast to the Mississippi, hiding the illegal profits by laundering them in his legitimate businesses under the Castile Enterprises banner.

He was expanding his network when I first heard of him, buying off law enforcement in all of the agencies around Baltimore. His legal team was nothing to sneeze at, he had smart, efficient lawyers, adept at outmaneuvering and stonewalling the local and state attorneys.

He'd backed a few politicians as well, donating to their campaigns, purchasing influential people the same way he was buying up companies and commercial properties around Baltimore.

The door suddenly opens and Lin is standing in front of me. I look up at him in the briefest of seconds before I turn and run for the louvered dressing room doors leading out to the sales floor.

It's blocked by a man with a handcart loaded with boxes and I turn again.

Trapped.

I see the red exit sign above the door past the dressing rooms and I run for it, hoping it's unlocked, it has to be, it's a fire door, and I pull it open to enter a storage room stacked with boxes. There's another door to my right, and I race for it, hitting the panic bar and pushing through to the outside, the alarm is sounding, and I'm running left across the pavement and out to the street.

I hear shouting behind me, and I keep running along the roadway, looking for any place to hide, or to cut back through the mall to my Jeep, but there's no break between the stores, and nothing to my right, no houses or alleys, only a metal guardrail dividing the road from the open area behind the mall.

Headlights in the distance behind me now, I veer off the road to hide in the shadows behind the metal rail.

I vault over the barricade at a run, my feet hitting the ground behind it, and then they're sliding out from under me, I'm falling, and it feels like I'll never stop.

Until I hit the ground.

110

"Bishop." Elsbeth is tapping the back of my hand. I open my eyes to see everyone sitting there, looking at me.

Hatch picks up her phone and stops the voice recording.

"Did it work? Did you get anything?"

"Oh, yeah, we got something all right."

"Well?"

"Dammit, Bishop. You couldn't make this easy, could you." It wasn't a question and Hatch is shaking her head.

"What?"

"Castile."

I think I stopped breathing.

At least, I felt like I had. Or maybe it was more like taking a sucker punch in the gut, and the wind was knocked out of me. Either way, it took a minute to come back from that.

"Bishop?" Tess leaned forward, concern etched on her face.

I reach for her hand and give it a squeeze. "I'm okay."

I looked at Hatch. "Really?"

She nodded. She knew who he was. "I've been chasing him for nearly three years," she tells me.

Elsbeth was shaking her head."Well, that sure was something. It worked, Bishop, you remembered what happened to you. Maybe that will open up the floodgates."

I nodded.

"And, just to confirm this with witnesses present, you're still gonna let me take a little piece of your brain to study, right?"

We all stared at her, wide-eyed.

Elsbeth chuckled, then slapped her thighs and bounced to her feet, smiling as she began collecting the empty wine glasses. "So, does anyone have any bad habits they want hypnotized away before we go to supper?"

111

Tess was turning down the bedcovers when I walked into the room. It was late when we got home and the weather had turned colder in the dark, the crisp smell of snow in the air as we made our way from the car to the carriage house. I pulled a second comforter from the closet and unfolded it, draping it across the foot of the bed, Tess silently nodding agreement that we might need it in the night.

She crawled into bed, and I made my way around to her side, pulling the covers up and tucking them around her before leaning down and kissing her on the cheek. She seemed surprised at that, but didn't say anything.

"I'll be right back."

I don't know how to describe what I was feeling then, and I didn't know if the session with Elsbeth had left me that well-rested or if I was still running on the adrenaline surge that I'd had upon hearing the name I'd given while I was hypnotized.

I can tell you that Castile is the quintessential story of the diamond in the rough, the young boy who'd made it out of his dirt-poor circumstances to become the polished, smooth-edged businessman, the hero in every rags-to-riches story ever told.

How he got there is covered in layers of deception and dishonesty and, quite frankly, death and the destruction of anyone who got in his way.

His reputation on the street is the stuff of nightmares, he takes real pleasure in pursuing and catching his hunters in snares of his own, making examples of them for anyone brave enough--or stupid enough--to try to capture him.

I had escaped his trap once, I think it made me an even bigger prize to be had, but word was that, while I had shot and killed Krieger, he had killed me as well.

In our Memory School sessions, Tess had happily shared that my safety there in Tenley had been insured by Krieger shooting me in full view of his body man, who would send that info back to Baltimore.

So, as far as the Company was concerned, I was dead and gone--again--and no longer a problem to be handled.

I have a monster under my bed, though, his name is Castile, and while I could let sleeping monsters lie...

...where's the fun in that?

112

I crept into bed and pushed my way through the covers to Tess.

"Oh, you're so warm." I nudged my cold nose against her neck.

"And you're freezing! Stop! That's just mean!" She laughed, I was pressing my feet against her legs, pulling her tight against me so she couldn't get away. "Have you been outside?"

"I wanted to smell the snow again. And the floor is cold."

"Slippers."

"What about them?"

"We need to get you some."

"Okay."

"Fluffy pink ones."

"No."

"Yes."

"I won't wear them."

"Okay, then, some old-man slip-ons."

"Tess, no!"

"But your feet are like blocks of ice."

"And I have you to warm them up."

She chuckled and shook her head. "I didn't sign on for that."

"Yes you did, when you said 'I do.'"

"There are limits."

"And I'm pushing them."

"Yes, you are."

"But you love me."

She didn't answer back, not immediately. In that moment, I was afraid I had truly breached a breaking point, but she turned over in my arms and looked at me, half her face cast in shadow.

"I do love you, you know I do. And it scares me sometimes, how much I love you."

"Tess..."

"Listening to you this afternoon, Bishop, I can't describe it. I was scared for you, even though you were sitting there in front of me, I was afraid of losing you. And then I realized that I did lose you, in a way. You're right when you say you're not the woman I married. That fall took her from me.

"I will always love the Bishop you were when I married you, but tonight I realized that I love this Bishop, too. I don't know if I'm strong enough to do the things you've done, to be as brave as you in facing death, but I know that you will not go without a fight, and that, to me, is the most important part of you. Your sense of justice is what drives you, and I think it will most likely get you killed, but if that happens, you will go down swinging on your own terms. And I can't stand in your way."

I pulled her against me and softly kissed her.

"I love you, too, Tess."

I couldn't have stopped those words from falling from my lips, they had to be said, let loose so that she could hear them. I don't think I'd said them to her even once in all of this, but I had to now, I needed her to know.

"I love you. I love you for your kind heart, your grace, how you've withstood the hardest soul-killing moments one human could ever face and still be as warm and loving and strong as you are. I don't ever want you to be hurt again and I know that that is completely unreasonable, especially since I am the one who could hurt you the most.

"It makes me sad to think about that, but you've thought about it too, and knowing this will keep me from second-guessing, from hesitating or holding back in that split second when I have to push forward. Knowing that you understand will help keep me safe."

We laid there wrapped around each other, quiet, listening to each other breathe.

The wind was picking up, sighing as it blew across the roof and under the eaves.

She dropped off to sleep before me, and I whispered to her in the darkness.

"Good night, wife."

113

I awoke to an oddly-bright room, a diffuse glow from behind the window shade. Tess was still sleeping and I crept out from under the covers, pulling on a pair of sweats and my flannel shirt over my T-shirt before jamming my feet into my sneakers. Leaving the bathroom through the living room door and pulling the bedroom door closed as I passed by, I made my way into the kitchen and stopped in astonishment as I looked through the double window.

The white was nearly blinding in the early morning sun, the entire yard was covered. There were no spaces anywhere that did not have snow--the wind had made sure of that. And I chuckled as I saw Rosie and Sophie dashing about, playing tag in the middle of the yard, Rosie bursting through the drifts and sending the powder up in a spray as she broke trail through the pristine whiteness.

I put on coffee then made my way outside, taking in the muffled quiet. No traffic noise, no birds or squirrels chirping or chattering, just the two dogs huffing quietly when they tagged each other in their game, as if they also were aware of the unusual silence.

They caught sight of me and the game was over, they were ready for their breakfasts, having built up quite the appetites in their playing. Making a beeline for the porch, the two dogs barked and jumped on me, their wet paws leaving cold prints on my sweatpants, before nosing through the doggie door and into the house.

"Oh, no, wait," I called as I rushed in behind them. They skidded on the tiled floor, their wet paws still holding clumps of frozen snow. "Get back here."

They came back to the mudroom and I pulled two towels from the dryer, dropping one over Sophie like a horse blanket then picking up Rosie and wrapping her round wet body in the other, scrubbing her dry and picking out the snow berries from her paw pads.

"My goodness."

I looked up as Tess peered out the window. "It's beautiful."

"Isn't it?"

She looked down to Sophie nudging her. "You're all wet," Tess laughed, reaching down and briskly rubbing her with the towel still draped over her back. "Oh, Sophie, you smell so good! You've had a snow bath!"

They were dry and eating when I looked over at Tess sipping coffee as she gazed out the window "You know what? I'm starving. How about you?"

"Gawd, yes, I could eat."

"Let's go out."

Tess looked at me, smiling and shaking her head. "You just want to drive that Jeep in the snow, you don't fool me."

I hung my head, but there was a smile on my lips. "Oh, absolutely!" I laughed at that. "Admit it, you're as excited about getting out in that as I am!"

She was grinning like a kid on a snow day. "Johnson's is always open, even in weather like this."

"Breakfast," I growled, drawing out the word.

We both took off for the bedroom in a rush to change clothes.

114

About twenty minutes later, we were pulling into the parking lot and I spied Hatch's pick-up truck parked near the door.

"Look who's here."

Tess smiled and we carefully made our way along the icy sidewalk, glad to get inside, spotting Hatch sitting with a rather attractive but unfamiliar woman at a booth towards the rear of the diner. I caught her eye, but she shook me off, and I grabbed Tess by the arm before she started over to her.

"They don't want our company," I let her know when she turned to see why I'd stopped her.

"Who's she with?" Tess's eyes were narrowed.

"I don't know and it's none of our business. Let's get a booth on this side."

We walked over to the other end of the diner, far enough from the door that the chilly air wouldn't be a problem as people came and went.

We'd ordered when Hatch made her way to our booth, taking a seat next to Tess. "Hey! Y'all didn't come out in all this just for eggs and coffee, did you?"

"Of course, it's just what we do when there's two feet of snow on the ground." Tess bounced her shoulder against Hatch as she answered.

"Sorry, Hatch, she's a bit snarky now that she's had a cup of coffee," I laughed.

"So, who's so important that you're out in two feet of snow?"

I had to smirk at Tess, she wasn't being too obvious with that question.

"Honestly? Baxter."

I sat blinking, my forehead knotted. "Me?"

"Yeah. I played the session you had with Elsbeth for Hennings. She's headed to Virginia Beach to follow up on a couple of leads, and I thought she could use the info. It actually turned out to be a big help. I hope you don't mind."

I nodded. I'd have done the same thing. They wanted Castile, too.

Maybe they didn't burn with it, but still.

"Well, I'm gonna go, I've got to get back to Penny." Hatch stood up. "Y'all have a good day, enjoy the snow."

We said our goodbyes in turn, and I watched Hatch walk over and pay her tab, then head to the parking lot.

"I'll be right back." I got up and followed Hatch.

"Hey!" I called as I got onto the sidewalk. Hatch looked up, puzzled, then came back and joined me.

"Be honest with me."

"Okay."

"You're still working for the DEA, aren't you." It wasn't really a question.

"Baxter."

"C'mon, Hatch."

She hung her head, pursed her lips while she considered her options.

"Hatch."

"Okay, okay. Listen, you can't tell anyone, not Tess, and definitely not Penny."

"What? Why? What's going on?"

She stuffed her fists deep in her jeans pockets and stretched to her full height. "I'm here because of Penny."

"I know. You love Penny."

"No. I mean, yes, I love Penny, but..."

"But?"

"There may be a hit out on her."

"*May* be?"

"Well, not a hit, exactly, more like a bounty. She cost Castile a lot of money and a helluva lot of drugs when we pulled all those trucks off the highways. Since then, there's been some chatter that she's wanted, there's a price on her head. Even though she's not named, she's identified as 'Individual Three' in the agency reports of the bust in Richmond, and well...we...have a mole."

115

I was incredulous.

"There's a mole in your investigation?"

"Okay, so, we're not sure, exactly, where the mole is..."

I grabbed Hatch above her elbow and manhandled her back into the diner, shoving her into the booth next to Tess.

"What's going on?" Tess looked back and forth between the two of us, not sure who to focus on.

"Tell her." I stood beside the table, leaning toward Hatch. "Tell her what you just told me."

"I was just telling Baxter that...there may be...a..."

I rolled my eyes and leaned forward, whispering, "she still works for the DEA, there's a hit out on Penny, and there's a mole in their investigation."

Tess's coffee cup stalled halfway to her mouth, which had fallen slack as she heard my news. She closed her mouth and put down the cup, her forehead puckered as she considered what I said.

"Can I get y'all anything?" Bridgette was standing next to me, topping off my coffee with the fresh pot she carried with her, looking over at Tess.

"Just our breakfasts," I replied, a bit short. "It's been a while."

"Be nice, Bishop," Tess admonished. "It's late, the wait staff has changed shift."

"Sorry. Our orders are in, could you check?"

Bridgette filled Tess's cup. She turned to Hatch. "And what about you? Wait, weren't you just..." and she looked over at the other end of the restaurant.

"Yeah. But another coffee, if you don't mind." Hatch replied.

I sat down across the table from the two as Bridgette headed for the kitchen. "Anything else we need to know, Hatch?"

She shook her head. "No, no, that pretty much covers it."

"You're a good liar, Hatch." Tess didn't look her way. "Really good. Maybe better than Bishop. And that's saying a lot."

"Hey, now."

She gave me a little smile to let me know that she wasn't being mean. "Okay, Hatch, tell me about your little rodent problem."

116

According to Hatch, for the past four months, someone was giving the targets a heads-up whenever the DEA planned a raid, leading to empty warehouses and offices when the teams of agents arrived on-scene to execute the search warrants. It didn't happen every time, but it was embarrassing and costly enough when it did that the higher-ups were getting pissed.

"Internal Affairs has even gone through the personal financials of every agent involved in every part of this mission and they've come up empty. And it's been terrible for morale, no one trusts anyone, everybody's on edge..." Hatch sat back at that, exhaling loudly before she took a swallow of coffee.

I nodded, thinking of my life in Baltimore after I'd discovered my partner's involvement with Castile's operations, the paranoia and distrust I couldn't shake in my day-to-day interactions with the other officers in my precinct. I looked across the table at the two women as I tossed a bit of salt on my omelette. "I understand your pain, Hatch."

"What do you think, Tess?"

"I think you'd better tell Penny."

Hatch was sadly resigned as she shook her head at that. "She'll be looking over her shoulder from now on."

I added ketchup to my hash browns. "And I understand *her* pain, Hatch. She can stand her ground." I lowered my voice and leaned toward them. "Or she can relocate with WITSEC."

Hatch looked at me as she considered that. "She'd never leave her dad. And she loves her house. And her job."

"And she loves you, Hatch. Penny will be fine. She's tough, she's smart, and she's armed--that makes her dangerous. She saved Kane's life. Remember?" Tess was completely serious and the questioning look I gave her reminded her that I didn't know what she was talking about. "I'll tell you about it later," she said, nodding.

117

We parted ways in the parking lot, slowly making our way back home when Tess pulled out her phone.

"Hey Joe, we need to talk."

I nodded, hearing Tess's side of the conversation while she brought Fowler up to speed. We hadn't exactly been good at keeping him in the loop when it came to sharing information. He needed to know that everyone he was working with regarding my disappearance, from the Whitmore PD and any other interested party on down, could be sharing info with Castile's organization.

Tess signed off the call acknowledging Fowler's words of caution and that they'd talk more in the department in the morning. She sighed and leaned back in her seat, looking at the snow and marvelling at how the streets and houses and parks looked so different with everything covered in the white powder.

When we got home, we positioned ourselves under a blanket on the couch, choosing a movie and settling in against the cold. Tess laughed, saying it felt like old times, telling me that we had spent plenty of days doing exactly this when I'd first gotten to Tenley, and later, after we were together again and newly married.

I smiled as I put my arm around her and pulled her close, her head resting on my shoulder as the opening notes of the movie's score played.

It's easy to see how I had fallen for her. We share a quiet comfort, there are no hoops to be jumped through, no expectations of anything more than what we already share.

It was a perfect day.

118

Because of the snow, classes were cancelled, so just after two o'clock the next day, Tess, Joe, their partner Whyte, and I were sitting in the Tenley PD conference room when Hatch and Penny joined us, taking their seats at the table as I began telling everything I knew about Castile and his activity in Baltimore.

Joe was nodding as he made notes while Whyte sat quietly, also jotting down details, clenching and unclenching his jaw as he considered what a deep-dive investigation into Lin's business ventures would entail, since he was taking charge of the financial side of the probe.

When it was Hatch's turn, she laid out what the DEA had found in their Task Force investigation. Castile's corporation and subsidiaries owned a number of warehouses just off the primary North-South interstate, the corridor connecting the uppermost reaches of Maine to the southern coast of Miami and intersecting with east-west highways into the major cities just this side of the Appalachians.

Hatch said they'd located a small prop jet Castile owned and that the plane was noted to fly in and out of a number of municipal airports at intervals, usually preceding pop-up events throughout the area.

The pop-ups are the most interesting.

They're used to establish contact with the local commerce groups, providing connections to real estate and small business owners in the towns and cities the Company is looking to expand into. The handshakes and backslaps lead in turn to bigger financial and real estate dealings, with the commercial development and resulting new jobs lauded as 'good business' as the local economy grows.

Everybody wins.

Fan-fucking-tastic.

Penny sat quietly, listening to all of the information, and when we were done, she sat up in her chair, leaning her elbows on the table as she said her piece.

"Oh, they're gonna hate us. I mean, c'mon, there are people working throughout these states in jobs they wouldn't have if Castile hadn't shown up. He's not a exactly a snake-oil salesman, taking their money and running off into the night, the towns are profiting from this as much as he is."

"He's supplying the drugs some of those people are wasting their hard-earned money on, and he's cleaning that money by recycling it back into their paychecks, buying up and renovating properties that they'll never be able to buy on their own, so they're stuck in rentals--*his* rentals. He's gonna own everyone's lives, from their jobs to the roofs over their heads.

"We're going to have a helluva time convincing people that he's bad news. You know that, right? No one is going to appreciate our killing the goose that lays the golden eggs, no matter how tainted those eggs are, from the mayors to the wage earners losing their jobs when we bust the company open."

Whyte looked at Penny, blinking and shaking his head, his lips curved in a small smile. She had absolutely nailed the situation.

We were quiet while we considered all of that.

"Hatch." Tess softly called to her across the table. "Tell her the rest of it."

Hatch's discomfort was hard to watch, the way she shifted in her chair, not able to look anyone in the eye.

"Hatch."

"Tell who what? Me?" Penny looked around at all of us. "What aren't you telling me?"

Hatch sighed, taking on a look of resignation. She took Penny's hand.

Penny's eyes grew wide with uncertainty, her voice nearly a whisper. "Hatch?"

"Penny, we have good intel that...well, there's chatter..." Hatch stopped and took a breath. "You really pissed Castile off. He's put a bounty on you. He wants you."

Penny didn't move, except for her eyes narrowing as she considered Hatch's information. "Dead? Or alive?"

"Ha, ah, well..."

We were all looking at Hatch. It was a question worth asking. Worth hearing the answer to.

"Ten thousand dead. One hundred fifty thousand if you're delivered alive."

Penny leaned back in her chair. "Well, then, I at least have a chance."

She didn't blink.

Tess had told me about the night her fast thinking saved Kane's life.

Penny Harris is the smartest, toughest woman I know.

Hatch and I were making our way out the rear exit of City Hall when I spotted Dennings headed in our direction.

"Shit. Wonder what he wants."

"Who is he?"

I took that opportunity to introduce Hatch to the man, since he was now standing in front of me, leaving out the fact that Hatch was DEA. It was better to withhold that info, I thought, especially since we didn't know who could be playing on Castile's team.

"Yeah, okay, whatever." Dennings waved the introductions off. "I'm glad you're here, it saves me from having you picked up."

He seemed disappointed by that.

Obviously, his poor attempt at intimidation, in my opinion.

"Why don't you just come along with me, Miss Baxter, I have some more questions for you."

What could he possibly think I know?

Except this time, after having the session with Elsbeth, there *were* things I knew. And I knew that I really didn't like his tone.

Hatch looked at me. I don't think she liked his tone either. Or him in general.

We both turned and the three of us walked back into the department, Dennings bringing up the rear. The desk sargeant, George, called into the bullpen for Fowler, who led us back to the conference room we'd so recently vacated, but not before sending Hatch to get Tess.

Fowler, Dennings, and I took our seats and I assumed an open position--nothing crossed, both hands open on my thighs.

Dennings pulled out his phone and tapped the red record button, logging the date, place, time, and names of those present.

"Okay, Miss Baxter, on the night in question, you accompanied one Justine Daley to Whitmore to obtain crates and crate pads for Dr. Sharon Biggs from Dr. Sam Tedder's clinic." He looked up from his notes for my confirmation.

In our previous encounter, I'd had no recollection of the events of that night, and I had no knowledge of anything that had happened prior to my waking up in the Whitmore County Hospital. I thought it best to stick to that to see just what the detective had uncovered in his investigation.

"That's what I've been told."

"You still have no memories of that night."

I shrugged and shook my head.

"Out loud, please, for the record."

"Oh, of course. For the record, Detective, I have no recollection of my actions the night of December 6th."

Tess entered the room as I was repeating 'for the record,' and she passed a puzzled look to Fowler.

Dennings paused here to add Tess to the attendance, then continued his questioning.

"You accompanied Ms. Daley into the Baljean's fashion store, where she collected her weekly pay, and you followed her out. You returned within two hours, alone, and took a shirt from a display rack, entering the dressing room with that merchandise."

Now, that surprised me. "I did? I picked out a shirt? Really? What did it look like? I mean, I can't imagine my finding anything there that would be a part of my particular fashion style, all things considered, Detective. Would you, Tess?"

She knew not to laugh but the corner of her mouth drew up a bit as she considered it, leaning towards the table and Dennings' phone. "No. No, I don't. Do you have anything to support your claims, Detective Dennings?"

Ah, my wife comes through.

She's turned the tables on him, doing a little investigating of her own. He paused, I watched him weigh his options. Does he play his cards close to his chest, or does he turn a card up?

"We have video of Miss Baxter entering Baljean's, and then carrying merchandise into the dressing room, reportedly a shirt. Or a blouse...whatever."

He was showing some exasperation at this point. "We do not have video of her leaving, however, and there is a record of the emergency exit alarm in the adjacent area being activated within three minutes of her entering the dressing rooms."

"So what, exactly, are you asserting here, Detective?"

Now Fowler was enjoined.

"Baljean's has asked us to investigate a trespassing that occurred on their premises involving Miss Baxter, and we are following up that request with the subject in question."

"Trespassing. By a potential customer? Was anything stolen? Was there any property damage that requires filing a claim? Dennings, what, exactly, is the intent of this investigation?"

"We're gathering information at this point in the investigation, Detective Fowler."

120

Fowler stood up, leaving no doubt as to the end of the interrogation. He looked across the table at Dennings. "If there are no damages, nothing to make a claim on, no laws broken, then I don't understand the purpose of pursuing this line of questioning, or this investigation, any further."

Dennings squared off with Fowler. "Detective Fowler, in the past two months, Baljean's has suffered property losses of thousands of dollars and we are actively pursuing any and all requests from them to level charges of theft in the matters we are investigating."

"Wait, all of this is because Baljean's thinks I stole a shirt? Are you kidding me?"

I knew that it really wasn't, Dennings knew I was in the store and he wanted to know what I might have remembered about that night, if he could get me to admit I'd been spying.

I also had a really good hunch as to who'd been stealing merchandise from the store, but I was keeping that to myself.

Continuing to play dumb was my best defense.

"Really, Detective, I am not the customer Baljean's is in business for. You're wasting your time, my time, everyone's time here." I was standing now, joining Fowler.

"I can certainly see that, Miss Baxter, you are absolutely not their target customer, by any means. I still have you on camera entering the store, the dressing room, and you did not leave the way you came in. Why is that, do you think?"

I shook my head. "I don't know."

I dropped back down in my chair, still shaking my head.

Dennings huffed out loud, then snatched his phone up from the table, stopping the recording as he slid it into his pocket.

"I don't know what you were doing in there, but I can assure you, Miss Baxter, if I find that you are lying to me, there will be consequences."

He turned and yanked open the door, then stormed through it, Fowler right behind him.

Tess stared across the table at me. "He really doesn't like you."

"I get that. Wonder why?"

That was rhetorical.

And then she turned serious. "Something's not right with him, Bishop."

"I was thinking the same thing. He's a little wound up about all this, isn't he? Makes you wonder, doesn't it."

That wasn't a question, either.

121

Fowler came back into the conference room with Hatch in tow. Penny was in a meeting with Captain Huff and the Watch Commander, reviewing the first month's use of body cams by patrol officers. Whyte was at the Whitmore Courthouse, tracking property titles and deeds purchased by Tri-County Real Estate.

"Okay," Fowler took his seat. "First impressions. Go."

"They know it's me on that video. Dennings didn't know where I was before I was found in the ditch during our initial interview. Is it a coincidence, or did Dennings know more than he was letting on the first time he questioned me?"

Tess went next. "Why did it feel like he knew where to start looking?" We were quiet while we thought about that. "Hatch, I wish you'd been here, I think someone has leaked Bishop's session with Elsbeth."

Fowler looked at Tess. "Her session with who?"

"Oh, uh, yeah, Bishop's been hypnotized, I guess we should have told you."

"Ya think? So, do you have the recording? Mind if I hear it?"

"Sorry, Joe." Tess looked a little ashamed about that. "Really. Hatch?"

Hatch was quiet, her concern apparent as she chewed the inside of her cheek, but she glanced at Tess and nodded.

"Has he interviewed Justine? Dr. Biggs? I would think that they'd have told me about it, if he had--don't you? Maybe because the video captured my movements it just feels the same, but he didn't say that Lin had caught me listening in the doorway, he didn't say anything about anyone in the store. Maybe we need to see the video for ourselves, put a little heat on his investigation to see if he's on the up-and-up."

Fowler nodded at that. "Let's do that. Let's see what all he's got on you."

I think Fowler just wanted to get in Dennings' face, to be honest, but I was more than willing to see that happen.

122

I left Tess and Hatch at City Hall and headed back towards the carriage house. Driving through town, I pondered Dennings and his line of questioning, wondering if he actually had taken a statement from Dr. Biggs and Justine. Turning off of Main, I rolled on past the house and headed towards the animal hospital.

Making my way in, I smiled at Margaret, who positively beamed at me and rounded the desk to pull me into one of her full-body hugs.

"Baxter, it's so good to see you!"

"Hi, Madge, you too!"

I was suddenly confused, I didn't know where that name had come from, but I was put at ease when Dr. Biggs came through the door from the lab, her head down as she scanned a clipboard.

"Madge, would you mind calling the lab transporter, I've got some samples that need to go out today."

She looked up and spied us both standing there, still holding each other, and she tipped her head, an odd smile on her lips.

"I'm...sorry. Am I interrupting...something?"

We realized the compromising position she'd found us in, but I took it further.

"As a matter of fact, yes. Could you give us a minute?"

Biggs shook her head, smiling, her eyes wide. "The exam rooms are open, maybe you'd like to move whatever this is into one of them."

Madge laughed and hugged me to her again, then let me go. "Sorry," she feigned, regretfully patting my shoulder. "Duty calls."

"Next time, then" I offered, and we both laughed.

"So, Baxter, what brings you in? Do you need something?"

"Just a minute of your time, if you have it."

A delivery driver entered, carrying a pizza box and a large brown bag. "Dr. Biggs, good to see you!"

"Hello, Jeanine, how's the baby?"

"Big. Hungry. Growing by the day."

They smiled at each other as Biggs tipped her with some folded bills. "Thank you so much."

"And thank you," Jeanine replied, pushing the money into her pocket. "Always a pleasure!"

As Jeanine closed the door behind her, Dr. Biggs picked up the box, leaving the bag behind for Madge. "Are you hungry? Come join me for a snack while we talk."

I nodded and we headed for her office.

123

We'd both eaten a piece of pizza before Dr. Biggs sat back and looked at me, her elbows supported on the arms of her chair, wiping her hands with a napkin.

"I think you should know that I had a visit from a Whitmore detective by the name of Dennings this morning, Baxter. He had some questions about you, about the night you went missing."

"That's why I'm here."

"Are you in trouble?"

"No. Well, okay, maybe. I mean, really, once the investigation is done, it should all be nothing. I was just in the wrong place at the wrong time. What did Detective Dennings ask you?"

"I think he was mostly verifying the events of the evening leading up to your accident. Why did I send you to Whitmore, did I know what time you got back, did you go alone--nothing specific."

I nodded. It was a standard investigation interview.

And then I remembered the common link between the clinic and Baljean's.

"Is Justine here?"

Dr. Biggs shook her head as she leaned up and tapped some keys on her keyboard, eyes focused on the monitor on the corner of her desk. "No, she's not on at all today. Sorry. I can call her," she offered as she reached for her phone.

"No. No, that's okay, thanks. I'll catch up with her later." I smiled and stood up. "Tell Carole I said 'hi' and I'll see her tomorrow."

"Will do. Give Tess our love, please. We should have dinner some time soon. I'll talk to Carole and see when we can do that."

"Certainly. Sounds good." I turned to go, was at the door when she called to me.

"Baxter."

"Yes, ma'am?"

"Stay out of trouble."

I nodded.

I really wasn't sure I should make that promise out loud.

124

I texted Justine from the clinic parking lot and got a response seconds later telling me that she was on her way home. 'Home' to her is Biggs' and Carole's house and I turned away from town and drove in that direction, arriving ten minutes later.

She met me at the front door, smiling and welcoming me in.

We made our way to the kitchen, and were standing at the center island, the corner of the counter separating us as she passed a cup of coffee to me.

"So, Baxter, what's up?" She smiled, a curious look on her face.

"Well, there's a Whitmore detective that's investigating my accident and he seems to think I was up to no good that night. I think you may be on his list of interviews and I was just wondering if you'd talked to him yet."

"His name is Dennings, right?"

"Yeah. Has he already interviewed you?"

"I have an appointment to meet with him in Whitmore in an hour."

"Okay. Well, would you mind letting me know when you're done? I'm just curious."

She tipped her head as she considered what I was asking. I watched her face and a look crossed it, but it was quickly covered by her smile, now a little smug.

"Baxter, has he got something on you? Did you do something you shouldn't have?"

"I wouldn't say that, but I think we've got a difference of opinion in the matter."

"I don't know why you went back, I don't think I'm going to be much help to him, but Baxter, you must realize..."

She paused, still holding that smile. "...he doesn't know that, so I could tell him anything, give him something to use against you..."

I'm pretty sure the confusion was written all over my face and her face reflected her seeing it, the glint of amusement shining in her eyes.

"...unless you find a way to...ah, guarantee that my information on your behalf is in your best interest." She stepped around the island, pressing against me, looking up into my eyes as her hand stroked up my forearm.

Her meaning became crystal clear.

"That's blackmail!"

She smirked at that. "You can call it whatever you want. I'd call it 'insurance.'"

I scoffed at that.

Justine leaned into me, pushing me back against the counter as she ran her hands down my sides, sliding them behind me and pulling my hips to her.

"You give me what I want, Baxter, I keep your secret safe."

"What are you talking about, I don't have any secrets."

Her hands still on me, she moved them down to my buttocks and squeezed, pressing her fingers just between the cheeks as she inhaled, the air passing through her teeth sounding like a hissing snake.

A warning.

She looked me dead in the eye, smiling, as her tone mimicked a cartoonish damsel-in-distress. "Oh, Detective, I'm so glad you're here, Baxter has been forcing me to steal from the stores, threatening to hurt me if I don't sell the pocketbooks and give her the money."

Fucking hell.

I was stunned, my mind immediately weighing the odds that Dennings would latch onto that and have me arrested by sundown.

They were not in my favor.

She was watching my face, still smiling as she pulled me down by the collar of my shirt, pressing her mouth against my neck, her tongue flat as she tasted my skin, and then she sank her teeth in, hard enough that I gasped, knowing that moving, trying to pull away, would only make her tighten her hold.

I stood frozen, pinned against the counter as she kept me there, taking her time in letting me go.

It was an abject lesson in surrender, and she held the reins.

125

She chuckled, I felt the rumble as much as heard it.

And then she abruptly let go, pushing me back.

"So, what do you say, Baxter? Feeling lucky? Want to gamble against me?"

She grabbed my collar again, and then my hands were up, taking hold of her wrists, squeezing until she let go, turning us both so that she was now against the counter, looking up at me as she tried to wrestle free of my grip.

"It's you. You're the one. You've been stealing from the stores, I saw the merchandise in your trunk that day at the college."

She was laughing as she fought me, twisting against me, trying to pull away, but I held her firm.

Her voice betrayed her, it was stressed as she struggled. "Just who do you think he'll believe, Baxter? Huh? You? Or cute lil ol' me?"

I released my grip, pushing her away at that, and she just kept that smile, shaking her head as she rubbed each wrist in turn.

"Thank you so much, hon, you just sealed your fate," and she held up her wrists, now dark red, the bruising from my fingers already starting to show.

She'd played me and I'd fallen into her trap.

126

I stood staring at her. "Why?"

She just shrugged, laughing. "I told you, Baxter, I just like to have fun. Fucking with you is fun. I warned you, though. I told you that I'd make you howl when I caught you. Meet me in the parking lot at Baljean's at nine o'clock tonight. And remember--there will be serious consequences if you don't show."

I wiped my hand over my face.

"Okay, this is where you leave, Baxter. Run along now. Nine o'clock. Don't be late."

I don't remember making my way through the house, getting into my Jeep, or what highway I was on before I pulled over into a parking lot and put my face in my hands.

What.

The.

Fuck.

127

I sat there trying to figure a way out, to somehow prove that Justine was lying about me, but I had nothing. She was right, Dennings would never believe me over her.

This girl had me up against the wall and she liked it that way.

I needed someone to back me up, a partner to help me trap her.

I burst out laughing. I knew someone who could best Justine in a battle of wits.

I pulled up into the City Hall parking lot and texted Penny, told her I needed her and to not say anything to Tess. She came out the back door, looking puzzled as she made her way to my Jeep.

I unlocked the passenger door and she got in, turning sideways in the seat to look at me. "What's going on, Baxter? What have you gotten yourself into n--holy shit."

She leaned over and pulled my shirt collar away from my neck and practically yelled "Who did that to you?"

"Justine."

"That *bitch*."

I nodded.

"Why?"

"Control issue, I think. Maybe her idea of foreplay."

"Geezus, Baxter. Don't let Tess see it, she'll think I did it."

"How am I supposed to do that? Wait--why would Tess think that?"

"Because of the last time."

"The last time?"

"Oh. Yeah. You don't remember..."

"Remember *what*?"

"When I bit you."

"You've bitten me? *When?"*

"Uhm, it was when you first got here..."

"Why?"

"We were having a fight."

"We were fighting and you *bit* me?"

"Well, it was more like we were having sex while we were fighting. Or fighting while we were having sex. And you were angry too, dear, don't think you didn't leave me with a few aches of my own."

She waved her hand in a dismissive manner. "Look, it's water under the bridge, Baxter, everyone got over it, and it all worked out. Now, what's going on with Justine?"

I told Penny about Justine's plan to blackmail me. She got really quiet after hearing it.

"Damn. That's just evil. Nine o'clock, huh? Okay, I can work with this. What we really need is her confession that she's setting you up."

She nodded at herself and blew a breath. "You need to wear a wire. And I've got just the thing."

She jumped out of the Jeep. "Well, come on." She motioned towards the City Hall doors.

I got out and fell in behind her. "But Tess will see this."

"Like you said, how are you going to hide that? And we need her help."

Tess was intently staring at her screen and tapping at her keyboard when we entered the bullpen.

"Okay, Tess, pull the plug on the space game and give us your attention, please."

Tess rolled her eyes at Penny's remarks before she looked up, surprise on her face when she saw me.

"Bishop, what are you doing here?"

Penny had picked up her camera and was pulling at my collar as she snapped a photo. I looked down at her, the question on my face.

"Just documenting the evidence."

Tess was on her feet in an instant.

"Who did that? Who did that to you? Penny!" She glared at the woman.

"Oh, no, don't hang this on me, Tess, not this time."

"Then who?"

"Justine."

"That *bitch*."

"That's what I said," Penny nodded.

"Why? Bishop, what were you doing with her?"

"I went to see her about her interview with Dennings, he's going to question her about the night I got lost."

"How did you even let her close enough to get her teeth into you?"

"Tess, I honestly did not expect her to attack me."

"Do you want to press charges? You could, you know."

"No, of course not! That would hurt Carole and Dr. Biggs more than Justine."

We sat down and I told Tess about how I'd seen Justine selling merchandise out of the back of her car, how she was covering her own ass by blackmailing me, demanding I sleep with her in exchange for a clean statement to Dennings.

"The thing is, Justine made me think of something Dennings said when he was questioning me earlier today. He said that the store owners had told him they were missing thousands of dollars in merchandise. Now, if you're selling counterfeit goods, would you really want to involve the police, have them snooping around your inventory if it's fake? I think Dennings is involved somehow."

"And that's why no one's getting busted?"

"And why he wants to know what I found that night that sent me running out that back door."

"Do you think he knows about Castile?"

"I don't know. Maybe. Maybe not. Maybe what he knows is limited to what's going on here and in Whitmore, that he doesn't know how big all of this really is. I think it's like most criminal businesses, anyone who knows who's at the top of the organizational chart is a liability, it's better to keep the different components blind to each other so no one can rat out the whole enterprise."

Tess was nodding. "Like local drug dealers. They know their suppliers and their buyers and that's it."

"Exactly. Once anyone starts digging, asking questions, it gets dicey for them. Knowing too much can get you killed."

"That's why Castile wanted you dead." Tess was quiet, it was practically a whisper, but I heard it and nodded.

"So, what are you going to do?" Tess sat down at her desk.

"Tess." I was hurt by her thinking I would sleep with Justine. "Do you even have to ask?"

"She's going to meet with her."

"What? Penny, no."

"Look, we put a wire on you, you get her to admit to stealing the merchandise and blackmailing you, and filing a false statement with Dennings. Right, Tess?"

Tess considered that. "That's not always easy to do, getting someone to spill their guts. You can't exactly ask leading questions without someone figuring out what you're doing."

Penny tipped her head at that and shrugged. "So then sleep with her."

"No!" I was up on my feet.

Penny held up her hand. "Geez, Baxter, what's happened to your sense of adventure? Did you lose that, too? You sex her, then get her talking when she's all relaxed and her defenses are down."

"Oh my gawd, pillow talk?"

She laughed. "That's what the best spies do."

I was chuckling and shaking my head. "That only happens in the movies." Looking over at Tess, I could see she was deep in thought.

"Oh, now, c'mon. Not you, too, Tess! No! I...I can't. It's...it's cheating."

She looked up at me, realizing the source of my distress. "Bishop. Really?" She smiled up at me, it was sweet and a little shy.

"Really?" She asked again, this time a little softer, a little breathless.

"Yeah," I squirmed.

"Now I'm lost," Penny threw up her hands. Her eyes widened as she hit upon the crux of the conversation. "Oh, well, *finally!* Did someone catch feelings?"

I was smiling, and the shyness of it mirrored Tess's as I held her gaze, her green eyes shining like a memory.

"Well, that's great, but it doesn't help with your problem, now, does it?

Tess was still smiling but her eyes were serious. "Bishop, you just have to get her talking. We need to know what Dennings has on you, how he fits in all this. I have a feeling that if he could arrest you, he would, and it would put you out of our reach."

I sighed. "Well, okay, then. Let's get this show on the road."

Penny practically squealed with delight. "I've got this great new mic, you're gonna love it. Comes with a camera so we can watch, too."

We spent the evening at the department, Penny testing her various cameras and mics, finally settling on one that had a significant signal distance and clarity.

At eight-fifteen, we headed for Baljean's in Whitmore.

129

I was in my Jeep, waiting in the parking lot of Baljean's, watching the doors for Justine.

It was nearly ten o'clock and I was having a one-way conversation with Penny and Tess through the wire I was wearing.

"Look, I don't think she's gonna show. We'll give her to ten o'clock and that's all, okay?"

Suddenly, an unmarked police car was racing across the parking lot blacktop, pulling to a stop behind me, blocking me in.

"Lisa Baxter! Show me your hands! Show me your hands!"

"Shit. Y'all? What the fuck." I looked at the rearview as I rolled down the window and put my hands through the opening.

"Don't move. Don't move or I'll shoot!"

I watched Dennings approach in my side mirror, gun drawn, pointed in my direction as he reached out and opened my door.

"Hands on your head and exit the vehicle now!"

As soon as my feet hit the ground, Dennings swung me around by the arm and shoved me against his car, pushing me down onto the hood and pressing his full weight as he leaned on me, patting me down and cuffing me before he turned me around.

He threw my phone on the ground, the battery cover skittering away. His face was twisted into a sneer. "You are under arrest for assault and battery," he announced as he snatched me up and walked me to the back of his car, shoving me into the back seat and slamming the door.

"Okay, guys," I whispered, "We're just gonna play this out and see what happens. You've got my back, right?"

I sighed.

Justine had screwed me.

130

Penny and Tess watched from across the parking lot with a close-up view on the hidden camera, had heard Dennings state the charges.

"What the hell?" Penny looked at Tess. "Let's go get her."

"Penny, we can't. He's arrested her, I have no say in any of this. Dennings will book her into the holding cells there at the Whitmore PD. He can hold her for thirty-six hours. And if he holds her without assigning charges as soon as he takes her in, she could be stuck in there until Monday."

Tess put an earphone in, trying to listen to the conversation between Bishop and Dennings:

"You have no idea who you're messing with."

"I'm not messing with anyone, Dennings, what the hell are you talking about?"

Dennings had started the car and was pulling away. Penny watched, then fell in behind him at a distance. Tess held Penny's phone, the transmission showing the back of Dennings' head as the car moved through the parking lot to the exit.

"Where's he going?"

The unmarked police vehicle was heading in a direction away from the central police department in downtown Whitmore.

Penny stayed a discreet distance from the detective's car, pulling off to the side of the road and cutting the lights when a stoplight would have put her in his rearview mirror. She fell in behind him again after giving him a headstart.

Reaching the outskirts of town, Dennings traveled down the bypass and looked like he was headed for the interstate when he turned off into a self-storage facility, stopping to tap in a code to open the gate and pulling through before it had reached the end of its track.

Penny went on past and stopped in the emergency lane, headlights off as she watched the unmarked police vehicle disappear around the side of the building. She put the little sports car in reverse and backed up to the driveway as fast as she could, jamming it into first and shooting through the gate with mere inches to spare as the gate closed behind them, steering away from the main warehouse and behind a row of sheds across from the front door of the business.

"I've lost the feed."

"Look up in the right corner of the app and hit 'scan.'" Penny steered the speedster behind the adjacent building holding a row of the largest storage units the facility offered

Four different screens opened in a cluster on the interface. "Well, huh."

"What?"

"I'm picking up the facility cameras." Tess scrolled the views. "Oh, and Bishop's camera."

She watched Dennings walk Bishop down a hallway and stop in front of a garage-style door, wincing as Dennings shoved her face-first into the metal, leaning against her while he unlocked the padlock. He took hold of her once again as he pulled the door up, then shoved her through the opening before rolling it back down.

"Wait! Wait! Wait! Dennings! At least take off the cuffs! C'mon! Don't do this!" Bishop's voice was muffled by the closed door.

"Listen, *Lisa*, you're pissing me off and I'll shut you up the hard way if you keep it up. Not another peep or I'll put you to sleep."

Bishop went quiet with that, leaning against the metal door, listening to Dennings walk away.

"Penny, Tess, if you can still hear me," she whispered, "I need help."

131

Penny had tucked the little car at the end of the row of storage units, then she and Tess had darted across the parking lot to hide in the shadows at the front of the business, just a few feet from the door, waiting for Dennings to show.

They didn't have to wait long. They heard Dennings talking as he exited the business, his phone to his ear. Penny leaped to catch the door before it shut and slipped inside as Dennings walked to his car and settled in, still on his phone. Tess stayed hidden as he drove out of the gate, joining Penny when she opened the door and let her in.

"Bishop!" Tess whispered, "Bishop!"

Penny stopped and looked at her. "Why are you whispering?"

Tess opened her mouth and then, "I don't know."

"Baxter! Baxter! Hey, Baxter!" Penny's voice echoed off the rafters.

They were walking down the first hall when they heard the banging from the second hallway, sending them running in that direction.

"Baxter!"

"Bishop!"

The banging was from a unit near the middle.

"We're here, Baxter, just hang on!"

Tess was looking at the padlock on the latch. "Well, if we had my car, we could use my bolt cutters."

"Pfft. Just give me a minute. And you really shouldn't watch, Tess, you've gotta maintain your innocence."

Tess looked down at Penny as she pulled her wallet from her jeans pocket. Penny looked up at her as she pulled out the set of lock picks.

"I'm serious. Look away, Tess."

Tess crossed her arms and turned her back to Penny. "Where did you get those? They're illegal, you know."

"Yes, I know. They were a birthday present. And you don't see a thing." Penny worked the picks in the lock. In a matter of seconds, she was handing it to Tess.

"Where did you learn..."

"I dated a locksmith. She taught me. My relationships are-- *were*--about so much more than just sex, Tess." Penny laughed as she leaned down and grabbed the metal handle at the bottom of the door, rolling it upwards.

Bishop was standing there with a sad, sheepish smile on her face as the two women looked in.

"Aw, Bishop."

She nodded at that as Tess made her way in and unlocked the handcuffs with her key. "I really wasn't expecting that."

"Yeah, we know. Now come on, we've got to get out of here. I don't think Dennings was planning on leaving you here 'til morning."

They made their way to the door, Penny peeking out to check the parking lot.

"Okay, let's go, but go fast just in case."

The three ran for Penny's car. The two-seater was cramped with Tess sitting on Bishop's lap, but Penny managed to get it in gear, triggering the gate and hitting the gas as soon as there was enough clearance to get through the opening.

They took the highway back to the shopping center for the Jeep, Bishop picking up the pieces of her flip phone and handing them to Tess, both of them frowning.

"Have I told you about how this phone saved your life?" Tess lamented as she put it in the glove compartment.

Bishop shook her head.

They followed Penny back to her house on the lake. Bishop would need to lay low, and hiding at Penny's was the best bet.

132

Hatch was sitting on the loveseat as Penny made coffee. Tess and I were at the bar as we all told Hatch our takes of the evening's events.

"So, what you're saying is that Dennings essentially kidnapped Baxter, that he knows the goods are counterfeit, and he's working for Lin."

"Well, that last two parts are purely speculation. We haven't actually seen Lin involved in any of this, aside from what Bishop recalled in her session with Elsbeth." Tess added that exception as Penny and I nodded.

"So, what do we do now? What's going to happen when Dennings goes back to get me and I'm not there?"

Tess frowned as she considered that. "I suspect he's going to go looking for you and when he does find you, he'll arrest you for real and put you in holding in Central Booking to keep an eye on you."

"I think that's a pretty optimistic outlook, if you ask me."

We turned and looked at Penny.

"Y'all, nothing about this is 'law and order,' anymore. This is 'tell me everything you know before I kill you.'"

Okay, so, all things considered, there was something to that.

"I don't think he sees the whole picture, to be honest, I think he believes it's all local and that it only involves the stores with Lin at the top of the chain."

"Maybe we need to let this all blow up, see what Lin does with him." Penny offered her take. "Wish we could be there when he goes back. Honestly, though, can you imagine the look on his face when he opens that unit and Bishop's gone?"

"He's going to wonder who the hell got you out of that storage unit. And then he's going to wonder who's watching him." Hatch took the steaming mug Penny offered her. "Which means he could quail on us and we lose any opportunity to find out who he's working for and what he knows."

"Which means..." Tess looked at Hatch, certain that she knew what was coming next.

Hatch read her look and nodded. "We put Baxter back in and hope we don't get caught doing it, or that Dennings hasn't already found her gone. If he doesn't come back for her by morning, we get her out and go pick him up for a little chat, during which he'll deny everything that's happened. Taking Bishop out of the unit erased all the evidence of Dennings' wrongdoing."

We were quiet with that realization.

Until Penny burst out laughing. "Oh, gawd, I love my job. I just love-love-*love* it. And I'm so damned good at it!"

Tess was nodding. "I love my job, too, but what...?"

"It's all in the Cloud."

"What?"

"I set up that app to send everything it captured to the Cloud. Oh, lawd, Dennings is so screwed."

133

We rode back to the storage facility in Hatch's truck.

And sat looking at the locked gate.

I was assessing how to climb the fence with the three strands of barbed wire stretched along the top of the perimeter when Hatch laughed and shook her head. "Well, it's worth a try."

I turned and looked at her. "Maybe you think barbed wire is no big deal."

"No, no, not that. At least, not yet." She rolled up to the box with the keypad and tapped out four numbers. "I'm thinking we get three tries before we have company."

Before she'd finished that sentence, the gate began rolling open.

"How did you..."

"Remember when we rented that truck? To move Tess's stuff?" She steered her truck on through then drove to the end of the row of storage sheds like Penny had done earlier.

Tess and Penny responded, saying 'yes' as I looked at Hatch, shaking my head. "No. Where were you moving her stuff?"

"From her house to your house." Hatch put the truck in park and shut off the engine. "It was a longshot, but the owner is in the midst of a divorce and I'm betting that his wife managed the office. He was really frazzled the day I was here and I'm pretty sure he isn't likely to email or send out a bunch of letters with new codes in it every month, maybe even every quarter. And he hasn't." She turned and smiled at the three of us.

"Okay, so, get going, you don't know when Dennings is coming back."

"One problem." Penny piped up from the back seat. "The door has a code, too."

"Probably the same one as the gate. Enter six-three-five-eight. It's the owner's birthday." Hatch laughed at that.

Tess repeated that and we all three bailed out of the truck.

"See ya, Baxter." Hatch smiled and waved.

"Yeah, sure." I waved back as we started the run across the expanse of parking lot.

Tess typed in the numbers and we heard the lock open. Penny waved in Hatch's direction as she entered first and took us back to the unit, popping the lock and rolling up the door.

Tess picked up the handcuffs we'd left on the floor, moving behind me to snap them in place.

"I don't like this," she admitted.

"I know. Thanks for leaving me a little breathing room with those," I remarked.

She turned me around and kissed me. "We're going to be right here, Bishop, we're not going to let anything happen to you, okay?"

She was talking brave, but her face was betraying her. She was scared.

"I know, Tess. I'll be fine. Now go on, before you get caught in here and we all end up in a mess."

She nodded and kissed me again, then stepped out into the hallway as Penny pulled the door down. "You're gonna be fine, Bax, the camera and mic are still hot, we can see and hear you." Penny was earnest in her attempt to assure me, her eyes on mine as the door rolled down towards the cement floor.

I nodded in turn.

My mouth was dry as the darkness fell and I heard the lock snap into place.

134

I managed to shuffle along the door to the wall, sliding down to sit, my shoulders and arms aching a bit from being pulled behind me. I closed my eyes and opened them, trying to adjust to the darkness, lessened only by the tiniest bit of light entering from along the bottom of the door.

It wasn't much, but you'd be amazed at how well your eyes adapt to what you initially think is total darkness. I could see the shapes of the boxes stacked at the back wall and I remembered glancing at them when Dennings first pushed me into the space. There was nothing outstanding to recall, they were plain cardboard boxes like the stacks I'd seen in Baljean's store room.

"Hey, someone, make a note, would you? See if you can find out who this unit is rented to. And then see if that person is connected to Baljean's or Lin's businesses in any way--even remotely. Okay?"

I paused as if I would get a response to that and it felt a bit odd.

Kind of like praying out loud and expecting to hear an answer.

I shifted and laid down on my side on the ground. My arms and shoulders were aching, my ass hurt from sitting on the cold cement, and I really wanted whatever was going to happen next to happen so we could get on with it.

The waiting was just pissing me off.

135

Hatch was standing watch at the edge of the building. It was nearly two o'clock, over two hours since Tess and Penny had put Bishop back into the storage unit, and the cold air was making her ankle ache. She was ready to trade places with Tess when the luxury sedan pulled up to the gate, the driver reaching out and entering the code into the gate box.

Hatch called Tess on her phone. "We've got company."

"Copy," Tess replied.

Hatch watched as the car pulled up parallel to the door, foregoing parking in a space, the lights going out as the engine was switched off. A very tall, very broad hulk of a man got out of the driver's seat and opened the door for a woman wearing a coat with a fur-lined collar, her hair swept up, the parking lot lights causing her earrings to sparkle.

"I can't tell if this is anyone we need to be concerned with. A rather rich-looking woman and what may be her bodyguard."

Penny was holding her phone, watching the feeds from the cameras. "They're inside, heading in Baxter's direction."

Tess relayed that to Hatch.

"They've stopped at Baxter's storage unit."

Penny pulled up Baxter's camera and upped the volume on the mic. Tess could hear the door roll up.

"We have contact, I see them on Baxter's feed. Whoa."

"What?" Tess and Hatch were immediately on alert.

"She's beautiful."

Tess looked at Hatch through the windshield, both of them smirking a bit.

"And she has a gun."

That wiped the smirks right off their faces.

136

"Ah, Miss Baxter, I am Alexandria Balantine. It is truly a pleasure to meet you. I heard such a lovely story about you from Alice Jefferson."

I had sat up, blinking in the flourescent light. I wanted to shield my eyes but, of course, I couldn't, so I limited my looking to quick glances between blinking as I adjusted to the brightness, catching a look at the small custom pistol she held on me.

"Who's Alice Jefferson?"

"The wife of one of my business associates. You rescued their daughter's dog from the streets, she'd been missing for months."

I shook my head again. "I'm sorry, I, ah, I've had a head injury recently, it's made a mess of my memory. Is that gun necessary?"

She looked at me, lips pursed as she considered my question.

And then she shrugged as she pocketed the pistol, nodding to the man standing next to her. He reached down and grabbed me up by the arm, and I'd swear my feet briefly left the floor.

"Easy, big fella," I cautioned. "That arm's attached."

He looked down at me. "For now," he sneered.

Oh.

Well.

Shit.

He pulled me out of the unit, holding me with one hand while he rolled down the door with the other.

Ms. Balantine closed the lock hasp through the latch and we all made our way outside.

I looked down the length of the parking lot but I didn't see the truck or anyone peeking around the corner. I could only hope they hadn't been found out, and that they were going to follow us, wherever we were going, because I was beginning to feel a little nervous about how this whole matter was playing out so far.

Especially since I had willingly put myself back into this situation.

137

The three women could see and hear the exchanges going on inside the facility. Tess was internet-searching Alexandria Balantine when she heard Bishop telling the man to take it easy.

"Bishop, careful..." she whispered.

"She's probably hungry. We should have fed her, she's had coffee on an empty stomach, you know how she gets," Penny remarked.

Tess frowned at that, but she nodded.

Hatch got out of the truck when they'd reached the door and she watched the man assist Ms. Balantine into the car, then walk Bishop around to seat her on the other side.

In the time it took for Hatch to get back into the driver's seat, the luxury car had swung around and exited the gate, heading toward the interstate.

Hatch drove the truck out of the parking lot, her eyes on the vehicle nearly half a mile down the highway.

"He's hauling ass," she remarked, hitting the gas to try to close the gap. "Let's hope I don't get pulled over."

The feed from the camera was beginning to pixilate and Penny was having a hard time hearing any conversation.

Tess found a local on-line business magazine detailing Ms. Balantine's accomplishments in the world of fine retail shopping in the Tri-County area, including her use of pop-up shops to gauge the local retail market as well as to stir interest in her stores when they opened.

"Well, huh. She is one of two owners involved in Baljeans and Ferranté. How about that..."

"Yeah, I kinda figured that with the Balantine part. What else ya got?" Penny looked puzzled. "That hardly explains why she's got Baxter and she's heading god-knows-where with her. What other businesses is she in? Who's her family? Where did she get her money?"

"Could you give me a minute, please, I'm just getting started."

"Sorry."

"Okay. This is from the Tri-County Business Association Directory. Alexandria Balantine recently settled here in the past year--doesn't say from where--she's on a number of boards in Tenley and Whitmore, she's a member of the Tri-County Chamber of Commerce, has season tickets to the Richmond Symphony, one daughter who goes to school in Vermont, and she's not married but is frequently seen in the company of...oh, shit."

Penny looked up at that. Hatch glanced over, too.

"She is frequently seen in the company of Lin Chen, a successful local business owner."

"Shit." Hatch concurred with Tess's assessment.

There was a fair amount of distance between the two vehicles, Hatch was trying to be inconspicuous.

"I wish I knew where they were going."

Tess tapped her screen. After a few seconds, she nodded. "Well. I think we're headed to Ms. Balantine's residence. It's about six miles to the exit, then another five down Taylor Road to Buxton Estates."

Hatch visibly relaxed at that. "I doubt they'd kill her on the grounds. At least, I wouldn't think so."

"Unless they have a room for that. Or they're going to hand her off to someone else."

"Penny, I'm trying to think positive about this."

"Not me. Worst case scenario all the way, then there are no surprises. So stay close, Hatch, don't get too comfy with the idea that they've invited Baxter out for a slumber party with tennis and horseback riding tomorrow."

138

The wrought-iron gates were already swinging open as our vehicle approached, the car's headlights showing the way up the curving driveway and through the small grove of trees and foliage providing cover from prying eyes. I lowered my head to see out the window as light from ahead passed between the trees.

Maybe I gasped out loud, but there was a frank beauty of an English country house ahead, the drive encircling a fountain at its center before passing the house and disappearing into another stand of trees.

I couldn't take my eyes from the structure as we drove by, and I met the eyes of my captor, who merely offered a demure smile as she acknowledged my response to the beauty of her home.

Now, though, we were entering another stand of trees as the concrete wove through the property and within a minute we had passed a barn, large and red, set back on the far side of a field, a good-sized paddock of white rail fencing outlining the area in front of the breezeway. More trees, then a small pond with a fountain spray of water at its center, and on a low rise behind it, a single-story house, white with green shutters, the front porch running the length of the structure, its roofline supported by four small round white columns in total across the front.

We came to a stop at the driveway's end. In the distance beyond the house, I could see what I presumed was the groundskeeper's shed, the large mowers and their attachments under a metal-roofed shelter next to the small cottage-like office.

I had no real reason to believe that anyone could see or hear me on the wire anymore, we were too far from the road to maintain contact, but I had to say something.

"Quite a piece of property you have here, Ms. Balantine, I especially like your guest house."

"Well, I do appreciate that, I'm glad you like it because, in a certain way, I suppose, you are my guest here, Ms. Baxter."

"And how long will I be staying?"

"That depends, Ms. Baxter. That depends."

Brutus had opened the door for Ms. Balantine, she was halfway to the door by the time he had assisted me out of the back seat and onto my feet, his grip making me wince as he jerked me towards the porch.

"Oh, c'mon, man, lighten up." I kicked at him out of anger and he shook me like a rag doll for that.

"Okay, okay..."

Ms. Balantine was standing in the open doorway by then and Brutus pushed me past her and into the small foyer. He unlocked and removed the cuffs then rejoined his employer.

"Make yourself at home, Ms. Baxter. Eat, drink, take a shower if you like, you'll find fresh clothing in the master suite. Try to get some sleep, tomorrow may be a long day for you, I think you'll fare better if you rest. Good night."

She smiled a little too sweetly, and walked out. Brutus followed behind her, pulling the door shut. I heard the deadbolt slam home, it was the kind of lock that required the use of a key from either side.

It should go without saying that my side did not have a key.

I sighed.

I am truly regretting going back in that storage unit.

139

Hatch pulled up outside the grounds of the Balantine estate, slowly rolling along the roadway as the three women looked at the twelve-foot high brick wall set five feet back from the pavement.

"Geezus." Hatch was shaking her head. "I would never guess there's a house back there."

"Right? No lights, nothing..." Penny was shaking her head. "If she's behind that wall somewhere, she's out of range. I've lost the signal."

Hatch followed the brick wall as it passed the estate, leading to a barricaded service road approximately half a mile from the ornate gates of the private drive.

Penny called up satellite images of the property on her cell phone. "Wow, that's a really big chunk of land behind that wall, y'all." She scrolled the screen. "I see the main house and what looks like a small house near the back of the property, a barn and maybe a shed?"

They were sitting at the service road when headlights lit up Hatch's truck and a searchlight swept back and forth over the vehicle.

"Uh oh." Hatch squinted into the rearview. "I think I see a light bar on the roof," she advised Tess. "Want to pull rank?"

"No, let's see who it is first, could be a security detail for Buxton Estates, I don't want to give away who we are just yet, they'll report it to Mrs. Balantine."

Hatch nodded as she watched the two officers approach the truck cab, one on each side, hitting the power button to roll down the window.

"Evenin', folks." The officer on Hatch's side was standing at the cab window, just behind Hatch's shoulder. "Are you having trouble with your vehicle? Do you need assistance?"

"No, sir, we were just talking." Hatch noted the private security service patch on the officer's uniform.

Tess had seen it, too, on the officer's uniform outside her window, and she decided to take a chance. "Actually, you can help us, I'm looking for my aunt's house, Alexandria Balantine?"

The officer on Hatch's side shined his light into the cab and leaned over to see Tess and she smiled at him and kept talking. "I expected to be here a lot earlier this evening, I was going to drop in and say hello, but it's been one delay after another getting here from Maryland, and now it's the middle of the night, and we were thinking we should get a hotel room and call Aunt Alexa in the morning just as y'all pulled up."

"Yes, ma'am, I understand. This is the Balantine estate service road, you passed the main gate about a half-mile back."

"See, I told you," Tess slapped at Hatch's shoulder, laughing.

"Okay, okay. Sorry," Hatch smiled and shook her head.

"Alright, then, thank you, officer, we're going to go check into a hotel in Whitmore and come back in the morning."

"I think that's a good idea, ma'am," the officer nodded then signalled his partner to return to the cruiser. "You folks have a good night."

He tapped his flashlight to his cap and left them there. Hatch watched the officers retreat, then cranked the truck and backed out, smiling and giving a little wave as she passed the officers, their patrol car falling in behind them and following them to the main highway.

Hatch turned the vehicle toward Whitmore, leaving the security team sitting at the intersection.

"What do we do now?" Hatch looked at Tess for her answer.

"We figure out a way to get onto that property."

140

I walked through the house, checking door locks to the side and rear exits as I reached the open kitchen and living area. Panels of framed crystal-clear glass formed the double windows, two in each casement, and I ran my hand around one to confirm that it was sealed tight.

Taking a mug from the cupboard, I bounced it a bit in my hand before launching it as hard as I could at the window behind the table.

I hit the ground as it flew back at my head and skittered across the floor to bang off the opposite wall.

I sighed, resigning myself to being Alexandria Balantine's prisoner.

I certainly didn't have to be a hungry one, though, and I opened the refrigerator, stooping to peer into the clear drawers.

"They're hermetically sealed."

I startled at the voice, banging my head on the refrigerator shelf. "Ow! Shit."

It really should have been no surprise to see her standing there.

She was drying her blonde hair with a towel, barefoot, dressed in a pair of navy sweatpants and a white oversized T-shirt. I could smell the fresh scent of a lavender soap. "Sorry, didn't mean to scare you. The windows--they're hermetically sealed. And, apparently, shatter-proof."

"What are you doing here?"

"Probably the same thing as you. Did Dennings pick you up?"

"Sort of. You?"

"Yeah. More like he kidnapped me and brought me here."

"So, he didn't put you in storage first?"

"What?"

I grabbed the mustard and the pack of corned beef from the refrigerator and began looking for bread to make a sandwich. Justine cleared her throat and when I looked at her, she pointed towards a louvered cabinet door.

Opening the cupboard, I was treated to the sight of loaves of bakery-style breads and rolls. I pulled out a loaf of sourdough and dropped it on the countertop. I looked over at Justine, my meaning clear as I cocked an eyebrow and pointed to the goods.

"Yes, please."

I added her pieces with mine and set to work. She opened the refrigerator and pulled out two bottles of cola, then tried to twist off the caps. It was my turn to clear my throat and point, aiming in the direction of the wall-mounted cast-iron opener, and she sheepishly nodded, then pried off the caps and set them on the table, taking a seat.

I joined her and we ate a silent meal together, not breaking that quiet until we were nearly done.

"Baxter, what do they want with us?"

She sounded scared and I knew she was. So was I, but I wasn't going to show it.

"I think they want to know what we know about their counterfeit goods. What I know about more than that."

Justine's lips pulled into a tight line and she shook her head. "I don't know anything about any of that."

"What did Dennings question you about? What did he want to know about you and me and the night I went missing?"

"He asked if I knew why you went back. I told him I didn't, because I don't, and then he wanted to know who was in the store when we were there, if you had said anything to me about going back. He got mad because I couldn't tell him anything, I don't know anything...and...and I just want to go home!"

She was on her feet and running to the door, trying to pull it open and getting nowhere.

I went to her and wrapped my arms around her, pulling her away from the door. I could feel her trembling and I tightened my hold, gently rocking as I tried to calm her.

"It's gonna be alright."

I listened as her rapid breaths decreased, and she steadied herself. She was still shaking, though.

"Baxter, they're going to kill us, aren't they."

It wasn't a question.

I think it was the answer, though.

141

I led her back to the table and sat her down without replying. Some things just don't need to be said out loud.

We finished eating and I spent the next twenty minutes scouring the house, looking for a way out, or even a way through, and finding nothing. There wasn't anything sharp to speak of--no carving or steak knives, no scissors, not even a pencil.

I went into the master suite and picked out a pair of sweats and a T-shirt from the dresser, heading into the bathroom for a quick shower.

I considered fashioning a shiv out of the new toothbrush, but I didn't have anything to sharpen it with, and whittling it down with my teeth was not an option.

When I returned to the bedroom, Justine was in my bed.

I really wasn't surprised to find her there.

I walked over to the other side and slipped in between the covers, then turned off the lamp on the bedside table.

"I just couldn't sleep alone," she whispered into the dark.

"I know. It's okay."

"I'm scared."

"Know what? Me too."

"I'm sorry, Baxter. For everything."

"Are you? Really?"

"Okay, well, maybe not for all the come-ons, I meant those."

I laughed at that in spite of myself.

"But I am sorry for telling Dennings you were blackmailing me."

I turned over and looked at her. "Do you think that's the only reason Dennings picked us up? Some stolen merchandise? What has he got planned for the two of us?"

"I don't know."

All I had were questions and I closed my eyes as I considered them, no closer to the answers than when this whole mess had started.

142

I woke with a start, disoriented. I wasn't in my house and the woman I held in my arms and draped across me was not Tess.

My situation came flooding back and my heart was banging as I realized that morning had come, along with whatever special events Alexandria Balantine had planned for us looming in the not-to-distant future. I was no further ahead in figuring an escape than I had been when I fell asleep too many hours ago, it was after eleven o'clock and I needed to get moving.

I slid out from under Justine and made my way to the bathroom to brush my teeth, thinking that a very large cup of strong coffee would be good. Looking around the bathroom, I wasn't entirely sure there weren't cameras, but I was still looking for anything I could make into a weapon.

Nothing of use had miraculously appeared overnight.

Once in the kitchen, I took immediate note of the high-end coffee maker and started a pot with the coffee from the cupboard above it. Scalding-hot water as a weapon was always an option, but I doubted I could make enough to stop someone with a gun.

Looking out the back window, I watched a man moving around the tractor attachments in the outbuilding by the groundskeeper's office.

He looked up, I'd swear he was looking my way and I waved, but he continued as if he didn't see me. I grabbed up the coffee cup still on the floor and began banging on the window.

Still no response. Not even a hint that he'd seen or heard me.

"I guess it's soundproof, too," I said aloud.

"Like space."

I jumped at that, and I turned to look at her. I hadn't heard her come into the kitchen, rubbing the sleep from her eyes.

"Dammit, you have got to quit sneaking up on me." I glared at her. "Like space?"

"No one can hear you scream."

"Well, gee, aren't you just a bucket of sunshine this morning?"

I poured her a cup of coffee, then opened the bread keeper to see if there was anything sweet.

"Oh, look, monster cinnamon rolls."

"Really, Baxter?"

"I love a good sweet thing in the morning."

She looked at me, her eyebrow raised and her lips pursed. "Oh, you do, huh?"

"Yep." I winked and smirked right back at her as I loaded two plates with very large servings. "Here." I handed over the goods.

Opening a drawer, I pulled out two individually-wrapped sporks, shaking my head as I looked at them. "They don't even trust us with forks. I suppose we could try to gouge them, except these aren't stiff enough."

I bent one nearly double without it snapping in two to prove my point before joining Justine at the table.

We ate and spent the next hour looking for anything we could use as weapons as well as possible exits. I shook my head at Justine as we met in the open sitting area by the kitchen.

"Nothing."

"Nope. You were right when you said it was hermetically-sealed. This place is tighter than a drum. But there has to be some way."

She just shook her head. "We've looked. This is the end, Baxter, don't you see? This is where Alex Cross goes out in a hail of gunfire, or Jim Rockford dies in a fiery blast, or when Derrick Storm takes a bullet to the head."

"Damn, girl, you have just got to stop with the happy thoughts. Please!"

I dropped down on the couch and turned on the tv.

"Really? You're just going to watch tv?"

"Well, like you said, there's no way out, and you're right, so what the hell else is there to do?"

She smirked. "I can think of something."

"Justine, for gawd's sake, stop it."

"Look, we could be dead in an hour, why the hell not? Nobody will tell your wife."

"Dennings would, just to hurt Tess."

I was flipping through the channels, not spending more than three seconds on each one, expending nervous energy the only way I could, short of actually bedding that annoying woman standing next to the massive flat screen.

Flip, flip, flip-- oh, wait...I turned back to a news channel and watched for a few seconds longer.

"That's it!" I crossed to Justine in three strides and grabbed her by the hand, pulling her toward the bedrooms.

"Finally!" She followed willingly.

I was looking up, trying to find it, I'd be surprised if there wasn't one, but for now I was thinking it was hidden. I pushed Justine into the second bedroom.

"Wow, unleash that beast, Baxter, just let it all out, baby, you won't hear me complain!"

"Check the closet, it's here somewhere."

"What? Check for what? What are you doing? I thought we were gonna..."

I cut her off. "The air vents are in the ceiling. There has to be a way to get up there. Maybe there's a door to the attic, but it's not in plain view, so check the closets."

I turned in the opposite direction to search the master bedroom.

"Dammit." No luck.

I heard her yell from the other room. "I found it!"

I ran to the second bathroom, she was standing next to the linen closet, pointing at its ceiling.

"Bingo!" I smiled at her.

"So we end up in the attic? Then what?"

"Well, help me get up on these shelves and through the trap door and we'll just see, okay?"

The shelves were recessed. I stood on the bottom and lifted the access door out of its frame, then used the shelves as a ladder, pulling myself up through the opening and sitting on the edge. I looked around the darkness, waiting for my sight to catch up, the light filtering up from the soffit vents under the eaves, with the thing I was hoping to find centered on the exterior wall not ten feet away.

The attic had a louvered gable vent. And it was big enough for us to fit through. I just had to kick it out. And try not to break my leg when I dropped to the ground below--likely a twenty foot drop.

I lowered myself back down and told Justine what I'd found. She nodded.

"Let's go." I was ready to boost her onto the shelves when I felt the air pressure change in the house, and I heard talking from the foyer.

"Uhoh."

"Baxter, we're not going to make it out of here, are we?" She looked like she was ready to burst into tears.

"Justine, I'm going to do everything I can to make sure we do."

144

Tess knew that what she was asking for was a long shot, especially since she didn't know who she could trust anymore, but she wasn't ready for the response her request elicited from Judge Thackery.

"Detective, you cannot expect me to issue a warrant to search the property of Alexandria Balantine without giving me sufficient cause. Your 'hunch' is just not going to do that."

"It's not a hunch, Your Honor, Lisa Baxter was last seen in Mrs. Balantine's vehicle heading in the direction of the Balantine estate. I have video surveillance..."

Tess followed the judge out onto the indoor tennis court, the judge stopping at the nearest bench and placing his equipment bag on it to pull out a towel and a can of tennis balls.

"Surveillance that does not include a properly-executed warrant. Detective, honestly, I'm having a hard time believing that this is anything more than a dispute between you and your wife. Are you the jealous type? Because I'm not going to get caught up in what appears to me to be a domestic issue."

"Your Honor!"

"Tess, I have never had a problem with your requests before, but this one is a little difficult to swallow. I cannot have you leading a team of officers onto the estate of a reputable businesswoman to look for your cheating wife."

He picked up his racquet and tested the strings, looking at Tess as he did. "And I will most certainly not have my past judgements called into question and placed under judicial review because I issued you a warrant to catch your wife in some kind of compromising situation with a pillar of this community--and one of my staunchest supporters!"

Tess shook her head, her lips drawn in a hard line.

There it was.

It was an election year and the judge was not going to piss off one of his biggest political donors for a lurid story of cheating and misuse of authority by one of the Tenley detectives.

So be it.

"Thank you for your time, Sir." Tess turned on her heel and stalked off the court.

145

We'd made it back into the living area next to the kitchen when Brutus and Mrs. Balantine entered from the foyer. I had Justine behind me, pushing us back until we were against the counter that divided the space.

I will admit that my eyes may have grown a bit wide when I got a good look at Mrs. Balantine in the light of day.

She is a truly stunning-looking woman, and I couldn't have guessed her age. Her brunette hair was brushed back from her face, her make-up simple, bringing out her dark brown eyes. She was wearing a cream skirt and jacket trimmed in the same deep brown as her eyes, matched with pale cream-and-brown heels, the silk scoop-necked blouse and three strands of pearls perfectly matched to the suit.

She was color-coordinated from her hair to her toes and I couldn't breathe.

"Whoa." Justine said in a whisper as she looked out from behind me.

"Right? I just learned I have a type."

She looked up at me and nodded.

Mrs. Balantine smiled, I don't know if she heard us or she was taking in the coffee cups on the table. "Oh, I'm so glad you're comfortable enough to help yourselves, that's lovely. Michael, pour me a cup of coffee, please, and let's get down to business, ladies, let's have a chat."

The suit she wore was lined and the soft swish of the material could be heard as she moved, taking a seat and folding her hands on the tabletop.

I looked at Justine and we both made our way back to our respective places. I waited for Michael to serve Mrs. Balantine and I sipped my cup as she sampled hers.

"Whoever made the coffee--well done!"

"Glad you like it. Now, Mrs. Balantine, what are we doing here?"

"I am so glad you asked. I have some questions for you, I need information, and I really hope you cooperate, because I just hate when things get...complicated."

"Define complicated."

"Oh, I'd rather not. Let's just say I'm all for cooperation without coercion."

I turned to Justine at that. "How about that. You need to take lessons from her."

I turned back to Mrs. Balantine. "Justine is quick to use the stick when the carrot doesn't work," I informed her as I pulled the collar of my T-shirt and showed off the bite mark, now dark purple and red in color.

"Oh, so Baxter's a stubborn one, is she?" Mrs. Balantine smiled at Justine, who nodded and smirked as she told the woman of her difficulty with me.

"Months of overtures--I told her I wouldn't beg. And then I had to start over when she smacked her head and didn't remember anything," Justine rolled her eyes.

"Yes, that reminds me, let's talk about your memory issues. Now, from what I've been told, you have no recollection of the past two years, is that true?"

I can only wonder exactly what she knows.

"Pretty much," I nodded.

So let's just see what I can learn first.

146

"Very well, Ms. Baxter, let's get down to it then, shall we?"

She got up from the table and stood behind me. Her hands were on my shoulders and she was standing close enough that my head was brushing against her breasts.

Her perfume was an amazing floral blend, not too sweet, not too cloying.

Memorable.

Expensive.

Honestly, it smelled delicious. It was making my mouth water.

She was making my mouth water.

Her hands moved from my shoulders, the flats of her palms stroking down my upper arms, pressing into my muscles, the heels digging in as she made her way back to my shoulders, kneading them with strong fingers and I felt the tension release immediately as she centered on the muscles in my neck.

"You're certainly tense, Ms. Baxter."

My ability to speak was impaired by her deep-tissue massage. "You can just...call me...Baxter. It's...just Baxter."

"Baxter. Really?"

I nodded.

"Okay. Well, then, Baxter, who do you work for?"

"I'm a full-time student right now."

"Oh, that's right. Law Enforcement. That still doesn't answer the question. Who do you work for?"

Her hands were still on my neck, still kneading, and then they slid down my arms and back up again, stopping just below my ears, her fingertips cool to my temples as she rubbed light circles on each side.

I sighed rather loudly with that.

This was certainly a carrot.

"Before, Baxter. Where did you live before you came to Tenley?"

Okay, so she either knows the answers and she's testing me, or she's fishing. I decided to stick to the WITSEC background, just to see if I could steer her around to giving something up.

"I'm from Rockville, Maryland."

"There, now we're getting somewhere. Rockville. You're sure about that?"

Crap.

She knows.

"Yeah," I chuckled. "I'm sure about that. Born and raised. Why?"

"No, no, still my turn to ask questions. What did you do in Rockville, how did you earn a living?"

"I worked in retail."

"Really. You don't seem the retail type. What did you sell?"

I turned and looked her in the eye. "Hardware."

She laughed.

So she's not oblivious to jokes about dykes and home improvement centers.

I stayed turned in my chair. "What, exactly, are you looking for, Mrs. Balantine?"

Her face took on a bit of a grimace, and she sucked air through her teeth before answering.

"Answers, Baxter. I need you to answer my questions, and I need you to be completely honest when you do."

"But I am being completely honest, why don't you believe me?"

"Because," she leaned forward, her cold eyes on mine, we were face-to-face and only inches from each other. "I know who you really are...Bishop."

147

Now the gloves were off and we both knew where we stood.

This was not going to be pretty.

"Michael, I need your help in here."

"No, she doesn't, Michael, because I have no idea what she's talking about."

Michael came into the kitchen and snatched me up with that one-arm lift he seems so fond of.

Justine rushed him, but he hit her with a backhand that I knew was going to leave a mark, leaving her a crumpled heap on the floor.

And then he was walking me back to the second bedroom, Mrs. Balantine following, locking the door behind us.

"You've been busy." I looked at the wooden arm chair in the center of the large bathroom, straps in place for my wrists and ankles.

Michael slammed me down in the chair and trapped my hand on top of my thigh with his knee, leaning on me while he buckled the strap around my other wrist. He applied the other three and then we were all staring at each other.

"Tell me everything you know about Castile Enterprises, and who you've told it to right now, Bishop, or this is going to get uncomfortable for you."

Oh, yeah, like I'm gonna do that.

"I don't know what you're talking about."

"No more lies." She nodded to Michael. He turned and picked up a syringe.

"Aw, no, not drugs...it takes me days to shake the aftereffects."

"I don't think that's going to be a problem for you, Bishop."

"What? Oh...hah, yeah, I get it..."

I felt the pinch and then the burn as it traveled up my arm. I could taste it in seconds.

"Oh, gawd, that's awful. What is it?"

"A little cocktail I devised, it's a wonderful combination, you'll see."

Suddenly, my mouth was dry and everything was bright and bold. My heart was pounding and my muscles were jerking. Sweat popped out on my forehead and I was panting to catch my breath.

"Holy shit..." Every fiber in my body was urging me to run and I jerked against the straps holding me in place.

My heart was beating like a freight train. And I got really warm, all over.

I closed my eyes to focus my breathing. The drug peaked and my heart was finally slowing, my limbs were loosening, and I was relaxing. I exhaled in a sigh.

A rather satisfied sigh.

"So, Bishop, how are you feeling?"

I could feel the half-cocked smile on my lips as I looked her up and down. She offered me a rather brash one in return, her eyebrow raised in knowing what I was thinking.

I was high on whatever she'd had me injected with, but it wasn't difficult to handle now, it was more like that rush when you've had just a little too much to drink. "I am feeling much better, Mrs. Balantine, thank you. That is quite a little cocktail you serve."

She nodded. "I call it the 'orgasm.' So, can we get on with it?"

"Fire away."

"Who do you work for?"

I looked at her, my turn to be skeptical. "You tell me."

"Bishop, if you don't play along, I'll have to punish you, and I don't want to do that."

"Oh, no more carrot, huh? Justine bites--what do you do?"

She nodded at Michael. He picked up another syringe.

"Oh, gawd, again?"

The pinch, then the burn, and I was hot, my chest burning, sweat running off my lip and into my mouth.

My muscles were twitching and I was very aware of my body betraying me with a hot throbbing between my legs.

I was straining against the straps, blowing through my mouth like a distance runner.

The sprinting portion passed. I looked up at her.

"What is in that?"

"A little amphetamine, and a lot of sodium pentothal."

"Truth serum? Are you serious? Who uses that anymore?"

"I do. So, what do you have to tell me, Bishop?"

"Well, first, let me just say that you are gorgeous."

"Thank you."

"Have you ever had sex with a woman, Mrs. Balantine?"

She laughed. "I've experimented, like most young girls."

My turn to laugh. "That's not a very good sampling of sex with a woman, Mrs. Balantine. Two girls, drunk, high, fumbling around with each other."

"And you're saying...?"

I looked her up and down through half-lidded eyes, that crooked smile on my lips. "I just want to mess you up."

She laughed. "Mess me up? What does that mean?"

"I want to leave your lipstick smeared, your hair tangled, and your clothes on the bedroom floor." My words were a little slurred and my head wobbled a bit. "You could have a shot and join me. This shit is awesome. You should sell it."

I laughed at that.

"What?" She was curious.

"You should sell it...get it?"

"Oh, yes, I see. You're funny."

"Glad you think so. Some people don't. Anyway, what else can I tell you? How about you tell me what you know and I will confirm or deny."

She leaned back on the doorjamb and crossed her arms, cocking her head as she appeared to consider that. Then she shook her head. "No, that's not going to work for me. Let's start with when you first figured out that your partner was dirty."

Sonofabitch.

Did she know everything? Was the mole in the U.S. Marshall's office? It felt like she'd read my WITSEC file, the unabridged one that held my statement to the State's Attorney.

And then I realized that I remembered making a witness statement.

In the hospital.

In Baltimore.

Two years ago.

This little truth serum session could be really hazardous to my health.

"What's to tell? He was taking envelopes from some guy he was meeting every week while we were on patrol. One evening, I followed him into the basement of a warehouse, he beat the crap out of me, shot me in the leg so I couldn't run, set the building on fire and left me there to die. I've been told that I shot him dead last year. The end."

"You know, that is a quite a good story, Bishop, and all true. Let's go on to the next round. How did you track your partner to Evan Castile?"

Okay, this is where it gets ugly. I can't give her anything, I don't know how much information she really has, and I can't name names or someone will get killed.

And what I really need most is to get the fuck out of here because I already know that this is not going to end well for me at all.

148

"Another, Michael."

"Oh, no, Michael, thanks, really, I couldn't, two's my limit..."

This time, I tasted something different, and the colors didn't just get bright, they swirled and spun. My head was buzzing, I wanted to run. I bucked against the restraints, I was too hot and a little nauseous.

Mrs. Balantine said something to Michael and he left the room, closing the door behind him.

She moved close to me and her lips were at my ear.

"Still want to mess me up, Bishop?"

I was sweating and revved up on the speedballs Michael was shooting me with, but there was something about the last one, it made me more than giddy and restless. I couldn't seem to stop talking, whatever I thought popped out of my mouth.

I was panting. "I didn't need drugs to seduce you, Mrs. Balantine."

She stepped back and smiled. "Now, now, Bishop, focus."

"What were we talking about, I forget."

"Baltimore. How did you connect your partner to Castile?"

Tess was right, I'd been hidden for a reason. I had fit all the pieces into the puzzle, connecting it all back to Castile, or I'd at least come very close, and now it was a matter of finding out who else knew what I knew.

I would die before telling her anything. At this point, though, I was going to die regardless.

I needed to stall, buy some time.

"Oh, no, now, see, that's a really funny story, but it's not a short one--you should have a seat, get comfortable. Before we go any further, though, what I want to know is..." and I looked up at her, suddenly confused and I laughed.

"...what was I saying? Oh, yeah. Whew, that's some stuff you've got there, ma'am." I took a breath and swallowed, my spit was like cotton in my mouth. "So, anyway, what's the quid pro quo here, Mrs. Balantine? Hm? What do I get out of this?"

"You are certainly in no position to bargain, Bishop, but for the sake of argument, what would you like?"

"Well, you've made it quite clear that I'm not going to live through this, perhaps you'll give me something to smile about before you have Michael punch my ticket?"

"The drugs aren't enough?"

"They're just the appetizer. I want the main course."

"And that would be..."

"I'll tell you everything you want to know because I just really hate leaving things undone, you know? I mean, I even make my bed every day, so I guess what I'm saying is...I want one more night."

She laughed at that. "I'm sorry, Bishop, I have an engagement this evening."

"Not with you."

She looked puzzled.

"With Justine."

149

It was a gamble that I was literally betting my life on. And I had to make it tempting enough that she wouldn't see the harm in giving me one more night locked in her guest house with Justine.

"Look, I may not remember what happened a year ago, but I remember everything you want to know about like it was yesterday, because to me, it *was* yesterday. Or last week. Okay, maybe a month ago, but you get my drift. I've got names, dates, times, places, what was being moved, who was there, who shot who..."

My voice trailed off as I watched her considering my words before adding, "And all for the low, low price of one night with Justine. You go and have your evening, I'll have mine, and we'll meet back here in the morning. We can have brunch, a little coffee...all very relaxed and civilized. I'll tell my story, maybe you could even fill in some gaps for me, and with all the loose ends neatly tied, I'll go quietly into the Light."

So, let me just say, right here and now, that I never, *ever* want to play another high-stakes game of any sort with this woman.

She has no 'tell.' Nothing twitched, nothing gave away her thinking as she considered my request. It took all I had to keep my eyes on hers, to not move, to not keep running my mouth.

Her loss would be nothing more than an evening of her time, and the clock was already ticking on her need to move me along in order to make her evening's engagement. I was hoping that my being difficult and uncooperative now, even with her chemical persuasions, was enough to make her reconsider and opt for the easier conversation tomorrow.

Finally, she pursed her lips and looked at her watch, and I knew I had her.

"Well, Bishop, you've made a compelling argument. After all, who am I to forgo granting your last request, hm?" She opened the door. "Have your night, then. I'll be back in the morning."

She turned and walked out and I listened to the soft sigh of her suit as she moved through the suite. Michael entered and let me loose, then left me there.

I felt the air pressure change as the front door opened and closed, and I breathed a sigh of relief, my head falling to my chest.

150

"Baxter!"

Justine raised my head in her hand and I looked up at her. She was looking down at me through one helluva shiner, the eye purple and nearly swollen shut.

"Oh, thank god! I was afraid you were dead!"

She found me still sitting in the chair in the center of the bathroom. I was trembling, and I wasn't sure if it was from the drugs or the bet-my-life gamble.

It was both, I think.

"Are you all right?" She stood looking at me with concern.

I shook my head at her question. "No. Help me to the bed."

I rocked up and managed to get halfway, and then her arm was under mine and around my back as she lifted me to a standing position. My head swam and I tipped with it, Justine staggering a little under my weight as she shifted and forced me upright.

"Deep breaths, Baxter, let it all settle before you try to go forward."

I did just that, spending another half-minute while I gained my equilibrium. I nodded at her and we made our way to the bed, she could feel me shaking as we moved across the floor and onto the area rug defining the bedspace.

She sat me on the edge of the bed then laid me back and lifted my legs onto it as well, pulling off my shoes, and I moaned a bit as I sank into the luxurious mattress. She drew a small comforter over me, her eyes widening when she saw the needle tracks on the inside of my arm.

"Baxter," she whispered. "What did they do?" She rubbed her fingers over the punctures and I jumped. "Sorry," she whispered.

"I'm going to sleep now." I couldn't help it, it was coming on too quick. "Wake me in an hour."

151

"Baxter. Baxter. Baxter..."

"What?"

"Baxter."

"What!" I opened my eyes, pissed that someone was disturbing the best sleep I'd had in weeks. Justine leaned into my view.

"Don't be ugly, you told me to wake you up in an hour. It's been an hour. And ten minutes."

I inhaled, loudly, slowly letting out the breath as I tried to clear my head.

Oh.

Yeah.

Fuck.

We're still in the Balantine guest house.

But I'm alive. Justine's alive.

We've still got a chance.

I sat up on the side of the bed, my head swimming a bit as I reached the fully-upright-and-locked position. Justine handed me a glass.

"Drink this. You'll feel better."

"What is it?"

"It's just water, Baxter. Now drink it."

I sipped, and the cool wetness hit my mouth, then the back of my throat, and I downed it, gasping when I was done.

"Gawd, that was good." I wiped the dribble from my mouth and chin.

"See?"

I looked at her, my head cocked as I took her in. Her face, a little cockeyed from the swelling and discoloration covering the right side still showed her worry, and I knew then that she was sincerely concerned.

"You ready to get out of here and go home?" I smiled at her, trying to convey some sense of assurance that we were going to do just that.

"You have no idea."

I nodded.

"Alright then, let's see what's going on outside first, see if there's anyone stationed close by to keep an eye on us."

We split up then, she took the front rooms, looking out the windows for anyone standing guard, or parked in a vehicle and watching.

I looked out the back. Nothing to see there either. We met in the central hallway.

"Let's do this."

I climbed up into the attic crawlspace and did my best to kick the vent out, but my muscles were still feeling the remnants of the sodium pentothal. I leaned back and called through the hatch.

"Come on up, I need your help."

She made her way through and she copied my position, settling on the narrow boards next to me.

"On three."

I counted down and we kicked against the vent, repeating the action until we felt it start to give.

"One more."

The frame sailed out and we both leaned up and watched it land on the ground below, skewing crooked as a corner joint hit first.

I rolled up onto my knees and peeked around the edge of the opening to see if anyone had heard us and come to see what the noise was about.

Nothing.

I looked down, concerned with the drop below. "That's a little more than what I was thinking."

Justine looked out. "Whoa."

"Yeah."

I made my way back to the hatch and reached down, pulling up some nicely folded linen sheets, handing one to Justine.

"Uh, Baxter, these really don't work as parachutes, haven't you seen the videos?"

I chuckled. "I know, silly, open it up and give me a corner." I crawled over to the exhaust pipe from the bathroom vent and tied my sheet around it, jerking to test the square knot, nodding as it tightened and held.

I made my way back to Justine and tied the end of her sheet to mine, tossing the other end through the vent opening.

"Wrap your arm through it, that's your brake. When you're down, get low and stay close to the house."

"I'm going first?"

"Well, I'm going to be holding this end to keep it from tearing or coming loose so you don't bust your ass from halfway up, because then you won't be able to run, okay?"

Her forehead knotted as she considered that and she nodded. "Okay."

She moved to the edge, turning onto her belly and wrapping her arm through the sheet, then followed it feet-first through the opening. I had braced my legs against both sides of the gap as she made her way down and I fell back as she reached the ground and let go. Sitting up on my knees, I looked down at her giving me the okay sign as she moved towards the back of the house.

My turn.

I wish I could say it was smooth, but without a counterbalance, the sheets pulled apart just as I passed the half-way point of my descent. I hit the ground with a thud and fell on my ass, the sheet ghosting out and covering me.

"Well, that was graceful," Justine smirked, shaking her head.

"Shut up."

I tucked the sheet up close to the foundation and made my way to Justine.

"I haven't seen any movement at the shed," she reported. I nodded at that as I squinted towards the low building, looking for a car or truck to steal.

No luck there.

We crouched and made our way to the opposite end of the house. I was flat on the ground as I peered around the side and looked down towards the barn.

There was a red dually pick-up truck parked just outside the paddock, a small enclosed cargo trailer hitched to it. On the other side of the fence rails, three people stood looking at a reddish-brown horse, the reins held by one of the three.

Justine looked around the corner with me. "There is a god," she whispered. She was looking down at me as I met her eyes. "That's Biggs. And Tracey."

My eyes were wide as saucers.

Huh.

So.

Maybe she's right.

Maybe there is a god.

152

We had a lot of open land to cover if we were going to make our ride out of there, and I wasn't sure how we were going to do that and not get caught. Then again, I wasn't sure if the person looking over the horse with Biggs was someone who knew we were being held against our wills, but if he was, he'd have a helluva time trying to take all four of us captive.

Their visit ended and the man took the reins from Tracey, leading the horse towards the barn as the two women cleaned up, gathering their supplies and packing their tools.

"Go."

We took off at a run for the truck, jumping up onto the floorboard of the crew cab's second row of seats, staying below the windows as I quietly pulled the door closed.

We both blew sighing breaths, and I think Justine was even a little tearful.

I nodded.

I knew how she felt.

153

Biggs and Tracey were in their seats, Biggs had cranked the engine, turning the truck and trailer towards the maintenance shed and what was probably a service road. I didn't want to draw their attention yet, not until we were well on our way off the property.

Neither she nor Tracey had noticed we were in the back seat and I was just about to lean up and let them know we were there when the truck slowed to a stop. I looked over at Justine, who was looking at me, fear in her eyes. I gave a slight shake of my head.

The dually was jacked up off the ground, making it easier to get through high water or over rough terrain, no one on the ground could see into the cab.

Biggs rolled down her window and leaned out. "What's up, Mr. Baker?"

I could hardly hear him, tucked up on the floor with my back against the seat. The conversation was mostly Mr. Baker talking, Dr. Biggs listening, until Biggs interrupted the monologue, telling him that she had another patient to see and that she'd call him in the morning to schedule an appointment later in the week, powering up the window to formally end the conversation.

The truck was rolling again, bumping up onto a paved road and heading for the tree line. "Geez, once he gets wound up..."

The two women laughed at that and I could see Tracey nodding.

I leaned over and pushed my head up between the two seats.

"Hey, y'all."

"Holy fuck!"

I don't think Dr. Biggs was inclined to cuss, but that flew out of her mouth like she was an old pro at it, and I was reminded of how calm she is in a crisis because she didn't drive the truck and trailer into the trees.

"Baxter! What...?"

"Hi, Dr. Biggs."

"What are you doing in my truck? How did you get in there? How long have you been there? What's going on?"

"Hi, Sharon."

"Who's that?"

"Justine," I answered.

"What?"

"Dr. Biggs, just get us out of here, okay? And would you call Tess for me? Now?"

Dr. Biggs tapped a button on her steering wheel. "Call Tess."

We could hear the ringing through the speakers, Tess's voice a welcome sound to my ears.

"Dr. Biggs?"

"Tess, it's me."

"Bishop?" The whisper revealed her uncertainty that she was actually hearing my voice.

"Yeah. It's me. Justine and I are with Dr. Biggs, can you pick me up? We're going to the..." I looked up at Biggs, the question on my face.

She looked down, her eyes quickly taking me in. "Tess, I'll bring her to you."

"I'm at the department, call me when you get to the parking lot."

"Fine, we'll be there in twenty minutes."

Biggs ended the call, shaking her head as she looked up into the rearview mirror. "Didn't I tell you to stay out of trouble?"

She didn't wait for me to answer, following her first question with another. "Are you going to stay on the floor?"

I was so tired and so relieved that I couldn't pull myself up on the seat. "If you don't mind."

Justine heard that and slid up onto the bench, laying prone across it, her eyes closed.

Her head was turned to me, and I studied her. Leaning up, I brushed her hair from her face, tucking it behind her ear, then lightly cupping her swollen and bruised cheek with my hand.

I was inches away. "Hey."

Her eyes opened.

"Thank you."

"For what?"

"For looking out for me when I needed you."

"You wouldn't have been here if I hadn't been so stupid."

Okay, there's some truth to that. Still, though...

"Well, then promise me you won't do something that gets you into a predicament like that again."

"I promise."

"Good enough." I took my hand away and leaned against Dr. Biggs' seat back, closing my eyes and listening to the all-terrain tires whine as we rolled down the highway towards Tess.

154

Tess, Fowler, and Whyte were waiting in the lot when we pulled up, throwing her arms around my neck and pulling me tight against her.

"Are you okay?"

"Yeah, I'm fine."

She held my hands as she leaned back and looked me over, seeing the bruising around the needle punctures in my arm.

"Bishop, what did they do?"

Twenty minutes later, I was sitting on the stretcher in the Tenley hospital emergency department as a CSI tech took a sample of my blood for evidence. Fowler had rushed us out there, calling ahead to have beds open and waiting. The CSI handed the tube off to the lab tech and Whyte accompanied her to the lab to monitor the processing and to maintain the chain of custody.

Justine was taken for x-rays. For a few minutes, I was left alone, and then Ginnie entered, closing the door behind her.

"How're you doing?" She smiled down at me as she wrapped a blood pressure cuff around my arm and pumped it up, her stethoscope in her ears. I waited until the air had hissed out of the cuff to answer.

"I'm okay. Tired." I paused. "Ginnie, Mrs. Balantine shot me full of speed and sodium pentothal--'a lot' of pentothal, she said."

"Yeah?"

"I remembered some things...from two years ago. And my head, it feels like...it's funny, I can't describe it. It's like...like I'm wired and everything's going off at once...and everything is still a little...shiny."

Ginnie smiled at that, but there was sympathy in her eyes. "Hon, you ever do drugs?"

I looked at her, weighing my answer. "I smoked some pot in high school, but nothing like this."

She nodded. "I can call Dr. Sampson if you think she should see you."

"No, that's okay, I don't think it's anything she could do anything about anyway."

"If it doesn't get better, call me. Okay?"

"Thanks, Ginnie."

"You're welcome, Bishop."

I had sat up and swung my legs over the side of the stretcher by then. Standing in front of me, she took my face in her hands and kissed me on the forehead, patting my knee before gathering up her equipment and moving to the door.

The feelings that evoked almost caused me to burst into tears.

It was the way I had always imagined a kid would feel after their mother had bandaged their scraped knee and kissed them 'all better' before sending them back out to play.

The drugs were definitely still in my system.

155

We spent the afternoon and early evening in debriefing as Justine and I recalled the events of the last twenty-four hours to the three detectives and Hatch.

Tess and I'd eaten, I had showered and was lying on the couch, settled under the blanket with two very attention-starved dogs stretched out across my body.

We were back in WITSEC mode and there were officers stationed at Biggs' house to protect Justine. Hatch had informed her DEA chief, with more agents moving into the area.

Tess picked up my legs and situated herself underneath the three of us, smiling and shaking her head as the girls panted their happiness.

"They'll get down shortly, it'll get too hot."

"I know."

I nodded. Of course she did.

"Are you really okay?" Her concern puckered her forehead and narrowed her eyes. "Should I call Ginnie and have her take another look at you?"

"No, I'm fine. I just need a good night's sleep."

"I felt so inadequate, I was no help to you at all. You might as well have been a hostage in a foreign country. There was nothing I could do, Hatch had called for an extraction team, but you know how fast that was going."

I laughed at that.

Tess shook her head. "Judge Thackery thought I wanted a search warrant because I'm a jealous wife and I was trying to catch you cheating."

I hollered at that. "With Mrs. Balantine?"

Then I thought about Mrs. Balantine. "Okay, well, she's, uh...she's okay."

"She's 'okay.' Bishop, she's gorgeous."

"If you say so."

"You don't?" She poked my foot. "You liar. I saw her."

Now it was my turn to laugh. "Yeah. Well, and the drugs didn't help."

"Are you confessing? Did you make a pass at Mrs. Balantine?"

I blushed and avoided looking at her.

"You did!"

"Not in so many words. I was under the influence. The drugs, they made me a little...hot and I couldn't stop talking..."

I stopped talking.

Tess sat looking at me, shaking her head, her eyes shining. "I'll bet you were something."

"Oh, yeah, I was a sight to behold all right, strapped to a chair, all hot and sweaty."

Her eyebrow raised at that. "Strapped to a chair. All hot and sweaty. That's kinda...hm..."

I blushed again. "Oh, you'd like that, huh? Drugs, hon, remember? Honestly, I was hitting on her like a horny sixteen-year-old."

"You didn't."

"I remember telling her I wanted to mess her up."

She chuckled. "I know what that means."

"Oh? From personal experience?"

"Yes. And that's all I have to say about that."

"I'll tell you some of my worst pickup lines if you tell me yours."

She laughed, shaking her head. "I wish..." and she stopped.

I waited, but I had to prompt her. "You wish. Wish what?"

"I wish I'd known you when you were younger. When you were in Baltimore."

"Oh. Well. Huh." I looked away at that.

"You don't like that thought?"

"I don't think you'd have liked me."

"Would I have been on *your* radar then?"

"Yeah, I'd have noticed you."

And I really would have, but I also would've probably corrupted her and moved on.

And then she wouldn't have liked me.

She might even have hated me. Like a few others.

Neither of us said anything for a while after that. We were content to just sit and look at each other.

Then, "You ready for bed?"

"I am exhausted."

We adjourned to the bedroom and she settled in under my arm. I pulled her close and sleep came quickly.

156

It was a little after three o'clock in the morning when I set the letter for Tess against the coffee pot, same as she'd left her letter to me that morning she'd gone to Richmond.

I'd slept for what felt like a full night, but I'd only been down about four hours. I had awakened with a start, my heart pounding, and I *knew*--I could feel it.

It was time.

Kissing the girls and giving Smokey a good head scratch, I grabbed up my duffel and took the keys to Tess's sedan from the hook, then quietly let myself out, locking the door behind me.

Her car had half a tank of gas. It would take me a good ways up the road before I'd need to top it up and grab a coffee, some snacks.

I looked through the windshield at our house, quiet in the dark, and I sighed. I could turn back at this point, Tess would be none the wiser, but I started the engine instead and pulled away from the curb, heading towards the four-lane on the outskirts of town.

Time to wake the monster.

Dear Tess,

I can't spend my life living like this. It is not the life I want, it is not the life I want for you.

For us.

It is better I face Castile instead of waiting for him to come for me, never knowing when he may be around the next corner, or when he will catch me from behind.

Or when he'll take one of you instead.

Third one's the charm, you know. It's time to end this.

And Tess--

I remember everything.

All of it.

I would look for you in every lifetime and I would die sad and unfulfilled if I didn't find you.

I meant that.

I still do.

I love you,

Bishop

157

Making good time, I accessed the interstate outside of Richmond just after four a.m., taking the first off-ramp for gas and breakfast. I had my order spread out in front of me when she slid into the seat on the opposite side of the booth.

"Are you sure this is what you want to do, Bishop?"

She was small in stature, thin, her long black hair pulled into a neat ponytail. Wearing a navy blue windbreaker over a white sweatshirt, the tawny color of her skin was muted by the winter's lack of sunshine. Her dark, almond-shaped eyes held steady on my face as she took a massive bite of a huge hamburger fixed with all the trimmings.

At four o'clock in the morning.

Did I tell you she had dark eyes? Awesomely dark. Two deep pools of unfathomable darkness.

Dark, yes, but friendly, if you can imagine the contradiction.

"Well?" She prompted me to answer, taking another huge bite of that burger.

I leaned towards her, low to the table, my eyes narrow. "What are you, DEA? FBI? Oh, wait--WITSEC? Are you a U. S. Marshall?"

Her lips curled upwards at their edges as she swallowed, then pulled a fry from the stack in front of her. She tilted her head, one eyebrow up now as she waited for my answer.

"Are you absolutely sure that you really want to do this?" She asked again, accenting the question by waving the fry back and forth. She popped it in her mouth, talking around it. "And just exactly what are you going to do when you get there? How close do you think you'll get to Castile before someone shoots you?"

I closed my eyes, my head falling back on my neck as I groaned.

"Do you even have a plan?"

"I do."

She smirked and shook her head. "Whatever it is, it's not good enough. Look, if you insist on starting this war too soon, I've been instructed to tell you how it will all end. And it won't be pretty. So I'm going to read you in, Bishop, and then you can decide for yourself."

158

Tess was holding my letter when I walked into the kitchen.

She stared at me and I tried to read her, but she was cycling so quickly I couldn't keep up. I didn't have time to even guess, she was on me in two short seconds, accentuating her words with pushes against my shoulders.

"You don't get to make decisions that affect us both like this!"

Her eyes on fire, her words unmistakable in their intensity. "We're *married*. This is *us!* We make decisions *together!*"

I kept my voice low as I worked to defuse her anger. The déjà vu was there, but so was the memory as I took her hand and pressed the back of it against my chest, over my heart.

Once again I was looking down into her eyes as I made a promise to her, making it the same way I'd made that very first one to her in this kitchen, on a day that felt so long ago.

A lifetime ago.

"Tess, I'm not going. Okay? I'm here and I'm not leaving you."

She leaned back, still angry, and then her palm was on my cheek.

"Bishop," she whispered. "I see you. I *see* you. You *do* remember."

She grabbed my jacket and pulled me to her, wrapping her arms around my shoulders as if she was drowning, and then she cried out and kissed me, hard, sending that white-hot fire coursing. She was in my blood, I could taste her, and I held her tight, my mouth on hers as I moved her through the kitchen.

My turn to crash us against the wall, pressing up against her, my hands under her shirt and roaming over her, so familiar, I knew her well and I set her off, leaving her shivering in the wake of my fingers as they slid over her.

She moaned and I heard her words. "Bishop," she whispered. "Please..."

We turned the corner into the bedroom. I guided her backwards until her knees buckled against the bed, and then I was on her, rolling her over on top of me, pulling off her shirt, holding her up to take her breast in my mouth, tonguing and lightly sucking her nipple into hardness.

Her skin was hot, her breaths coming as short huffs as her tension grew.

I turned us, and now she was beneath me.

Looking down at her, her bright eyes were skimming over my face, the lids heavy with want, I was suddenly overcome with an array of emotions for her, this woman I love, so much at once that I couldn't stop the tears from forming in my eyes.

"I love you, Tess, I love you. Forever and ever."

Both of us lost now to everything but each other, my heat grew with hers as I shared everything she felt, and I led her to the top of the summit, then fell with her as she came under me.

I left her long enough to pull off my clothes, then rejoined her under the covers, sharing the remnants of her heat between us.

159

Laying there in my arms, in the quiet of the early morning light, she reached out towards her bedside table. "I have something for you," she smiled, a bit shy, showing me what she held in her hand.

It was my wedding band, the mate to hers, the gold shining in her palm.

"I didn't know if you wanted to wear it...before."

I looked at it and I knew right away. There was no quibbling argument to be had in my head, and I held out my left hand to her.

She slid the ring onto my finger, pushing it into place as we kissed, wordlessly sharing that singular promise to each other once again.

I raised my hand up, turning it this way and that as I inspected the look of that gold band on my fourth finger, a sight I had never imagined I'd see.

It was natural, though, to see it there, and I felt I had come from a far-away place to find it, to find her, and to have her put it back where it belonged.

I love you, Tess, and I will look for you in every lifetime.

I promise.

The line clicked as the call was picked up.

"Agent Shaw."

"Director."

"Is Bishop back in place?"

"Yes, Ma'am."

"Good. Well done."

"Thank you, Ma'am."

The Director smiled. "That will be all. For now."

The call disconnected.

We weren't exactly sitting on a mountain of evidence, most certainly not enough that did us any good when it came to making arrests.

Whyte and Fowler had gone to Colton County Chief Judge Alton Bailey and obtained a warrant to search the guest house on the Balantine estate, using my affidavit claiming kidnapping as cause, backing that up with a statement from Dr. Biggs affirming that she had transported us from the property to the Tenley PD.

It was an uphill battle, according to Fowler, since the Chief Judge had already heard from Judge Thackery about his encounter with Tess.

"Gentlemen, this had better not come back to bite me on the ass," he said, signing off on the order. "Or I'll be doing some chewing of my own."

They nodded in turn, but neither was willing to make any promises.

An hour later, Penny was looking through the viewing screen on her video camera as Fowler drove onto the property through the open gates, now being tended by two maintenance workers.

She also documented the serving of the warrant on Mrs. Balantine's attorney, who met them on the driveway, informing the officers that Mrs. Balantine was unavailable for an interview as she had left earlier that morning for an extended trip with an open-ended itinerary.

The primary focus of the search was the guest house, which was found to be pristine in its condition, including the louvered attic vent, already replaced.

Penny was still recording through the police sedan's rear window as they drove away from the grounds. Her last image was the Tri-County Real Estate 'For Sale' sign, now attached to the bars of the iron gate as it shut behind them.

Detective Dennings had also disappeared.

The Whitmore PD Chief of Detectives advised Fowler that when the officer hadn't shown up for work and didn't answer his phone, a patrol was sent out for a wellness check.

Dennings' apartment was found unlocked, still containing his belongings and furniture, but his personal vehicle was not parked in its assigned space. An APB was issued, with no reports of any sightings.

The three Tenley detectives believe that Dennings has gone completely off the grid and is on the run.

Or he's dead.

All things considered, and knowing what I know, I'm inclined to agree with the second choice.

162

I made a call to Elsbeth McKay later that week. I wanted her opinion on the drugs Mrs. Balantine had shot me with and the return of my memory.

Elsbeth reported that she had used sodium pentothal in therapy sessions for patients unable to access their most profound traumas, but not combined with amphetamine, though it was certainly something to consider, and, if I wouldn't allow her a piece of my brain, would I agree to a scan?

I did, in the interest of science and her therapy patients, so we all journeyed to Richmond.

Afterwards, the five of us invaded Lily's restaurant on the city's outskirts, inviting Detective Miranda Miller of the Fighting Fourteenth Precinct to meet us there, and we were feted with the best Chinese food I have truly ever had, concurring with Tess's assessment that it was, indeed, better than Lin's Buffet.

Lin's restaurant is certainly out-of-bounds now, none of us wanting to push our luck, all of us laying low and staying close to home.

I'm pretty sure WITSEC is very happy about that.

163

By the end of February, Biggs was becoming downright giddy. Softball practice would start the second week of March, with tryouts and player evaluations, and she began to infect all of us with her happy demeanor as we shed the winter blues and began preparing for the season.

Now in her role as Coach Biggs, she sent out emails to the team members and we heard her call of "Play Ball" the same way one hears the chirps and chatters of birds in the trees announcing the coming of spring.

The team met at the field the following weekend. Some of us were hosing down the bleachers and seats, the rest walking the outfield to pick up stones and rocks that had worked their way to the surface, uncovered in the wetness of the snow and cold rain.

I smiled as Coach reminded us to pay attention, that any pip by a ball would be our fault as we walked six abreast in a familiar grid-pattern, mimicking evidence searches from my other life.

The sun was warm, the ground smelled fresh, and new, and I stopped to pick up a hefty specimen, looking over to the track across the way, smiling at the woman with the steady stride leaning into the far turn of the oval.

My wife.

Beautiful and kind and strong of heart.

I love her so much that it hurts.

Hearing shouting, I broke away from watching Tess, spotting Penny on the lower deck of the bleachers, threatening to spray Hatch with a blast of water from the hose. I smiled and shook my head as Hatch charged anyway, throwing her arms around the smaller woman, pinning Penny as she lifted her up and kissed her, both of them laughing.

Coach had rolled a large charcoal grill out in front of the home dugout. Justine was unloading the contents of two coolers, setting the rolls and fixings on a fold-out table as Carole tended the burgers on the rack, the savory aroma reaching us in right field. The smoke just above our heads, we all had our noses up like dogs on the scent.

There is nothing more promising than the smell of hamburgers cooking over a charcoal fire.

At the end of our meal, Carole and Biggs brought out a large sheet cake decorated with candy softballs, bats, and mitts, to commemorate the start of another season. Each square was garnished with a single birthday candle, Carol and Biggs smiling as they passed out the pieces, then lighting each of the wicks.

"Today marks the beginning of the fourth year of the Pride," Coach Biggs informed us. "You are the best softball team in the Tri-County League. Thank you for making this the most fun I could ever ask for, I truly love you all. Now, make a wish and blow out the candles."

Tess was sitting next to me, smiling, her arm wrapped through mine, and I leaned into her as I looked around at everyone I love in this world.

What do you wish for when your life is perfect?

I closed my eyes and blew.

164

A week later, my WITSEC handler fell in beside me as I walked to my Jeep parked on the campus lot.

"There's a problem."

"The problem is going to be that my wife will hear I'm keeping company with another woman. We have got to stop meeting like this."

"Keeping company...do people really still talk like that?" She smirked.

"Welcome to the Old South," I replied. "Just cut to the chase, Shaw."

She stopped walking, leaving me moving on without her. I stopped and turned. "What is it?"

"You can't go home."

"Baltimore? I know."

"No. Your home here."

I crossed the space between us in three strides. "Why not?"

I was nearly on her, but she didn't flinch. "Your wife has done something unexpected."

"Okay..." I waited for the punchline.

"No one knows how this happened, how they made contact."

"Shaw, what is it?"

"Castile's wife."

"What about her?"

"She's in your living room."

My eyes wide, I shook my head.

No, I wouldn't imagine anyone could have predicted this.

"It'll be fine." I turned and headed back to the Jeep.

"Bishop, you can't go home."

"It'll be fine." I reiterated, now in the driver's seat, talking to her through the open window.

"Bishop...!"

"She won't hurt me."

"How do you know?"

"Shaw, Mrs. Castile's birth name is Jillian Lorraine Bishop." I put the Jeep in gear. "She's my sister."

I rolled up the window and made my way out of the parking lot towards home.

So.

Baltimore has come to Tenley.

The war starts here.

Whew!

This one was fun, huh!

If you have enjoyed reading any of my books, please spread that joy and tell your friends, but most especially--and this is important--please take a minute to leave a starred review on Goodreads (if you're on an ereader, you don't have to write anything to do that, just turn to the last page, swipe one more time, click the stars and hit 'submit').

Or if you want to leave one on Amazon later, you could drop a little note on the book's sale page next time you're shopping (you don't have to write a lot there, but they do kinda expect words. Except--and I'm not absolutely sure about this--maybe you can just use emojis).

If you're a blogger or a reviewer and you want to write a post about the books, I thank you very much, please tag me in, you can always contact me at therealb.d.gates@gmail.com for further discussion or questions.

Lastly, you should follow me on Twitter (@BDGates4real) just for fun (I'm friends with a lot of other #lesfic writers, you'll hear about new and upcoming books of theirs, but we also get really goofy sometimes), or you can join me at BDGatesBooks.com for news and information as well as sneak peeks of the fourth and final book in the Bishop's Run series.

I would really enjoy hearing from you.

Love to all,

BDG

Made in the USA
Columbia, SC
29 September 2023